Communion Town

Communion Town

A City in Ten Chapters

Sam Thompson

W F HOWES LTD

This large print edition published in 2013 by
W F Howes Ltd
Unit 4, Rearsby Business Park, Gaddesby Lane,
Rearsby, Leicester LE7 4YH

1 3 5 7 9 10 8 6 4 2

First published in the United Kingdom in 2012
by Fourth Estate

A CIP catalogue record for this book is available
from the British Library

ISBN 978 1 47122 559 8

Typeset by Palimpsest Book Production Limited,
Falkirk, Stirlingshire
Printed and bound in Great Britain
by MPG Books Ltd, Bodmin, Cornwall

For Caoileann and Oisín

This city is Epidamnus while this story is being told:
when another one is told it will become another town.

PLAUTUS

CONTENTS

PART I

COMMUNION TOWN

D o you remember how you came to this city, Ulya? Think back, because we need to agree on what happened right from the start. I want to help him out as much as you do, believe me. I know you're worried, and in your place I'd be the same – but I can promise you that conditions are actually quite tolerable in there. So let's approach this calmly. When I've said what I have to say, I'm going to offer you an opportunity, and I hope you'll feel able to respond.

It was early morning, remember, when you and Nicolas arrived. Did your spirits lift at the first sight of what you'd travelled so far to reach? A world of grey dawn twilight and blackened stone above, rainwater dripping from the girders, pigeons sulking in rows and strangers spilling from carriages to gather on the concourse, disoriented. Even at that hour the Grand Terminus was full of migrants anxious to enter the city. They formed queues for processing, shambling in their soiled clothes, their heads twitching at the noise of the tannoy.

I picked you out of the crowd right away. You weren't like the rest: with most of them it's obvious,

3

you can see it all in their faces as they offer up their papers for inspection, clutch their belongings and steal glances at the carbines of the watch. You and Nicolas, though, you were different. I have an instinct for these things, and I'm seldom mistaken in the end.

You mustn't be surprised if I seem to know a good deal about your life over these past months: maybe more than you know yourself. The fact is I've been here all along. You won't have seen me, but I've kept a discreet eye on your progress. So why don't I go ahead and talk you through the way I see it? Then you can correct me on the finer points, fill in the details, let me know your side of the story. How does that sound?

No one wants to spend the first hours of a new life in an interview room, so let me apologise for what you went through that morning. I hope you feel you were treated with due sensitivity and respect. After they'd taken your photographs and left you waiting for a while, the door was elbowed open by a short man fumbling with a sheaf of papers. He had a preoccupied, officious manner, I'm afraid, and I certainly wouldn't have chosen him to welcome you to the city with his damp scalp, his rumbling stomach and his tie that kept twisting around to expose its underside. He didn't even introduce himself. As for you and Nicolas, you avoided eye contact and kept your answers minimal. Who could blame you?

It's unsettling, isn't it, being asked to tell your

story over and over, when as far as you're concerned it's perfectly straightforward. The little man never said he didn't believe you, but I know you felt that he was listening for a contradiction, waiting for you to slip up. He sighed as if your responses were somehow disappointing. He left the room, then came back, and you had to try again: Where have you come from? How did you travel here? Do you have friends, family, means of support? Can you prove that you have reason to fear immediate danger in your place of origin? Thoroughly tiresome.

At last they issued you with temporary permits to remain in the city, and a list of appointments to attend in the coming days: to apply for your identity cards, to request help with subsistence and accommodation, to make sure we didn't lose track of you. By the time they let you go, you must have been hungry, thirsty and aggrieved – I know I would have been – but neither of you showed it. Now, you might think this wasn't much to go on. But I've learnt to trust my intuitions, and I could tell that you and Nicolas were going to need my help.

I realise this is all very inconvenient, and I appreciate your patience. You can't imagine what involvement he might have with Communion Town, but that's all right – we'll get there. Would you like a glass of water before we continue? You need only say the word. Everything now is strange and uncertain, Ulya, I understand this, I really do, but keep in mind that you and I can help each other if we choose.

For what it's worth, I think you did just about everything you could. You tried gallantly to hold it together, but there were certain aspects of your life in the city that you could not have foreseen. It's always clearer in retrospect. Think of the first time you walked into the apartment you had been assigned out in that half-empty tower block in Sludd's Liberty. I'll admit it wasn't everything you might have wished for, with the stains on the ceiling and the smell of blocked drains. There was no furniture. Nicolas prodded with his toe at the great chrysalis of ripped-out carpet lying in the middle of the room, then gave it a kick, releasing an odour of damp.

You were uneasy, of course, seeing the reticence he had preserved so well at the Terminus already beginning to come apart. You had an inkling he would need to exercise more self-control in future. I have to say I agreed. Yes, I was there with you – at least in the sense that matters most. I'm good at not being seen, and in my job locked doors aren't a problem.

What could you do? You were concerned about him, naturally, but you had your own adjustments to make, as every newcomer must. Nowhere is exactly as you think it's going to be, and when you settle in a strange city you soon find out there's more to learn than you suspected. You know what

I'm getting at. You remember it: the day you saw your first monster.

You had been at the Agency all day, trying to see someone about your claim. You'd reported at nine a.m. sharp, as instructed, then queued until four in the afternoon to have an irritable clerk glance over your documents. Afterwards you crossed town to the depot in Glory Part where you queued again to redeem your food stamps. Then, burdened with cans of preserved meat and UHT milk, you rode the city metro west to the end of the line and a forty-minute walk through Sludd's Liberty.

They have an unfortunate reputation, those banlieues where the old streets are overshadowed by never-completed tower blocks stalled midway through the process of being torn down. Most people I know wouldn't venture out that way. On your route home stood one half-demolished high-rise with the open sockets of bedrooms and bathrooms visible from down in the street. Another tower, still whole, was trussed up in scaffolding, and the wind sang through the structure of metal poles, wanting to fling pieces down at you.

You walked by vacant lots behind chain-link fencing and under the arterial flyover. You passed a cherry tree in blossom, and an off-licence like a bunker, locked down with steel shutters. You skirted a rubblescape where mechanical diggers scraped the ground and a builder in a fluorescent jacket trudged along with a hod on his shoulder,

7

while another picked his way over heaps of bricks, slowly and helplessly, as if it were the wreck of his own house. Three more sat in a circle, like practitioners of some ancient folk industry, using hand-tools to chip mortar off bricks.

You did notice these things, didn't you, on your daily trek through the outskirts? It's important we pay attention to the details, because I want to understand what it was like for you in those first days and weeks. I want you to persuade me of it, Ulya. I really think I'd be letting you and Nicolas down if I didn't try my best to see things from your point of view.

As you neared the tower block, you became aware that something unusual was happening. Most of the time the inhabitants of Sludd's Liberty went about their errands furtively and alone, but now a group had formed on the dilapidated high street: women and children from the high-rises, men from the bar on the corner, some of the youths who hung around in the recreational areas and a couple of the homeless people who frequented the district. A city watchman was there, too, and the doctor who ran a clinic here once a month. In spite of the group's diversity, something united them, a recklessness sketched across all the faces. They had clustered around the entrance to a short blind alley that ran down beside a fast-food restaurant, their body language tense.

Drawing closer, you caught sight of what they had cornered. I'm sorry you had to go through that, but

I suppose in truth it was a rite of passage into our city more significant than any Agency interview.

Can we try to describe what you saw? We could say it was pale and ragged, that its movements were oddly askew and that you felt sure it was broken or deformed in a way you couldn't quite identify. We could say that your stomach turned, and you grew dizzy as the urge to stamp the thing out of existence struggled against the need to flee as far away from it as you could get; that you would have done anything rather than let it touch you. But in the end all we can say is that what confronted you was *wrong*, so intrinsically wrong that just by being there it was committing an outrage against us all. It stared back at you with ghoulish immodesty, clutching a lump of rotten matter which it had fished out of the bins.

I know you recognise what I'm telling you, Ulya, because I've had those encounters myself. You might spend a lifetime in the city and never glimpse one, if you're lucky, but few of us escape the occasional reminder of their presence. They're bolder in areas like the Liberties, but even in Cento Hill or Lizavet or Rosamunda you can never be sure they won't slither without warning out of the crevices where they hide. Walking to work you might hear a verminous scrabbling underneath a bridge. Travelling on some deep line of the metro you might catch fleeting sight of an ill-fitting parody of a face, smeared and pallid in the dark beyond the glass.

There are several names for what they are. Some people call them ingrates or the abject, the *pharmakoi* or the *homines sacri*. But you might as well call a monster a monster.

For a long moment the people of Sludd's Liberty confronted the thing. Then someone groaned, and someone else threw a stone that crashed into the bins. The trapped creature giggled and cowered and the watchman finally fumbled at his holster as the others cast around for weapons. But then it leapt forward, and as the crowd recoiled it slipped past with loathsome speed to vanish into the nest of alleys towards the foot of the tower.

After that there was nothing to be done except lay down the stones and sticks, exhale, shake heads and trade reassurances. Everyone was voluble at once, talking and laughing, eager to tell everyone else the story of what they had just witnessed. They turned to you, inviting you to join the conversation.

But you didn't, did you? That was a pity, I think, because for a person in your position it's worth taking every chance to become more integrated with the community. Still, you'd had a shock. Under the circumstances, no one could really hold it against you that you ignored their exclamations and hurried away alone, back to the apartment in which you could hear several generations of a large family quarrelling on the other side of the wall.

★   ★   ★

All right. He's on your mind, so let's talk about Nicolas. There's a strong resemblance there, did you know that? The same dark eyes, always watchful, never telling.

You may find it difficult to believe, but I have a good idea of how it hurt when you realised you had lost him. I wish I could change it, I really do. And I know you can't help holding the city a bit responsible. You can't help feeling that if the two of you had never come here then everything would have been different. I just hope you won't let it colour your impressions unduly – because there's so much to celebrate about this place, and we mustn't forget that. Of course sometimes it can seem excessive, too huge, with its fathoms of brick and iron and its endless capacity to churn out litter and exhaust fumes, and too sad, with its sleepers in stairwells and Cynics plotting in respectable suburbs. But that's the price we pay for the sheer vibrancy that surrounds us. I don't think I could ever leave.

You know what I like to do? I like to go out running. It's so easy to lose touch with the simple, indispensable things, just the world around us, but running keeps me in the city in a fundamental way: the texture of the ground under the feet, the flow of the air around the body. I run first thing every morning. You can picture me lacing up my shoes in the dim space of my flat with dawn coming up in the windows. My place is over in Loamside, so I head past shut shops and cafés and across the park, I dodge the gangs of men hauling crates along the streets as the gaining light scribbles colour and texture into the world, and soon I smell brine and I'm on the seafront, buffeted by gusts of wind, with crows blowing around above the mud like cinders off a bonfire.

Actually I'm a serious runner. Not one of your fair-weather joggers, anyway: you'll find me out there every morning without fail, heatwave or hailstorm or dead of winter. I'm never going to win any marathons but, you know, that doesn't matter. It means something to me. When I think back, I get the feeling I've spent the better part of my life in this city pounding the pavements and river walkways and cycle paths, pushing through the pain barriers, keeping up that steady rhythm on one unending run, looping from Three Liberties to Green Stairs, from Syme Gardens to Glory Part, never stopping, with first light setting the pace.

This morning it was very fine. I ran along the path with the sun breaking through the mist, and I paused to catch my breath, paced up and down, leant on a bench and stretched my calves. Further down the seafront a pair of forms thickened out of the visual hiss and shot by me, one before the other, freewheeling. The light was lifting off the water in nets and chains of dazzle, and a gaff-rigged sloop was cutting around in the bay, jammed in between the elements, gearing the sea and the wind together, taking the strain in its ropes and the hands of its crew . . .

I'm digressing, aren't I? You'll have to forgive me. I think you know what I'm trying to say.

When someone means that much to you, you don't have many choices, do you, much as you may pretend you're free to do as you like. That other person is threaded into you as deep as your own soul – you hold his image in your mind, always, and you hope he keeps an image of you, because in the end that's the only place where you can live secure and complete. You know that if you were to vanish from the world it would be in that person's thoughts that you lingered, for a while at least, after you were gone. So I understand what it was like, those times he went off alone into the city without quite explaining his plans. Do you remember the night, less than a month after you arrived, when he came home late with two black eyes and a bloody nose? You were frightened for him but he shrugged off your questions. Already he seemed to be breaking away.

It's true he didn't reveal much, but I do feel that I came to know him, in my fashion, in the time we had. Have you noticed how each of us conjures up our own city? You have your secret haunts and private landmarks and favourite short cuts, and I have mine, so as we navigate the streets each of us walks through a world of our own invention. And by following you into your personal city, I can learn a great deal of what I need to know.

Of course I can't approve of his decision to seek

out unlawful employment. I have to make it very clear I think that was the wrong choice. But at the same time I understand how people in your situation can find themselves facing an unenviable range of options, and so I watched with some sympathy as he crossed the city every night for his illicit shift in the kitchens of the Cosmopole. I can assure you, incidentally, that the relevant authorities will be taking a keen interest in working practices at that particular establishment.

Nicolas's personal city was dingy and utilitarian – he would always take the fastest route to his destination, however squalid or threatening the streets – but there was an honesty about it, and a certain pride as well. He lived in a city populated exclusively with his equals. If he never acknowledged the grand department stores on Vere Street or the fin-de-siècle facades of the Palace Mile, it wasn't because of his broken shoes and four-day beard but because he found their hypocrisies unacceptable. Once, in the Esplanade, a motorcycle tore past him along the pedestrian precinct, sounding its siren to clear the way for a cavalcade of police jeeps and VIP cars to roar through, followed by more bikes carrying more weaponised, shiny-helmeted men. The passers-by formed naturally into lines of spectators, but Nicolas swore under his breath at the arrant incivility of it.

He preferred cutting through the back streets of the city centre. In those alleys, which seem to contain all the litter that has been swept out of the boulevards, he knew where he was going: his stride became longer and easier and he'd nod to the waiters out for a smoke or slip the odd coin to a sleeping drunk. After work at the Cosmopole, most days, he stopped off to treat himself to breakfast at a place called the Rose Tree Café. Did you know that? Then he'd walk to the Communion Town metro and disappear into the underground crush to fight his way back to Sludd's Liberty. Half his wages must have gone on metro tokens but there was no alternative if he wanted to snatch a few hours' sleep each afternoon.

Communion Town: strange, isn't it. Nowadays it's hard to remember a time when those two words weren't loaded with horror. The season has hardly turned since it happened, and yet to think of the days when Communion Town was merely the jostling heart of the Old Quarter, and its baroque subterranean maze of a station nothing more than the hub of the city's transport, is to recollect another era.

I was nearby at the time of the event. There's no denying the diabolical ingenuity of what the Cynics did that day. The city was unprepared because no one had imagined they could go so far. At the moment they chose, the station was flowing with the usual early-evening mob of shoppers, revellers, hipsters and tourists – ordinary people, self-absorbed and carefree, sunburnt from the first real day of summer we'd had. It doesn't bear thinking about, does it, finding yourself

15

trapped down in the guts of the metro and slowly realising what's going on.

I thank my stars I was above ground myself, walking through another part of the Old Quarter to meet friends at the cinema. Have you ever been on the margins of an event like that? The awareness that something was wrong came over us like a change in atmospheric pressure. Without quite knowing why, strangers turned to each other, asking for explanations and swapping instantaneous rumours. There's a certain thrill: you want to know what's happening, but more than that you want to know if it might still be going to happen to you.

You've seen the news footage of that day. I can't decide whether the television stations should have been allowed to release the images to the public at all. Perhaps we need to see these things, but it made me uncomfortable that just because the Cynics had managed to feed us those pictures, we went meekly along with it and watched, powerless to intervene, as the horrors unfolded in exactly the way they had planned. Sometimes I think that was the worst aspect of what they did – showing us. Who can make sense of the mentality?

In the days afterwards the weather was superb, deep skies pouring down hot light so strong that the parks stiffened with vegetation and the streets seemed unreal. We had slipped into a strange kind of time: a kind that, instead of passing, accumulated. I remember pausing one afternoon in a small triangular park below an office block, nothing but some trampled grass, a drift of daisies and a rusted-up fountain, and having the most curious sense that as long as I stayed on this spot the city would remain poised and safe, not a mote in the air moving. When I passed that way again I couldn't find it.

We all did our best to return to normal life – to do so, we assured each other, was nothing less than a principled stand – and soon enough the commuters were again streaming in and out of the ornate arches of the Communion Town metro. The city doesn't stop, however appalled. But I had a suspicion that the busy citizens were no longer quite so convinced by the performance in which they were taking part. I couldn't shake a sense of – what? I suppose the fragility of everything we were about.

On the streets the city watch were swollen with seriousness, their automatic weapons perched high on their chests and their eyes scanning. Life was less convenient than before: it was common to have your way blocked by bulky torsos and protuberant holsters, and to be instructed to take an alternative route to your destination. Most frustrating. I don't pretend that my experiences correspond with yours, Ulya, but we all have mixed feelings about how things have been lately.

The watch stopped me once on Impasto Street when I was already late for an appointment, and I swear they enjoyed making me wait. They were lumpish types, two big raw hams in uniforms, and when they saw I was getting impatient they visibly settled down to savour their task. They took their sweet time establishing where I was going and why. I showed my identification, but they ignored it, conferred for a while, then told me to touch the wall and patted me down. I barely restrained myself from asking ironically whether they thought I looked like a Cynic; who knows where that might have led. At last one of them laid an oversized palm between my shoulder blades and pointed back the way I had just come.

'You see that street, sir?' he said. 'Would you mind walking down it?'

I spent the whole night going over those words. I took a late run to calm down. Maybe it doesn't hurt to be reminded now and then that the city can clobber you whenever it likes, but the odd thing, it occurred to me as I pushed myself forward with my head bowed under the streetlamps, tarmac filling my vision and grit scraping between my soles and the pavement, was that just for a moment I *had* been on the side of the malcontents. As I had walked away I'd been half-mad with resentment. That can't be right, can it?

I ran through the small streets around my place, encountering cars, dark and crouched with their headlights up, waiting, their intentions obscure. It was one of those stifling nights when the lamps only smear the murk and, run as I might, my past opened up underneath my feet: I found my legs

18

working in emptiness and I drifted like a balloonist over the depth of my personal time, seeing straight down to the bottom. Long ago, I felt, I had been the victim of some fleeting violence, of no great importance to the perpetrator but enough to leave me bent and scarred, sculpted casually into what, now, I'd always be.

When I got home I was glad I'd left the flat in darkness. My eyes had adapted, so I opened the windows and left the lights off while I drank a bottle of beer, listening to warm rain beginning to fall. The spattering steadied to a hiss, spreading coolness through the air and releasing the smell of school football pitches from the park across the road, and as it grew heavier it made a sound-map of the trees and glass roofs nearby. I swigged a cold mouthful and placed the bottle on the table: a bubble swelled and broke at the lip, and a tiny catastrophe of froth worked itself out in the neck.

I'm telling you this because I want you to see that in the end I'm like you, Ulya, trying my best, getting by, hopefully getting it right sometimes. I'm not some faceless administrator. I'd hate you to think of me that way, because we have the potential for so much more, you and I.

If we're to make sense of the predicament in which Nicolas finds himself, we have to try and imagine his state of mind in the months and weeks prior to the events at Communion Town. I hope you don't find it impertinent, me telling you this. I feel

I'm claiming to know more about him than you do yourself. His motives were basically good, I do believe that, but the fact is he was reckless on occasion.

That café of his was a run-down warren, crammed in around the back of Communion Town station; and cheap food or not, I would have preferred not to see him spend his time there. Grease clung to the plate-glass window, deposited by the clouds of steam that filled the interior, and you could tell at a glance that the plates would be grubby and the bacon and eggs swimming in fat. Even so it was always packed in the early mornings. Nicolas sat down to his breakfast elbow-to-elbow with students in dishevelled finery after a night on the town, tram drivers and rickshaw kids at the end of their shifts, backpackers fuelling up between hostel and railway station, civil servants heading for the offices of the Autumn Palace. There were immigrants who had just finished cleaning those same offices, or who were on their way to the building sites across the river; there were men with nose-rings and women with shaven heads who looked to have been up all night, dancing violently in cellar clubs or publishing underground magazines. There were less identifiable types, too. A lot of talk went on in there and I found it impossible to make out any single conversation above the spluttering griddles and clashing cutlery. But I knew it was not what Nicolas needed, given his propensities. Too often through that clouded window I saw him in impassioned discussion with some near-stranger, their heads together. It bothered me, I have to tell you. I could never quite decide what he was thinking as he swigged his tea and walked out to Halfmoon Street, vigorous and stern-faced, to plunge back into the metro.

Communion Town station itself was a city in miniature, with a specialised urban ecology flourishing in its tunnels, a functional society from the ticket sellers and engineers to the lavatory attendants and platform-arabs. Daily, after his night's work and his grease-soaked breakfast, Nicolas shouldered his way through the station's Upper Hall to board the ancient lifts down to the platforms.

Most people on the metro will look straight through their fellow commuters and out the other side, but that was a skill Nicolas didn't seem willing to learn. He studied the traders of the Upper Hall with tight-lipped intensity; he made no attempt to hide his interest in the sallow man with the too-small suit and the dabs of tissue paper stuck to the shaving cuts on his throat, who tirelessly informed the commuters that the misfortune soon to come upon them would be a punishment for their degenerate lives; or the personable youngster in the cagoule who handed out leaflets advertising walking tours of the Old Quarter, saying welcome, folks, you're very welcome to our fine city, but make sure and look to your valuables, ladies and gentlemen, there are criminals about so make sure your valuables are secure! – so that hands moved for assurance to certain points on bags and bodies, and the leafleteer's beady-eyed associates, slouching nearby, knew where to concentrate their attentions.

At least I can set your mind at ease about the night of the black eyes. He'd been foolhardy, nothing worse. He had witnessed a more or less everyday spectacle in the Hall, a gang of roaring boys who had encircled another youth and, amid laughter, were spinning him around by pricking his behind with their knives. Well, you know what Nicolas is like. He had waded in to put a stop to it, and had been rewarded with a crisp headbutt and a discharge of abuse from the bullies, in which their victim joined.

That didn't put him off, though. Whatever he saw, he took it personally. I couldn't quite make him out; he would scowl at the skinny youths who hauled their rickshaws past the front of the station to pick up rich couples. He'd give filthy looks to such harmless types as the five middle-aged monks who strolled through the Hall in their saffron robes, all with close-shaved heads, rimless spectacles and digital cameras, or the undergraduates complaining languidly to one another about the length of the cashpoint queue: 'This is *abzurd.*' On the other hand, he always had a friendly word for the two smartly dressed women who ran the cosmetics kiosk, and for the leather-tanned, tattooed guy who could usually be found patrolling the Hall with a can of cider in one hand and the other thrust down the back of his tracksuit trousers. I can admire it, the instinctive conviction with which Nicolas responded to all that jostling life, but I'm sorry to say that it served him badly in the end. It's all part of the story of how you lost him to the city.

I wish his judgement had been better, we both do, but there was something wilful in his conduct. It was as if he wanted to put himself at risk. He had taken to buying breakfast every day for one of the other patrons of the Rose Tree Café, a person who it pains me even to describe to you. I knew his sort well, and I could not have imagined a less desirable companion. It's strange. I like to think I'm pretty tolerant, but with some people you just can't help how you feel.

He was often to be seen around the streets of Communion Town, this one: he was no older than Nicolas himself, but his face was ruined, a mask of putty on a skull, and he made a show of walking with a limp, cautiously, as if he were favouring a hidden injury. Nicolas, I think, had mistaken him for a genuine casualty of the city, taking pity on his sickly look, his unwashed clothes and scrawny frame, and perhaps on his attempts at dandyism: he actually affected a carnation in the buttonhole of his jacket, and his long hair had been clumsily bleached. As he sat down opposite Nicolas, he combed his fingers through the oily locks as if folornly hoping to be mistaken for a member of the opposite sex.

I could understand why Nicolas felt sorry for him, but he failed to see the arrogance behind the frailty. The fellow wolfed down his plateful each morning without a word of thanks. Then, after another mug of coffee, he would launch into a tirade, staring at Nicolas greedily and plucking at his cuff as he spoke, like someone imparting urgent secrets. He was a fraud, of course: in spite of his appearance I would not have been surprised to learn that he had a trust fund to support his loafing, his radical posturing. Now and then you saw him plaguing the shoppers around Vere Street, going from person to person like a beggar and delivering his spiel with an unnerving show of anguish. He held the sleeves of his targets as if his life depended on getting them to believe whatever line he was spinning.

A fraud, but a dangerous fraud for someone in Nicolas's situation to associate with. I fumed to see him deceived, and wanted to tell him that this personage was laughing up his sleeve at the fine joke of it. Nicolas could be so unworldly. I watched them through the grease-fouled window, hazy figures leaning seriously towards one another. I could only guess what lies were being told in there, but, if what happened later was anything to go by, I fear very much that he believed them.

You saw the nature of the situation better than he did. I'm only sorry you couldn't help him understand. I'm thinking of the afternoon you took him picking blackberries down by the canal. The brambles beside the cycle path were dense with shiny black flesh, so you and Nicolas took plastic supermarket bags and struggled in among those alien castles full of cobwebs and dead matter and tiny sharp barbs, threaded through with nettles and loaded with decayed, insect-ridden fruit, some of it soft enough to turn to pulp at a touch and much of the rest pinkish and shrivelled. You walked home scratched and stung but your bags were heavy and wet with purple juice. I often think of you like that, the two of you, blackberrying in a revealing light that lay longways across everything, stirring up the colours of the hedges and the banks and resonating off the water. Sludd's Liberty had retreated from you. The evening moon was up, and behind the city and the trees the sun was setting in a sky like a sheet of cold copper marked with the single dent of a hammer. One of those sunsets that looks to be changing the world and no one is noticing.

I wish Nicolas had been able to learn that kind of lesson. But looking back, it seems now as though it was only a matter of time until he was mixed up in an incident like the one that followed.

One morning, as he crossed the Upper Hall of Communion Town metro station on the way to his shift, he noticed a figure sprawled on the tiles, full-length, with its body twisted, the side of its face flattened into the floor and its arms thrown loosely over its head. The sparse hairs of its beard stuck to the tiles, and its parted lips were within kissing distance of somebody's footprint. There was no sign of life. The prostrated form looked for all the world as though it had fallen from the rafters. Probably it had just dragged itself out of the shadows in the night – suffering, perhaps, with one of the diseases to which its kind is prone.

Where it had come from didn't matter. There was no doubting what it was. The commuters stepped around it without registering its presence, and those breakfasting a few feet away at the aluminium tables of the Transit Café never gave it a glance.

Nicolas, though, not only looked openly at the comatose thing, but stopped and squatted beside it. I felt my innards reorganise as I watched. Even at a distance I could smell the foetor of the overalls and army-surplus jacket it wore. He felt for its pulse and leant in horribly close to its face. His movements were competent, and an idle part of my mind speculated on whether he'd had some medical training back where you came from. He brushed his fingertips lightly against the creature's eyelashes, and it stirred.

This was lunacy. Cursing my sluggishness, I broke in on the scene, hauled Nicolas bodily to his feet with more strength than I usually possess, and steered him away through the Hall. My heart was lunging and I had a sudden headache. He stared as I explained to him, as if to a child, that you couldn't *do* that – never, and certainly not in a public metro station. Through good luck no decisive line had been crossed, but I was genuinely angry at the position he had put me in. I hadn't intended for us to meet face to face like this. Fortunately, he didn't seem inclined to wonder who I was; but I couldn't conceal my indignation at his conduct. What, I asked him, had he been thinking?

Nicolas didn't answer. The creature had woken now, and he watched with what might easily have been taken for solicitude as it scrambled out of sight. He twitched his shoulder free of my hand and glanced in my direction before he walked away, but he didn't really notice me at all.

I want to be generous, and perhaps we can allow that in those early days he simply did not appreciate the implications of his actions. No doubt he was misled by the company he kept. In a sense he was guilty of nothing more than a failure of imagination: but if so, then the events that came soon afterwards surely granted him all the insight he could have desired.

What the Cynics did at Communion Town was simple in conception, intricate in execution, a nightmare in its outcome. At five-fifteen p.m. on the first Friday of the summer, the conspirators – a cell of only ten men and women, as we now know – took control of the mechanical and electrical systems of the metro station, and crippled the lift shafts. At the same time, down in the station's innards, they caused a series of ancient fire doors, six-inch slabs of iron which had been out of use for a century, to grind shut. Twenty-seven members of the public were imprisoned, unable either to return to the surface or to escape on to the platforms. They had been sealed without food or water into a buried tangle of tunnels lit by stuttering bulbs. The city above could watch them through the security cameras that the saboteurs had left operational, but all other lines of communication had been cut. The emergency services were baffled by the obsolescent structures that had been layered down through the generations of Communion Town's growth beneath the city. The wiring had fused and melted, the doors were impenetrable, and any incautious attempt to dig out the trapped citizens was liable to cave in the entire catacombs.

These developments should have been enough to show Nicolas that the city contained more dangers than he had supposed, and stranger motives. But it was only as Saturday passed with minimal progress towards a rescue, and a second midnight approached, that the true nature of the Cynic design became clear. The citizens waiting down there in the tunnels, who by now must have been exhausted and dehydrated and their psychological condition increasingly frail, would have heard the first mutterings, rattles and scrapes, and would have seen the first flutters of movement at the edges of their confined world as, in greater numbers than anyone can have witnessed outside their ugliest fancies, from the ventilation ducts and drainage grates and disused access hatches and all the other dark corners and cracks in the surfaces of things, the monsters arrived.

The barbarism of it is hard to credit. The imagination baulks. We'll never begin to guess what it was like for the victims, but what choice do we have except to go over the details, transfixed by the fate that was engineered for them, trying and failing to grasp its reality?

When I last spoke to Nicolas, I asked him what he thought about the conspirators and the way the city dealt with them after their arrests. As for myself, and I'm not very proud of this, my first instinct was that they were being treated far too kindly – but then, of course, I know that's not good enough. I know it's by extending to the Cynics the respect and decency they deny to others that we show our difference from them. We offer them the chance their victims can never have. We don't cast them out, however abhorrent their point of view may be to the values that underpin our way of life. Instead, we take them in. We engage with their ideas and challenge them through vigorous rational debate. We let them know that, in spite of what they've done, we're with them, and we won't give up on them until we have helped them find a way out of the error in which they are mired. Patiently we show them that we'll never let them go until they understand, and until they have been understood.

We tell their stories.

I said as much to Nicolas, when I faced him across the table in a room not unlike this one. I said to him what I'm saying again now: I can help you, but I need your help. I want to believe that you're on our side, that you're serious about embracing the welcome this city has offered, but I need you to make me sure. All you have to do is convince me, I said, and this is your opportunity.

But what was the response? None. He had nothing to tell me. He lowered those dark brows as if he were embarrassed on my behalf.

The sad thing is I wasn't entirely surprised. I hate to say it, but I've spent a long time watching over you and Nicolas, doing all I can to help you make the adjustment to your new life – and what have you given back? I ask myself that, Ulya, and to be honest I don't have an answer.

I'll tell you something. You'll find that there comes a point when you can give up on the regret, at long last – on the hurt of not having kept what you had. But then you hesitate, because letting go means giving up the last piece of ground, and if you did that you'd be surrendering, you'd be allowing yourself to turn into a different person. I can't help you make that choice. Each of us has to decide for ourselves.

Think of Communion Town. Can we say how we would have behaved, if it had been us in the place of the citizens as they were surrounded by those things? Things that, in spite of what they were, gave the uncanny impression of having a coordinated and even a compassionate purpose. They were carrying plastic canisters of clean water and packets of all-but-fresh food pilfered from the refuse bins of supermarkets. They offered these gifts with nods of encouragement and gestures of hospitality.

I don't think any of us are in a position to moralise on what ensued. All we can do is state the facts as we know them: that after a night and a day trapped underground, every one of those people accepted food and drink from the monsters without hesitation. It's clear in the security footage. You can watch, if you have a strong stomach, as an overweight man still wearing his jacket and tie crams his mouth with a hunk of bread that has been torn for him by one of the *homines*, and as a young woman cups her hands, the most natural thing in the world, to catch the water that one of them is pouring for her.

They must have known the consequences of what they did. By the time the would-be rescuers succeeded in bringing the lifts back to life and prising open the fire doors, there were no human beings left in the tunnels for them to save. Nothing was left down there except the pests, the meaningless creatures that slink with the stray cats and cockroaches in the underparts of the city, and those were fit only to be driven off into the dark with oaths and stones. There are twenty-seven more of the wretched things now than there were before.

★   ★   ★

31

I'm not going to hide my disappointment with Nicolas. He had the chance to improve matters for himself and he turned it down, in the petulant, deliberate way that he has. For reasons that frankly elude me, he prefers to leave everything up to you. But I'm not too sorry, because, it occurs to me now, you were always the one who fascinated the most. Nicolas had his pleasing qualities, certainly, but you, Ulya, you've always been the mystery. You know, I believe that since you came to this city you've not shown anyone a glimmer of what goes on inside. Did you give yourself away, perhaps just once? I don't believe you did.

But you've been holding yourself apart for too long now, refusing. I'm here, but I can't help unless you let me. Think of this as your true arrival in the city. Do you remember how, once, soon after that first glum morning in the Terminus, you spent a long time by the seafront, lost in thought? I was with you then, too, though you didn't notice me. A storm was setting up offshore, and you must have been cold in that cheap plastic raincoat, but you walked there for an hour. I don't know what it looked like to you, but to me the sky was a cavernous auditorium, its hangings dark and threadbare and its plasterwork falling apart before our eyes. The sea was full of the anticipatory movements of an audience; rustling programmes, shushing itself, waiting for the spotlight to snap the boards into existence under your feet. I sniffed the chilly, promising air and felt a tingle of excitement, and I was on the point of calling out to you. But I knew it wasn't yet time, and so I waited, and now at last the chatter has turned to attention and the hush is beginning to stretch, and you have to decide if you're a singer, a magician or a clown.

We can make a beginning here. Yes. I feel a special moment approaching. I'm hanging on your words. Now take your time. Breathe in.

PART II

PART II

THE SONG OF SERELIGHT FAIR

I saw her on the street today. Another pedestrian pushed in front of me and she was there, already moving past, carrying a takeaway espresso and grasping the strap of her shoulder bag. She'd bought a smart new coat for the autumn, and her hair was cut above the shoulders, but it was the old shade of red again. I ducked towards a news-stand as if I were studying the magazines. She'd prefer that, I thought. She had somewhere to go. For the space of a single foot-step, there was nothing in between us but air, and I could have spoken to her without raising my voice, but then the space widened and rush hour commuters filled it, pushing us further and further apart. I followed her for a short distance, just to see if I could stay close, but she outpaced me and I lost her as she boarded a tram. As I watched her disappear a song came into my head, an old song I used to know. I've been singing it to myself ever since.

The first time we met, she was climbing into a rick-shaw. It was a bitter night and the two of them had

37

just emerged from the yellow mouth of the Communion Town metro, breathing steam and protesting at the cold. She seemed merry and disputatious, and her boyfriend, a big man in leather gloves and a fine wool overcoat, was finding her difficult to manage. She resisted for a moment as he helped her into the seat. Spots of snow were softening on their coats and in her loose hair. I thought I recognised her from somewhere.

'That's what he's here for,' I heard the boyfriend say. He leant forward, slapped my shoulder and told me an address in Cento Hill. As he settled into the chair, reaching an arm around her, I lifted the bar and took the strain.

If you wanted to pull a rickshaw, you rented it for the night from one of the toughs at the rank off the pedestrian mall. Once he had secured the cash in his money-belt, dropped the chains onto the pavement and told you to have it back by six, you hauled the chair, with its canvas hood and bicycle wheels, around to the galleria to wait for students and tourists to come out of the night-clubs. You could usually cover the hire and more besides, if you were good at spotting the ones who'd leg it without paying, and those who'd show you a knife and take your night's earnings. Most of the drunks were harmless, but many found the idea of riding a rickshaw hilarious. They would give false destinations or direct you along a labyrinthine route and collapse in mirth when you arrived back where you had started; or they'd simply yell encouragements and fling their rubbish at the back of your head. I had a small melted hole where someone had flicked a cigarette butt into the hood of my jacket. On a good night you could make a decent profit, especially if the weather was foul.

Soaked to the knees, my plimsolls frigid, I splattered through the snowmelt with his voice droning behind me. Damp flakes funnelled down between the granite facades, showing in the streetlights before blotting themselves out on the pavement.

We were halfway to Cento Hill when the rickshaw wrenched itself sideways. I narrowly avoided slamming my chin into the bar as dirty iced water slopped over my ankles and metal grated on stone. One of the wheels had slipped into a pothole. I caught my breath and leant into the bar to test how badly we were jammed.

The rickshaw stuck, then shifted abruptly, and I staggered forward to save myself from falling. Turning, I saw that the boyfriend had climbed out. He beckoned to me, and said:

'Do you know what these are?'

He sounded very calm, very self-controlled.

'These are brand new Jas Copeland loafers. Have you any idea how much they cost?'

His breath fogged my glasses.

'Is it unreasonable to expect that you should be capable of doing your job without destroying my property? Do you think that's unfair? More to the point, are you intending to compensate me for the damage?'

I didn't reply, but I had a notion I wouldn't be getting paid for this run.

'I thought not,' he said. I could tell that this conversation wearied him very much. 'Hold out your hand. The right one. Palm upwards. Come on, get on with it.'

Without knowing why, I found myself obeying. I watched my right hand reach out to offer him my palm. He took off his belt, wrapped half its length around his fist, and tugged, testing its strength. Then he stopped. She had climbed out as well, and was finding her footing on the treacherous pavement.

'Wait a mo,' he said, his tone changing. 'Where are you going, we're nowhere –'

She ignored him and picked her way around the mired rickshaw. As she went past, she leaned close to me and said: 'You shouldn't let him speak to you like that.'

The crystals fell in behind her as she walked away.

Ten days later at the Institute of Humane Sciences, a lecture had just ended and the central hall was blocked with students, their voices flooding the barrel-vault roof which had previously echoed only the squeaks of my rubber soles. My daytime job was for an agency which supplied me with dark green overalls and sent me to the university, where

I worked my way around the corridors, lecture theatres and seminar rooms, wielding long-handled pincers and pushing a cart stocked with cleaning products and refuse bags.

The students drank coffee from tall paper cups and had a lot to say. The girls' hands flashed and the boys squared up to each other jokily with their chins raised. I trundled along the edge of the hall. This, I had realised, was where I had seen her before, and since that snowy night I had glimpsed her almost every day, arguing eagerly with other students, carrying books out of the library or, often, quarrelling in public with one tall youth or another – it pleased her to embarrass her admirers. As I caught sight of her now, though, she was glancing around, fiddling with an unlit cigarette, not quite listening to her friends.

Without warning she turned her back on them and strode towards me. I fumbled hastily in my cart.

'You can't keep staring,' she said, 'and then have nothing to say to me.'

Her friends, their circle still open from where she had broken away, watched us. I was at a loss and said nothing. Her eyes looked sore, as if she'd been out late somewhere smoky, but they remained fixed on me, insisting on an answer.

'What are you going to do, then?'

Her bedroom was up in the roof of one of the grand old Cento Hill tenements. Lying tangled in

41

a sheet, watching the snow dot the pane above my face, I thought about the daft bounty of the universe. This warm, shambolic nest, with her paperbacks heaped on the mantelpiece, photos of her family tacked to the walls, her guitar leaning in the corner, drawings her friends had made for her and postcards they'd sent, many-coloured underthings trailing from the dresser drawer: yesterday I couldn't have begun to imagine it. A stray hair on the pillow tickled my cheek: it was crimson with a dark inch at the root. The toothpaste-streaked sink was lined with lipsticks, mascara tubes and contact lens paraphernalia. Her eyes troubled her, I had learnt, but she refused to wear her glasses.

I struggled among the sheets until I was propped up on my elbows, and let my laughter pass as a silent shudder. A wave of sleepiness followed, and I considered giving into it. I breathed in the spicy fug. The city lay outside like a vast gift for which I had always only needed to ask. A song was playing. I'd never heard anything like it, but the twangling music was just another miracle of the afternoon, and I let it run through me, the singer drawling about silver saxophones, the Queen of Spades and a dancing child with a flute.

Bitter smoke had been on her breath. My mouth had never tasted like this before, so sugary and rank. My head never ached so dashingly. The sight of her buttoning an oversized old shirt, five minutes ago, standing on tiptoe to see across the rooftops, had rinsed my memory clean. She was making tea and I had no idea what would happen when she came back.

Up in her room, we listened to more old songs. A woman made her acoustic guitar buzz and thrum, and sang in a warbling contralto about romantics and idealists, poets and artists. *Silvertongue, you have placed your plans In your sweet, sweet nature and your hard hands . . .*

When the album had finished, I lay in silence, lingering at the edge of that world. It was late. She was dozing, her face hidden by her hair. The only light came from a decorative jar of red glass in which she had lit a candle-stub. Soft shadows pitched on the wall. My glasses lay on her bedside table, my jeans on the floor.

Without much thought I sat up and leant over for her guitar. I had never held one before now, and its lightness surprised me. Cross-legged on the bed, I tried how its curve lay in my lap and how I needed to support the neck. I touched the strings, one by one, then together. It hadn't been played in a while, I thought. I turned the screws, as I'd seen the buskers do at the galleria, until the notes sounded right. I fitted my fingers to the fretboard and let the strings speak softly, then strummed, as quiet as I could, with the pad of my thumb. I didn't know how to play, but my finger-tips began to move up and down the frets, exploring.

After some experiment I found a clean chord, and then another. I adjusted a finger and the chord opened up, suspending itself; then I lifted the finger entirely and discovered the minor.

Still quietly, very slowly, cautious not to damage the delicate find, I strummed a sequence of shapes. A tune was buried there. I hummed along with the chords, picking it out. It was a simple song, one I must have heard recently – I didn't know where or when. I felt my way through, learning how its simple phrases went around, and how they changed in the middle, then changed back. I played it again, and instead of humming, I sang, letting the small sound vibrate in my sinuses and the top of my throat. I didn't really know the words but I sang the syllables that seemed to fit. My tongue had never stepped so well around my teeth and palate.

My palm stilled the strings. She shifted drowsily.

'Keep playing.'

The next time I stayed over she went out early and left me sleeping. Later in the morning I found myself in her kitchen with the two girls who shared the flat, old friends from back home. They brewed coffee and insisted on cooking me pancakes, then swapped indulgent smiles as they watched me eat. The flat smelled of cigarettes and perfume. They lolled on the kitchen chairs, clasping their bare feet in their hands to touch up the polish on their toenails, and tugging their fingers through

44

their tangled hair. They didn't seem to mind discussing their private lives in my company.

'. . . *still* in love with me.'

'Oh, yuck.'

'So that's . . . fun. Yeah.'

'And this was the one . . .'

'Cried when I said I didn't like him that way.'

'Not awkward at all.'

'He keeps sending messages saying *I think about you every day*. You know.'

'Oh dear.'

'So I'm quite glad I'll be away in the summer. Give him a chance to maybe find someone, you know?'

'You poor thing.'

As they talked, a new way of life revealed itself. Theirs was a complicated youth, a fine game: they were free to do as they liked yet they lived at the mercy of lawless passions. Their relationships were troubled with their fathers and mothers, their sisters and boyfriends. They knew how to trade just a kiss for a kiss. They named strange nightclubs. They were jaded and sweet-natured, in and out of love, adventuring in the contradictions of their own emotions. No love affair could last, but what beautiful, bruised hearts they had. I took it all in, stirred to find I was capable of such sophistication. They knocked their cigarettes on the rim of a saucer and poured me more coffee, which I did my best to drink.

Later the doorbell buzzed and two young men

arrived, beefy types in striped scarves and good coats who walked in without breaking their conversation, their voices ringing importantly through the flat. They looked like members of the same sports team. One of them went to one of the flatmates, sliding a thumb into the waist of her jeans, and she wrapped her arms around his neck. When they caught sight of me both men stopped in their tracks just long enough to assess the situation; then they relaxed, and their eyes slid past me. I left soon after.

I would happily have spent all my time in the slovenly female warmth of her room, sitting on the bed with the guitar in my lap, working out one song after another from her collection, or lying face to face on the pillow, my hand on her hip, watching her lips form words while her music, turned down low, murmured *were they in love, or only in love with a song* . . . On mornings when I woke up in her bed, I was perfectly indifferent to any fate I might meet that day. I wouldn't have minded if on my way home I had been mown down by a tram or shot through the heart by a vengeful rival.

One morning she sat up and gave me an appraising look.

'It's my cousin's birthday tonight,' she said. 'I want you to come.'

While she was at class I visited a department store and bought, for a startling price, my first suit. The fabric was scratchy, the trousers too long, the shoulders far too broad, and the whole outfit hung off me, but I supposed I'd get used to it, and to the constriction of the domino-patterned polyester tie which had come packaged with the shiny charcoal shirt. I couldn't stretch to new shoes, but maybe my plimsolls would go unnoticed.

We rode out to Rosamunda by tram, and found ourselves in a suburb full of unobtrusive mansions behind evergreen hedges. We strolled the rest of the way to a walled garden. It was a private park for residents of the district, she explained; you paid a subscription. She spoke in low tones to a guard in a kiosk, while he gazed at me, sucking his teeth and rubbing a pimple on his cheek. He took a minute to think about it, but finally the gate opened on its pneumatic hinge.

We followed the path through the park, around landscaped hillocks and a miniature lake. For the first time this year the air was balmy. Pale green spikes poked through in the flowerbeds, and handsome iron lamp posts lined the pathway, their globes not yet lit. A game of tennis was finishing up. Other figures moved ahead of us towards the party. Beyond the lake stood a pavilion with a rococo conservatory, from which light spilled out to a terrace set with white iron tables. Decorous jazz wandered from the french windows, and as we drew closer there was the intricate murmur of voices and the chiming of glasses on glasses. The pavilion hung above the lake like the idea of another life, a future swimming in minty light and odoured evening air.

I would have liked to walk around in the dusk for longer, admiring the glow from a distance, but she was distracted. She undid her hand from mine and led the way in. Recently she had dyed her hair a chemical-looking carmine, and for a moment as she moved ahead she seemed quite unfamiliar. Bodies surrounded us. Lights flared. Someone called her name: the stream of the crowd caught and whirled her away.

The knot of my tie was pressing on my throat. Would it matter if I took it off? I couldn't see anyone else in one. None of the partygoers, it appeared, had made any effort to prepare, but all were elegant in their soft shirts and worn jeans, short dresses and block-heeled mules. They spoke with their hands and stood with tilted hips. The music – louche, swung instrumental standards – was provided by a trio in the conservatory. Everyone seemed to be absorbed in exceptional conversations; they scintillated, debated, gossiped and flirted; their eyes were never still.

What was happening here? I saw no clues. I dodged through the crowd and paused in the shelter of a grotesque ornament, a decorative cage containing a pair of artificial brass chaffinches. As the birds hopped along their perch, a tune played from inside each of their breasts, each just a couple of tinny notes, tricking in and out of harmony, over and over. They canoodled, blinking red glass eyes, then whirred against the bars, their wings flickering faster than I could follow. I listened to them, my head touching the wires of the cage, until I began to feel conspicuous again.

Behind the bar a cohort of waiters polished glasses and mixed drinks. They wore smart navy jackets and white breeches, and their faces had been painted with such care that they seemed masks of polite white enamel, each with an identical, gentle set to the lips. Their hair, dyed poster-paint yellow, was tied in braids and secured with tiny bows. Others, identical to the bar staff, slipped deferentially through the throng, positioning their trays beneath empty glasses as the guests' fingers let go.

All the waiters moved with the same practised discretion, wasting no gesture, spinning like weathercocks attuned to the needs of the partygoers, meeting no one's eye. They were silent, except for the music-box tunes that tinkled away continuously in their chests. Each of them, I noticed, had a slightly different melody; you could make them out, pinging and plinking away beneath the chatter. Each repetitive phrase interlocked with the others, and seemed to fit with the trio's jazz. I wondered if they could change tempo and key signature to match the local ambience. As they went past, I tried to lean close and hear better: perhaps it was the inbuilt rhythm and harmony of these small tunes that enabled them to serve everyone so gracefully.

The room's clamour swelled, everyone determined to talk loud enough to drown out everyone else. Jaws worked, lips pouted, eyes danced. An outflung arm caused a waiter to veer and weave, smiling, with a loaded tray. Beyond the windows it was solid dark. The noise and heat and alcoholic humidity had fused into a thick pane between me and the room. Beside me, a youth with dark smudges under his eyes was talking to a girl in a shiny black wig.

'How do you know her?' he was asking.

She sighed. 'How do you think?'

'Um. Right. So . . . what do you do?'

'*Do?* I dropped out, so I work in a shop. All right?'

'Right.'

There was a pause.

'Um, which one?'

A longer pause. Then: 'Dees. All right?'

'Draughtsman Gray? Very nice!'

'What's nice about it?'

'Well, it's – it's so exclusive . . .'

'Yeah, I work in a shop. Thanks for that.'

They fell silent, although neither moved. At my other elbow, a young man in blue-tinted spectacles was leaning on the bar, smoking a cigarette. When he glanced in my direction I pulled a neighbourly face. He considered me without hurry, then looked away.

The room darkened and swam and I realised that the party was a sort of paranoid conspiracy. These ruthless creatures were watching each other in perfect mistrust. They smiled little incredulous smiles. Was something wrong with my suit? Had I overlooked some social nicety? I was the only living thing in a place full of cunningly animated mannequins. I had no idea how long I'd been in here, but I needed to get away. I pushed off from the bar and began to sidle back across the room. I couldn't see her anywhere. I caught sight of myself in a mirror, a waxy face sprouting from an ill-fitting collar. Behind me a french window was open, and without further thought I escaped into the dark outside.

I took a breath, letting cool air flow into me, and crossed the terrace to sit on a wall. Twilight had submerged the garden, but evening was still bright above the skyline. A few partygoers were dallying out here in pairs and threes, but none paid me any mind. Seen from outside, the party appeared benign. I exhaled.

'You haven't spoken to me all evening.'

She sat down beside me.

'I'm glad you've been enjoying yourself,' she said in a pointed undertone. She was glaring at me. 'I was watching, you know. You should have seen yourself. I should have known better than to bring you. Oh, don't even try. You'll only make it worse.'

As she spoke, it dawned on me that I had never seen her so angry. Dumbly I understood that I'd got the evening wrong. All at once it was obvious: I'd got it all wrong, somehow, from the beginning.

I said nothing.

'It was so blatant,' she hissed. 'Don't you care what anyone thinks?'

I wondered what I had expected if not this. It occurred to me there were probably certain words I could say, now, that would change what was happening, but I could not begin to guess what they were. I stared down at my ragged plimsolls and wondered how I would get home tonight.

'Don't you dare ignore me!' She shook my arm. I looked up, and her eyes searched my face.

'Did you think for an instant about the position you've put me in? No, you couldn't care less, could you. It wouldn't even cross your mind. Don't you have any *shame*?'

She paused, slightly out of breath. Then her fingernails were in my scalp and our mouths jammed together. Her weight laid into me so that we tipped backwards and rolled off the wall into a flowerbed. After a frantic minute I struggled up and hauled her to her feet. I pinned her wrists in my hands and led her deeper into the park, to find privacy among the hedges.

New experience made me bold, and I began to frequent parts of the city I would never have dared before. I found myself walking at a slower pace, happy to get lost in the spacious maze of all these flower tubs and iron railings, these stained white pavements, locked restaurants, fire escapes and commercial accessways, these airy canyons whose windowsills were crowded with geraniums, these deep arcades where shopfronts glinted: chocolatiers and milliners and dealers in delightful bits of junk. One afternoon near the November Bridge I discovered a secluded square dominated by a grand café. I decided to go inside and spend a while writing in the notebook I had bought myself earlier that day. I thought I had an idea for a song.

Inside, the café was a single high-roofed space, full of wood and brass and potted palms, the customers in pairs or alone. Two or three figures moved among them with silver pots. As I sat, a waiter appeared and took my order: moments later a tiny cup of black coffee stood in front of me and the waiter was melting away again even as he answered my thanks with a bow. His ceruse-white face paint was flawless. The tinkling music-box phrase that accompanied his movements stepped continually from major to minor and back. An overweight customer, sweating into a double-breasted wool suit, watched him narrowly as he crossed the room.

I sipped my coffee and opened my notebook at the first page. The words, which had seemed to fit so well in my head as I walked along, were harder to get hold of now that the tip of my pencil was resting on unmarked paper.

The fat man drained a bulbous glass of some viscid, dark-brown liqueur, and signalled to the waiter for more and quick about it. His small features, which were dwarfed by the swags of his cheeks and chins, wore a congested expression. His pointed patent shoes rested wide apart under the table and his short thighs lay puddled over the seat of his chair.

As the bottle was brought to his table, the customer glowered stolid-faced in the other direction. From my vantage point, though, I could see his hand settling on the back of the waiter's thigh, and sliding upwards. There was a clatter: the sticky brown fluid had slopped across the table, and a couple of spots were spreading on the customer's shirt. The waiter pulled a napkin from his apron and pressed it to the tabletop.

The customer, chins quivering, slapped the bottle from the waiter's hand so that it bounced across the tiled floor, splashing gouts of liqueur. As the waiter stooped to retrieve it, he was jabbed in the behind by a pointed, polished toecap, hard enough to send him sprawling in the mess. The fat man resumed his seat with a righteous twitch of his trouser legs, his eyes darting around the other patrons of the café. My cup rattled in its saucer. No one moved. Conversations continued; the other waiters went about their business. I swallowed the last of my coffee, and hesitated. The waiter rose to his knees, his white shirt blotted with syrup and grime.

The door at the back of the café banged and a young man appeared, his feet clicking fast on the tiles. His tie was slung over his shoulder and his hair neatly gelled. He saw the urgency of the situation: he caught the waiter a ringing slap across the back of the head, then took hold of his ear, dragged him to his feet and propelled him through the rear door. Returning to the customer's table, bobbing and bowing, he began what promised to be a virtuosic apology. Another waiter brought a mop for the floor.

The espresso machine rasped, and on the other side of the café a pair of ladies exclaimed their agreement about something or other. I closed my notebook and stood up.

One afternoon she brought me to a grimy street behind Festal Place, to a shop whose window was full of fiddles, mandolins, ukuleles and banjos: glossy wood in every autumn shade. Inside, guitars dangled overhead like extraordinary fruit. The myopic, dandruffed shopkeeper seemed as doubtful of my business here as I was myself, but both of us went along with what she wanted. Hopelessly conscious of my ignorance, I pointed to instruments which he lifted down for me, and, sitting on a tall stool, I ran my hands over the strings, strumming and picking the most impressive-sounding figures I had so far managed to invent. Right away I realised how flimsy and ill-made the guitar in her bedroom was. These were real instruments, sound and responsive, sweet and resonant. They had no end of music in them if I could find it.

I chose a traditional guitar with an unusually small body, a maple veneer and an inlay of darker wood around the sound hole. Every joint and curve, every detail, was flawless. In my hands it had the strange feel of future intimacy. It seemed heavy for its size, but the lightest touch pinned the strings neatly to the fretboard. I hung back, holding the instrument in both hands, while she paid. I never learnt how much it cost.

The city had music wherever you went, I discovered. Walking home from work through Belltown Park, I heard a tuneful racket from the old bandstand, where two bearded youths and a pale girl were playing amplified folk tunes, singing close harmonies through tinny microphones. Most people were ignoring them or pausing for half a song and moving on, but I stayed an hour, listening with envious delight. A grey-haired woman and a small boy stopped in front of the bandstand, her arm around his shoulders and his fist bunching her coat; she gave me a sharp look, but then seemed to decide I was permissible. A gang of teenagers around a park bench whooped half-sarcastically after each song. As the band packed up, I left, wanting to approach them but not knowing what to say.

I went through all the music she had in her room, listening to the same songs over and over and shadowing them on my guitar, chord by chord, until I knew them by heart. For a while I was preoccupied with a dead singer who had a trick of double-tracking his voice on his recordings. His eloquent, subdued melodies were so distinctive they must have been coded deep down in his cells.

Daylight from your bedroom window, That was what we wore ... My own songs were diffident and wary, so far. I could finish the writing quickly – on more than one occasion, half an hour of panic, strumming and scribbling with my face inches from guitar strings and notebook, gave me the whole of a song – but I was slow to begin anything new. My voice was sweet enough but I could only hold it steady over a single octave. It would surely improve with practice, and I reckoned my vocal muscles were getting stronger already. The interval of two notes could divide your heart and the tug of words against rhythm could mend it: I'd stumbled on the means to say whatever was true in this life. I only wanted the skill to do it.

We went out to a gig, a showcase night for promising local acts that took place monthly in a Communion Town bar. We walked across the November Bridge, through the Esplanade and under the floodlit face of the Autumn Palace – the trams weren't running, for some reason, and in the central metro plaza we glimpsed a confusion of ambulances and police cars – then continued down the Mile, across Impasto Street and into a side lane where, past a bouncer and down a flight of stairs, the music had already begun. The band, a duo, consisted of a long-haired girl who squeezed dark, complicated chords from a concertina and sang, while an older man – her raffish uncle, we speculated – waggled his eyebrows and played the clarinet. As far as this duo were concerned, a song was a melodramatic story full of ghosts, criminals, murders and revenges, told in spiky rhythms and pungent key-changes. When I went back to my songs the next day, they seemed flimsy and humdrum, and it was obvious that they could never win the cheers and foot-stamps that the duo's rowdy ballads had drawn from the crowd. The very idea of playing in public made me ashamed: but, for all that, I knew I was not going to give up.

In her room, late, I let her persuade me to play. She never asked if the songs were about her. Perhaps they made her shy, as nothing else did, or perhaps she understood better than me what a song really was. I had to keep myself from demanding more assurances, wanting her to guarantee that they were good enough – for what, I had no idea.

After graduating she took a job raising funds for a small, well-connected development charity. Spring was waking the city up just then, opening doors and windows, warming the separate streets into a single organism. Time felt spacious. If you woke early, the day was there waiting for you, untouched. Each morning the pitched window above her bed turned a fresh card from the deck of clear skies. Even a lunch-hour was wide enough to get lost in, and a free afternoon contained all possibilities. The dusks kept lengthening and you felt that if you took the right path, up the wynds past a paper-lanterned tea garden into the Old Quarter, or along the river, towards the sky's end-of-the-world pinkness, you could follow the evening as far as you wanted and never reach nightfall.

I met her from work at the end of her first week in the job. The charity was based in a small city square whose limestone townhouses had been converted into solicitors' and architects' offices, advertising agencies and boutique business premises. She was bare-legged in a pleated dress. I had my guitar; I was seldom without it, now. We walked along Mino High Street, against a flow of young men with their suit jackets off and their ties loosened, and stopped for takeaway iced coffees.

As we left the café, she hesitated, handed me both of the cold plastic beakers and skipped back inside to visit the lavatory. I waited on the pavement, glancing over at a torpid down-and-out who sat with his forehead resting on his knees so that only his greasy wool cap was visible. As I stood there, a rusty noise like a sigh scraped from his chest. A few copper coins lay on the ground between his feet. I thought of adding to them, but my hands were full and I wasn't sure whether I had any change. I closed my eyes to feel the sun on my face, and smelt hot tar and rotting vegetables. I hummed a song from the park.

She re-emerged from the coffee shop, took her drink and slipped something into my hand. It was a scrap of cotton, still warm. 'Look after those for me,' she said, and held my eye for a few seconds.

A few streets away we found a bridge, and,

beside it, the top of a narrow brick staircase. I followed her down. The city's canals were a sunken world, dank and green, hanging below street level like a reflection. Bright algae lay just under the surface of the water, clumped around the remnants of shopping trolleys and rotten planks, while above the waterline vegetation flourished on worn structures of brick. We walked the towpath, pushing through curtains of weeping willow and stooping along the tunnels. On the other side of the canal the unkempt ends of back gardens sloped down to the water. She kept just ahead of me, twitching away from my hands and hurrying us down the dozing watercourse until we found a place where you could leave the path to enter a strip of undisturbed woodland. Beyond it was a meadow, a place to learn about bark's texture, damp earth and the taste of grass. Later I strummed my guitar.

One Sunday afternoon she sat curled on her sofa, reading *Under the Net* and threading the fingers of one hand in and out of my hair. I was cross-legged on the floor beside her, running through my finished songs. By now I had six or seven I was more or less happy with. As the city sailed towards summer, half the pubs in the central district were advertising folk-club nights, photocopied fliers for local gigs were pasted on every hoarding and bus shelter, and most coffee shops I passed seemed to contain a boy or a girl perched on a stool with an acoustic guitar. This evening I would play at my first open mic.

The one I'd chosen took place in the upper room of a pub on the Part Bridge. I'd gone last week, just to listen. As I practised, now, with my back against the sofa and her fingertips at my nape, I held in my mind the image of that dingy room with its low stools and tables and its corner stage one step up from the floor, under walls and ceiling papered with old theatre posters. Tonight the place would be packed with musicians pulling on pints and beer bottles, each waiting for a chance to perform. Some would be old hands who turned up every week, but others would be new. If you wanted to play you had to arrive early and sign up for your ten-minute slot with the pair of middle-aged men who ran the night.

Last week they had taken the first slot themselves, performing raucous, straightforward folk-pop with harmonica and twelve-string guitar, to the delight of the crowd. A mixture of acts had followed: shy singer-songwriters mumbled their private codes into their chests, picking sparingly at their guitars, while others, more extroverted, bashed at their instruments with no aim beyond getting everyone clapping along. One young man specialised in extended, string-snapping solos like a stadium rock star, and as he stepped down from the stage he held his guitar up at shoulder height to receive its due applause. A woman draped in green taffeta spent her allotted time with her eyes shut, using a wooden pestle to draw one continuous, weird note from a brass singing-bowl, and improvising in a high-pitched wail.

As I watched all this, it became clear that the stage was a bubble of delusions, and that these people had come here in pursuit of some mistaken idea of themselves. But then, halfway through the night, a mournful-looking, deep-voiced girl played a single song, honest and catchy and personal without a trace of self-absorption. While she sang I felt the presence of the whole city, live and real outside the beery room. Colours and textures opened in my head. Her lyrics were casual phrases, ordinary rhythms of speech with everyday flashes of anger, emphasis and silliness, as though she was just throwing together fragments of a conversation; but the words fell into patterns. Her playing riffled through me.

That was what I wanted, I knew, without articulating it to myself or really understanding why. I'd practised all I could. I'd borrowed her laptop to make demos, layering strumming underneath fingerpicking and working out harmonies to sing with myself. I had listened endlessly to these record-ings, alert to their flaws and frailties, correcting and polishing. What did I want with the offhand approval of strangers? I didn't know, but communing in secret with a laptop wasn't enough. Two songs were ready to perform but I was hesitating over a third. Was it tender and truthful, or would it make that upstairs room fall uncomfortably silent? I uncrossed my legs, stretched my socked feet across the carpet, and began to play through the intro again.

She laid her book down. I looked around to find her glaring at me, and the words of the first verse faltered on my tongue. She let her breath out in a disbelieving snort.

'You keep on playing that,' she said. 'I'm right here! What are you trying to tell me?'

I opened my mouth to explain that I had to practise for tonight, that I needed to work out whether it was ready to perform –

'Yes, the damn open mic night, I know *all about* it,' she said. 'So what? You think you can keep on playing that song, over and over, and I'll just sit here and listen?'

She had raised herself up against the arm of the sofa. I twisted around to face her, the guitar slipping from my lap with a soft discord.

'Don't interrupt me,' she said, 'I'm getting going now. Are you actually trying to torment me, is that it? Have I done something to deserve this?' Her eyes were bright with frustration and, I noticed with a shock, also with tears. One brimmed over, then the other, brushing trails down her cheeks.

'You just keep on playing those damn songs – and yes, they're fine, they're *beautiful* – you keep on playing until I start to think they're all just words and they don't mean anything. Or maybe you're doing it on purpose, seeing how long I'll smile nicely and keep waiting. Were you ever actually going to *say* it? It's nothing strange, you know! It's not difficult!'

She rose and crossed the room to steady herself against the mantelpiece, sniffed loudly and rubbed her face with the heels of her hands. She let out a big sigh. 'Sooz and Ceelie are leaving at the end of the month,' she said. 'I wanted you to move in, can you believe that? I thought you could move in here and it'd be just us. How stupid am I? I mean, how was I supposed to ask, when you couldn't – when you wouldn't even say? Never mind. Forget it.'

I was on my feet, the guitar still in my hand. I took a hesitant step towards her, but she turned away. My skin stung, my head pulsed with pressure, my vision darkened. Sunlight fell through the window and her novel still lay open on the sofa, but the room had been pumped full of cold water. I couldn't speak. Her eyes were hidden behind her forelock. My guitar, brushing against my leg, gave another gentle, tuneless twang, an isolated syllable of sound.

'You'd better go,' she said.

I didn't play at the open mic that night. After leaving her flat, I crossed the street and hailed a tram, but when I felt in my pockets I found I'd brought no money with me. I had to apologise and climb back down to the street. The driver swore as the doors slapped shut and the rubber wheels sneered away.

I set off on foot instead, and walked a long way, not noticing where I was heading but not wanting to stop moving. Eventually the daylight failed and drizzle began to mist down. No more trams went past.

I passed through negative spaces, beside railway sidings, under archways clogged with litter and past industrial lots where the floodlights blinded me with after-images of concrete and wire. All was darkness and halogen. I didn't know where I was. A long way off I could hear a major road roaring like the lip of a waterfall. Soon, I thought, I would surely merge into the limits of the city itself. But instead I began to hear sounds ahead, yelps and bellows, the coughs of machines, sirens, infra-bass noise beating away in cellars deep under the pavement. Around me the streets came to a comfortless kind of life, warmed by exhaust fumes, lit by pornography shops and nightclubs that had not redecorated in twenty years.

I negotiated a grille in the pavement belching steam that stank of fish and starch. A woman in a shredded anorak observed me, while beside her on the doorstep her companion tugged at his dreadlocks and, in time with the faltering ditty of his innards, croaked for help, unless he was saying some other word. In the gutter a slow trickle of fluid found its way around rotting fruit, broken glass and the remains of a dog. Kerbstones and railings took their definition from pink neon signs. Further along, a vagrant, dressed in sacking but with enough sense of propriety still to have smeared streaks of white stuff down her cheeks, wandered from person to person, holding out palsied hands, ignored. A youth spat casually in her direction. Overhead, half the windowpanes had been smashed.

I turned the corner into a broader street, but, before I could take another step, a man burst from a doorway in front of me, knocking me aside as he went sprawling full length in the road. Catcalls and laughter pursued him from inside the bar. The man cursed, rolled on his side and retrieved his hat. He hauled himself to his feet with the aid of a lamp post, peering redly out of a mess of cuts and bruises, one hand fumbling to straighten his ruined tie. Someone told him to sleep it off.

I gripped my guitar case. The street swarmed with citizens of the late night, jostling their way from one den to another in search of whatever it was that they needed. As they pushed past they moved me out of the way with cordial roughness, so that I found myself manhandled along the street by the crowd, smeared with its perspiration, smelling its armpits and breathing its alcohol breath. It was easier to accept the embrace than resist it, easier to go where I was guided. I felt that if I chose I could simply let myself be carried forward forever as a particle in the city's bloodstream, dissolving. I tasted hot fat marbled through the air around a cluster of stalls selling sausages, sweating pies and whelks. I was hungry but my pockets were empty.

Up ahead, somebody was whistling tunelessly. Surprised at how the cracked melody pierced the din, I craned to see where it was coming from. The whistler was pestering people, jinking back and forth to obstruct them, conducting his own performance with his forefingers. He was an emaciated creature with a long, bony face and a shock of pale hair which in the glow of mercury vapour could have been peroxide blond or prematurely white. He kept on repeating the same jingle, a few shrill notes forced between his front teeth.

Periodically he paused, grinned and held out an open hand to the crowd. No one responded, but he didn't seem to mind. He would caper lopsidedly along the street and whistle his phrase again. Drawing closer, he gave me a hostile glare.

'Keep moving,' he said. 'These ones are mine.'

His skin had a damp, unwholesome texture, as if its pores were clogged with powder, and his eyes were the hard and sunken eyes of an insomniac. I thought he might be suffering from some serious illness.

'This is my street. Get your own.'

Taken aback, I said nothing. Then I noticed that his eyes were darting to the guitar case in my hand, and I understood what he meant: what he thought I was and what he was telling me would happen. If I were to do as he told me, I would keep moving until I found a street of my own; there I'd find a place to sit and play, people would give me pennies and soon I'd be able to buy myself something to eat. At this vision of the future, sweat prickled inside my clothes and I felt an irresistible need to get away from this whistling scarecrow. I turned and walked.

'Hey, you.'

He was limping along after me. He walked painfully, pressing a hand to his groin and pitching sideways at every other step, but he could still move at speed.

'You!'

He grabbed hold of my sleeve. Although his clothes were wrecked, he wore a fresh carnation in his lapel, its tight green bud barely showing the white furled inside.

'Where are you going?' he said. 'What's the hurry?'

He grinned the ingratiating grin he used on his patrons, and whistled a couple of notes.

'Wait a minute. Listen. Listen, I had some songs.'

He was close enough for me to smell decay on his breath and see the clots of grime in the tangled white mop. His fingertips brushed my guitar case.

'They call me idle,' he said. 'They call me good for nothing. But I don't believe them. They don't know our calling, you and me. They don't know what we are.'

He nodded, showing me the gaps in his teeth.

'You see? I'm just like you. A flâneur. I walk through the city. I hear its songs and I sing them back, and all I ask in return . . .'

I wanted to walk away, but there was something

68

needy in his face, something desperate, that would not let me.

'I was a guitar man once, too,' he said. 'I made songs in my time. Such songs. Set them on their feet, they'd fly. You know what I'm saying?'

He tapped the back of my hand.

'I can tell you know. There's nothing like making a true song, a real one. It might take a lifetime but it doesn't matter. It costs you everything but you never think twice about paying. But then it stopped. I lost it. Something went wrong, and all the songs left me. It was a long time ago. I can't remember.'

His fingers rested on my hand that was gripping the guitar case. His eyes were fixed on the instrument.

'I wish,' he said, 'I only wish I could try once more to play my songs.'

I held tighter.

'I only want to borrow it,' he said. 'I think maybe it'll come back. Maybe I'll play like I used to. I only want to play one song.'

He was staring at me in what looked like dire need. I pictured the two of us sitting down on the kerb and opening the case, and then his ragged voice lifting and his fingers rippling over the strings to release unforeseeable music. I imagined him restoring the guitar to my arms, and rising with a new ease, relieved of his pain.

'One song,' he said. 'Give me one song.'

I pulled away, grimacing in apology, and started

walking again. Behind me the whistler began to shout.

'Who are you?' he bawled. 'Where are *your* songs?'

He was still following me, dragging along with his broken gait, and before I could get away he made a grab for the guitar. We tusselled, and as I wrested the case away from him he stumbled backwards and fell. Sitting up, he coughed and wiped snot across his face with the back of his hand.

'They're not your songs, boy,' he said. 'They're mine. You'll see.'

He looked up at me with the same sly surmise I had seen on his face to begin with.

'A mirror,' he called after me. 'It's like looking into a mirror!'

But I heard no more from him, because as I turned another corner I realised where I was. This was Serelight Fair. The night's journey fell into place: I'd been here often enough pulling rickshaws for stag parties, and tonight I had only failed to recognise the district's drunken thoroughfares because I'd come by a roundabout route. I was fifteen minutes' walk from Three Liberties and my own bedsit.

As I set off in the right direction, the past night already seemed less than real.

It was close to dawn by the time I got back to the bedsit, exhausted from walking. Looking around,

I saw that I hadn't been back here in days. Heaps of dirty clothes lay on the floor and the dishes in the sink showed spots of mould. I looked in the fridge but there was nothing to eat. Outside my window, the glass tube of a streetlamp glowed against the beginnings of first light.

I snapped open the guitar case, lifted out the instrument and settled on my bed with my back against the wall, wide awake. I strummed aimlessly for a while, and then wrote a new song. It took twenty minutes and was the best I had ever written. It was still built around those same few favourite chords, more or less, but inside them and between them I discovered new kinds of longing, new kinds of sweet and bitter regret, not having to dig but finding them in plain view as you might find precious flotsam after a flood.

As I sang, my sinuses seemed to fill with a clean liquid. My voice grew thick. I could feel something twisting and tightening in my chest, and as I played – feeling for the shape of the song, making sure of the rhythm, trying out a pattern of fingerpicking, tracing the melody of verse and chorus, locating the bridge, piecing together the lyrics – the sensation grew deeper until I could have sworn that the twisting had levered my chest wide open and whatever it contained had been plundered, that she'd plunged her hands in up to the shoulders and ransacked me hollow, leaving nothing behind.

The title came last. Everything that had happened

between us, I realised, had folded itself down into a single night's walk through the city, sleepless and heartsore, and so the song must be named accordingly. It was called 'Serelight Fair'. I played until it was perfect and broad daylight was coming in at the window. Eventually I fell asleep.

She liked to walk through the park after work, so I waited all afternoon near the gate, leaning against the railings where the joggers and dog-walkers passed. I watched for a long time, occasionally thinking that I must have missed her, or imagining that she had walked right past but I had somehow failed to recognise her. Mostly I thought about nothing at all.

But when she appeared there was no mistaking her. She was in one of the short knitted dresses she wore with coloured tights, and she looked serious, gripping her shoulder bag close against her, with eyes forward, forehead creased and mouth pursed. I could never have missed her. She was the more strikingly herself for being a stranger again, another pedestrian on her way home to a life you could only guess at.

I hurried after her, calling her name. Heads turned, and she paused and waited, but her face gave nothing away. Other homebound workers stopped to watch me approach, and a couple of the males, seemingly by instinct, moved forward a step or two as if they might need to put themselves in between us: but they weren't sure of what they were seeing, and as we came together they turned dubiously away.

We stood still in the flow of passers-by, chilly among bright flowerbeds. She looked drawn and polite, but then all the distance drained from her face and left only a question behind. In my head I heard an old country song from her record collection. *I swear that I won't make your exit slow, But won't you break my heart before you go . . .* I reached for her hand and she let me take it. She gave me a tired, convalescent smile, as though she knew what it was that I wanted to say.

She was determined I should see the house where she had grown up. It was in the south, an hour's train journey out of the city through gentle yellow hills. In the middle of a hot afternoon we alighted at a market-town railway station and climbed into a taxi. As we were driven out of the town along narrow roads banked by groves in which olive-pickers were working, my nose started running and my eyes began to itch. I blew my nose loudly into my handkerchief and was ambushed by a sneezing fit. When I looked over at her, stricken, she burst out laughing. Over his shoulder, the taxi driver said something jocular that I didn't catch.

The setting of her childhood and adolescence was a villa in the colonial style, built around a large central courtyard, with terracotta tile roofs and stucco walls the colour of baked earth. The first-floor windows opened to broad balconies. As we climbed out of the taxi, the front doors of the house opened, and for an instant it appeared she had brought me here to introduce me to her exaggerated, faintly parodic doppelgänger. The resemblance was strong, in spite of the older woman's cream linen suit, her mass of orange hair, her cinched waist and billowing bosom. She wore heavy, precise make-up, with lips and eyebrows marked out in shapes identical to her daughter's. They kissed three times on alternating cheeks and then the mother turned with stately poise to acknowledge me, holding out a hand, like something held in tongs, for me to shake. In the shadows of the hall behind her I glimpsed two pre-teenaged forms and heard sisterly whispers, but as we went in they fled with a slapping of sandalled feet.

Lunch was about to be served on the terrace, her mother said. I followed them through the cool house. Father would not be joining us for lunch, her mother added as we emerged into the light again at the rear of the house, since he had so much work to do.

The terrace looked across a silver-grey valley. All the olive trees I could see, her mother told me, belonged to the family. In the middle distance I made out the red rooftops of the town, stacked in the lee of a hill. A heavy wooden table in the centre of the terrace was already set with bread, cured meat, salad, wine and olive oil. I brushed my hand against hers, but something had annoyed her; as we sat down to eat, she rolled her eyes, letting her hair fall sulkily across her face as if she regretted coming here at all. Her mother carried on the conversation single-handed, telling me I would find it most interesting to be here at harvest time and, what's more, I was especially fortunate because a Boy Singers Troupe was in town – I must make sure to see them perform because it was a fine old tradition and I must seldom have the opportunity . . . While she kept up a glassy monologue, the two girls, to whom I hadn't been introduced, exchanged continual scandalised glances, nudging each other under the table and occasionally exploding into giggles.

Later, as I was unpacking in the guest room, the younger of the girls wandered in behind me. Turning, I found her gazing thoughtfully at my guitar; I wasn't sure whether she had noticed I was here. Peering past me into my suitcase, she mentioned that her father wanted to see me in his study. I didn't know where that was, but before I could formulate the question she ran a fingernail across the strings of the guitar and walked out.

'Come in and close it,' her father said, when at length I knocked on the right door.

He had a tall man's stoop, and inclined his head as though to favour a slight deafness. He looked healthy and weather-beaten in his open-necked shirt. His dark grey hair was receding but he wore it long at the back. I thought for a second that he was going to make some violent physical movement, but instead he pointed at a chair, and glared at his bookshelves as I sat down. The window behind him was open to the sunlight, tinted by the lemon trees in the garden, but the room was in shadow. Warm air drifted in, bringing faint melodies from the workers in the groves, and carrying unfamiliar pollens. A sneeze was gathering in my sinuses. He seated himself behind the desk.

'We might as well,' he said, 'speak man to man.' He gave a stony, protracted stare to the wall behind my head, challenging me to derive any ironies I wished from the statement, and let the silence swell. My eyes itched and my nose was starting to drip, but I cleared my throat to speak.

'Quite clearly,' he said, 'all this is calculated to infuriate me.' His diction was crisp. 'I shan't rise to it. As usual she's determined to prove something or other. Let her do as she likes, and see the outcome.'

He tapped the desktop with a thick fingertip.

'But you listen to me. If I should learn that you have in any way – *taken advantage* . . .'

His voice trailed off. He stared at me a while longer.

'Do I make myself quite clear?'

I nodded, not knowing what I was agreeing to.

'Don't think,' he said at last, 'that I can't find you. Wherever you go.'

I found myself thanking him, sniffing, wiping my nose, stammering assurances, as I made for the door. He had already turned his attention to some papers on his desk, and did not look up.

The next morning she took me out early to see the estate. We tramped down into the valley under a filmy sky, our breath clouding and our feet sending stones ahead of us along the hard track. She was cursing in exasperation with her father.

'He can't help himself, can he?' she said. 'It's all about him, every time.'

In the groves the trunks looked like bodies frozen in motion. In the midst of struggling to escape, they had metamorphosed, and now they signalled their acceptance of the new life by sprouting silvery leaves and hard purple-black fruit. We passed gangs of workers as we descended the slope. In harvest time, she told me, her father employed more than a hundred labourers. They travelled down from the city for a few weeks' work and received board and lodging in barns on the estate.

'They've been out here since before dawn,' she said.

We paused to watch one of the gangs at work. They wore overalls, rubber boots and headscarves. Their greasepaint was utilitarian, as if someone had slapped a brushful of whitewash across each face. The inbuilt tunes jingling away in their breasts sounded distant but clear through the acres of trees. They had laid nets and groundsheets, and were dragging at the lower branches with rakes to dislodge the olives. Others had climbed ladders into the upper branches, and balanced there, scraping the fruit down with their hands.

I rubbed my itching eyes and blew my nose. We continued into the floor of the valley, circling back towards the trail.

'They'll get a month's work, then they're packed back to the city or on to the next temporary contract,' she said scornfully. 'Sixty or seventy hours a week at less than minimum wage, no rights, no security. And if you listen to him you'd think he was doing them a favour.'

We were halfway back to the villa when the sound of an engine made us turn. A motorised buggy, splattered with dried mud, was coming up the track, pulling a short trailer covered with a tarpaulin. It rattled to a stop beside us and a young man swung himself from the seat. She made a kind of squeak, a sound I hadn't heard from her before, and threw herself into his arms. He lifted her easily off her feet. 'Hey hey,' he said.

She turned to me happily. 'This is Leo,' she said. 'We grew up together – you know, I've told you.'

I didn't remember that, but I nodded.

He leant over and caught my hand. 'It's a pleasure to meet you,' he said. His face was fleshily handsome between a chestnut tousle and a grubby red kerchief knotted around his throat. He wore knee-high boots and jodhpurs stained with grass and mud. A stubby leather truncheon dangled from his belt.

'We go all the way back,' she was saying. 'Leo's family has the next estate. The pair of us were always planning to run away together.'

'True. Nearly made it right across the valley, that time, eh?'

'Yes, till you made me come home, sissy!'

Leo gave a chivalrous shrug. The silence stretched. I got the feeling they might forget I was there, and exchange something too private.

'I didn't know you were home,' she said at last.

'Back for the harvest.' He nodded. 'Here, take a look.'

He beckoned us over to his trailer and lifted the tarpaulin to show what was underneath. On the ridged metal bed lay three of the workers from the groves. Their limbs were cramped and bent, as rigid as wood, and their fingers had twisted into arthritic claws. Two were quite motionless but the third shivered feverishly. Disconnected plinks, clonks and twangs sounded from their thoraxes. Under their crusts of white paint, the three faces were paralysed in expressions of bewilderment.

'Oh, dear,' she said.

'Mm hm.'

'What happened?'

'Nothing out of the ordinary. They get worse every season. Can't take care of themselves. They want to lay around in the Liberties half the year, then, come harvest time, ride the bus down and work fourteen straight hours. No surprise some of them fall apart. Don't have the gumption, and so we end up with this. Eh?'

He looked down at the quivering labourer, whose open eye held, perhaps, a fleck of comprehension.

'Don't you worry,' Leo said. 'These fellers are going to be fine. I'll take them up to the sheds, have a tinker, give them a beaker of protein porridge and they'll be well set up. You love that stirabout, eh? I do believe it's the reason you come.'

He grinned at the figures. Then he turned to me, becoming more formal, and gripped my hand again.

'I'm delighted for you. Make sure and take good care of her.' He winked. 'Or else I'll want to know about it! Now I'd best get these up the hill.'

He climbed on the buggy and gunned the engine, then turned to us.

'Listen, why don't you two ride on with me up to the sheds? It'll take you closer to the house. And, tell you what' – he nodded to me – 'while we're there I'll find you something for those allergies.'

There was just room for all three of us, if she perched on the seat behind Leo while I sat in the trailer, holding tight to the sides. We bounced up the track.

Later that day, as we walked through the town, we found a crowd gathering in the central plaza around a makeshift wooden platform. At the platform's corners stood poles decorated with strings of flowers and swags of coloured cloth, and just behind it a striped tent had been erected on the back of a battered flatbed truck. As we watched, a man emerged from this ragged tiring-house and stepped directly on to the boards.

'Most noble gentlemen, ladies, and my worthy patrons!'

He towered over the crowd, twitching a moustache that was stiff and pointed with wax, and lifted his mortarboard in salutation. He was bald except for a waxy tuft at the crown of his large egg-shaped head. Along with the mortarboard he wore a dusty black gown, but when he threw back the wings of the drab garment and placed his hands on his hips I saw hairy forearms, gleaming leather trousers, pointed white boots and a waistcoat of threadbare red velveteen over a naked torso. He grinned, showing long, stained teeth – horse's teeth. The crowd fell quiet as he raised his cane.

'My boys have but one desire, and that is to please you!'

His voice was an exaggeratedly clear, teeth-and-tongue baritone, penetrating and sustained like a singer's. You could hear the ornamental curlicues at the end of each phrase. The tip of his cane slit the air.

'For what have they travelled far through peril and privation? For what have they spent their tender lives in long study and hard schooling? For what have they endured the exquisite educations of which you are to enjoy the fruits? Why, for your pleasure alone. They feast or starve at your pleasure, gentlemen and noble ladies; they live or die, believe me, young masters and mistresses, as martyrs to your pleasure. And so, today, we present to you one of the old tales, which we call the tale of the little sweep.'

An unresolved chord rang out, and two diminutive figures appeared on the platform, one holding a mandolin, the other a flute. They were perhaps ten years old, in white satin suits, silver-buckled slippers and chalk-white faces with red spots at the lips and cheeks. They began to play an intricate overture, its complex harmonies twining around the simple music that tinkled from inside their small chests. As they played, they danced: their movements were minimal, never more than a step one way or the other, but they were so exactly controlled, so synchronised, that in their ornate costumes they seemed less like boys than dainty, elaborate works of mechanical artifice. Every move of a limb, every facial expression, was disciplined and stylised. Their large, liquid eyes kept focus above the heads of the crowd.

Four more children joined them on the platform, and with just a few gestures, rigid, exaggerated, yet graceful, they mimed a busy street scene into existence, singing in pure, unbroken voices in a language I didn't recognise. Their master had withdrawn to the edge of the platform, from where, his cane twitching like a conductor's baton, he began to narrate the performance, his voice resounding in the pauses between the boys' songs.

'The story goes that there was a poor sweep. This was long, long ago, gents and ladies, in the olden days and the historical times.'

As he spoke, another boy entered, his satin suit simpler and baggier. His movements were as artfully exact as his schoolmates', but to a different effect: he was expertly ridiculous. The titters started as soon as he appeared. Every detail, from his toes-turned-out walk to the way he slumped his shoulders and lolled his head, won laughter from the audience.

'This sweep was the lowliest man in the city. Every day he swept up the offal in the slaughterhouse, loaded it up on his cart and hauled it to the dumps outside the city walls. He was filthy and he stank worse than you can imagine – yes, sir, even you! People held handkerchiefs to their noses as he went past, spat on him and cursed him. He never complained.'

The sweep mimed dragging a cart, with enormous effort, across the platform. He evoked the invisible burden so well that you felt it: he strained against its weight, slipped, fell flat on his face and sprang up again like a piece of rubber. The other boys, impersonating scornful ladies and gentlemen, turned up their noses at him. I stole a sideways look at her face. She was laughing along with the rest of the crowd at the clownish sweep. The other performers slipped in and out of secondary roles using nothing more than skilful adjustments of their stances.

'Now, one day, as our sweep was hauling his cart through the streets there was a commotion ahead, and he saw a squad of eunuchs approaching, brandishing staves, driving the people aside. Behind them came twenty female servants as beautiful as moons, as elegant as fawns, and in the middle of them a fine lady more beautiful and elegant than any, softer and more languid of limb, her eyes darker and brighter. All the women attended on her.'

Still another child emerged from the tent: he was corseted into a white satin dress and crowned with a silver wig, and carried himself with a sinuous femininity that was balanced on the very edge of burlesque. The supporting cast turned themselves into eunuchs and serving-girls, and the sweep goggled amusingly at the lady. Two of the eunuchs supported her fingertips as she stepped daintily forward.

'As they went past, the sweep cringed aside – but the fine lady paused, looked at him, and raised her hand. The eunuchs came forward and seized him; they bound his hands and dragged him to their mistress's feet. She proceeded through the city with her entourage, and the sweep was hauled behind her. One or two passers-by began to protest at the rough treatment he was getting, but the eunuchs threatened them and they said no more. As for the sweep, he stumbled along in the mud, thinking to himself, this fine lady must have been sickened by the stink of me; if I am lucky perhaps they will only beat me, but perhaps I will die today and no one will ever know.

'They dragged him all the way up to the Fair Quarter, to Lizavet where the grandest houses stood in those days, and led him into a villa. As far as our sweep was concerned, it might have been the Autumn Palace itself. The eunuchs prodded him through an entrance hall, and frightened as he was he had to marvel at its columns and murals, its endless marble floor. But they did not stop here. They brought him into a bathroom – need I say that it seemed to him as grand as a ballroom? – and there, three pretty girl servants came in to him and said, take off your rags. He cowered, but at last obeyed and removed his tattered clothes. Wrinkling their pretty noses hardly at all, the servants washed the filth from his skin, scrubbed his horny feet and shampooed his matted hair. They brushed his teeth and trimmed his nails. Before long he smelt of orange blossom. Next they brought him a pile of silk clothing, blue as night and yellow as noon, and told him to put it on. But the sweep had never seen clothes like this; he touched the strange garments helplessly. Laughing, the servants dressed him.'

As he spoke, the master's eyes followed the boys' movements with what seemed harried desperation, and his cane danced as if every part of the performance depended on it. The children, still moving with that stiff, stylised perfection of gesture, surrounded the sweep, artfully protecting his

85

modesty as they mimed his toilette. They held their faces fixed in hyperbolic expressions as though they were masks. I wondered how much they had to practise. Next the servants brought in an invisible feast: the sweep could not believe his eyes, and his amazement redoubled when the fine lady entered and sat down to eat with him. The servants danced and the fine lady strummed a lute, then she led him away from the feast and lay down with him in a cradle of the other actors' arms. All the time the audience's hilarity intensified, until I wondered whether it could all be in appreciation of the children's skill.

'If I have died, then I am in heaven, said the sweep to himself. Or perhaps I am asleep and this is a dream, and my heart will break when I wake up. But when dawn crept into the mansion of the fine lady, the sweep found that everything was real. She was dozing in his arms, warm and perfumed.'

The master leered in my direction, I thought, and winked.

'When the sun was up, the fine lady said to him, take this and go to the baths, and come to me again this evening. The poor sweep did as he was told. He made haste to his hovel on the other side of town, and then looked at what she had given him. It was a silver-stitched handkerchief in which five gold coins were wrapped. Not knowing what to do with such riches, he buried them in the ground, and sat on the stoop of his house for the rest of the day, wondering what it might all mean. Evening was drawing in when one of the servant girls appeared, and said to him, come along, my mistress is waiting for you.

'Well, friends, what would you have done? The sweep went along with the servant and everything happened just as it had the night before. He dined with the fine lady and spent the night in her fragrant bed. It seemed to him that each hour lasted forever and that the night was over in a heartbeat. Time is strange indeed for a sweep in a lady's room. You might think he'd have trouble believing it was real, but you'd be wrong. Through that secret night, he knew very well this bedchamber was real. What struck him as unlikely was that anything else might be – that he had ever led his mule through the streets, that dawn was going to come, that there was a city beyond the curtain.

'And in the morning, just as before, she gave him a handkerchief full of coins and ordered him to come back to her in the evening.

'But on that third night, when the sweep, with more swagger in his stride than usual, walked up to the mansion, something was different. The gate beside the house was open, and he thought he could hear the sound of horses from the courtyard, and from an upper window the intimate laughter of a man and a woman. Still, he went up to the door boldly enough and knocked. He was answered not by the pretty servants, but by a couple of eunuchs who asked him brusquely what he meant by coming to the front of the house. When he could give no reply, they beat him and drove him away. He fled back to his own hovel, and there he nursed his bruises and sobbed the night through.

'Many days later, in the marketplace, who should he see in the distance, once more, but the fine lady and her entourage? Of course, he dared not approach her. That was the last he ever saw of any of that household.'

The actor playing the sweep was left alone in the middle of the platform, fixed motionless in a pose of comical longing and despair, his mouth turned down at the corners and his arm extended after the lady. The master paused with one eyebrow flexed until the giggles quietened. The crowd became more attentive.

'And do you know *why* all of this happened to this little sweep?'

He looked around.

'No?'

He looked from face to face.

'None of you know?'

They waited.

'Then you never will!'

Mirth surged back more loudly than before. The master gave a perfunctory bow, swished his cane through the air, and grinned around at his crowd. For a heartbeat his attention settled on me, and his moustache twitched as if to enquire why I was not laughing along with everyone else. But then the children reappeared to dance a faultless polka to the strains of flute and mandolin, all except for two of them, who threaded through the crowd with velvet bags held open. She dropped in a handful of coins, tousled the boy's head and led me away.

That night I sat in the guest room with my guitar beside me on the cot, listening through the house to the muffled sounds of her having a row with her father. My eyes and nose were not streaming so badly since I had taken one of the tablets Leo had given me this morning. A chemical stink had surrounded the complex of concrete outbuildings they called the sheds, and from somewhere inside I had heard groans, the abandoned sounds of sickness or despair. Leo had not invited us into his workshop. As we had walked away she had explained to me that visitors from towns and cities were sometimes disconcerted when they came out here, but that this was just ignorance and sentimentalism.

I couldn't make out her words or her father's, only their voices drumming through the house. Tomorrow we would be back in the city.

The next few weeks passed quickly for me, and soon I was living in her flat. I never thought to mourn my bachelor freedom. I took to the routine right away, seeing her off in the morning and greeting her when she arrived home in the evening, and felt no qualms about domestication. She was going through a busy time at work, so I bought groceries and made the dinner every night.

One morning she was dashing out the door of the flat, late for her tram; but as I kissed her goodbye, she paused, and reminded me she couldn't wait to hear my new material. We had agreed that from now on I'd concentrate on writing songs. Finally I could get down to work. For too long I had been full of possible songs, nestled deep down, frail seedlings which would stay for a while and grow if given the chance, or shrink away again if they were ignored. Now I could attend to them all.

I shut the door after her and turned to face the empty flat, tightening my dressing-gown cord. I had the place to myself all day, with nothing to keep me from my guitar and notebook and the multi-track program on her laptop. First, though, I got dressed and cleared away the breakfast things. I tidied the flat – I was positively house-proud these days – then sat on the sofa and eyed my guitar. Eventually I picked it up, tuned it, and strummed for a while. But nothing was happening, and the prospect of settling down to a day's songwriting filled me with dismay. I was becoming alarmed. The fact was that since we'd moved in together I had written nothing at all.

My old songs, when I played them through, sounded transparent, ill-made, full of clichés and dishonesties. 'Serelight Fair' was still the best I'd written, and it was wearing thinner every time I played it: what had been unbearably true seemed now like cheap theatrics. But when I tried anything new, the jotted lyrics and sketchy chord sequences crumbled to pieces on my guitar strings. I told myself I only had to hold my nerve and keep going, but I found that I didn't know how. My attention lapsed and whole days drained away, wasted. I was getting nowhere. The suspicion was creeping in that I had already written my songs, that I had no more left to write. I put the guitar down. Mid-morning already. What I needed to do, I decided, was go for a walk.

My daily errands had been growing longer and longer. Often I walked for miles all over the city, through somnolent avenues and deserted municipal parks with empty flowerbeds, or through the main streets where I was surrounded by office workers hurrying to and from their lunches. I told myself it was all part of the process: you couldn't write songs by sitting in a flat, you had to go outside, keep on looking at the world, find out what it was like. Once, in Communion Town, I had heard a shred of melody, and seen a tangle-headed figure whistling for unresponsive afternoon shoppers. I had taken a different street instead.

Now I pulled the latch shut behind me and headed for the river, to join the tourists and students who would be out on the boardwalk, watching the human statues and browsing the tables of second-hand books. I began to hum a song I'd heard not long ago, but I found myself repeating the same line over and over. *A thousand black umbrellas and a thousand hungry dreams . . .*

An hour later I paused to lean against the parapet beside an open quadrangle, edged by brightly graffitoed walls, where skateboarders were showing off among brutalist concrete sculptures. A short way off, a spindly pedestrian bridge spanned the river. The water crawled far below.

It was only after the first shock of recognition had made me straighten up and take a step or two away from the parapet that I realised what I had seen. She was approaching across the bridge. I didn't know what she was doing in this part of town so early on a weekday afternoon. If it was for work she hadn't mentioned it. I hesitated. My first instinct had been to hide, not to let her know I was out wandering around when I should be in the flat working on my songs. But that was ridiculous: no one had said I was supposed to stay indoors all the time. I began to walk along the boardwalk so I'd catch up with her as she stepped off the bridge.

But before I got close enough, someone else moved forward to meet her, a tall chestnut-haired figure. They embraced, and kissed on the cheeks three times. It was Leo. He was dressed more smartly than before, in a dark overcoat, but he carried himself with the same outdoorsman's self-possession. I could easily have waved, called out and joined them, declaring a happy coincidence, but I held back. I couldn't have told you why, but I dropped behind one of the signboards that showed maps of the waterfront and watched as she slipped her arm into his. As they walked off together, I followed.

They left the Old Quarter and walked south along the quays. I kept them in sight all the way down the promenade, where coloured flags hung between the lamp posts and the daytrippers were busy using up the last of summer, and into the emptier streets of an unfamiliar part of town, a suburb where the breeze had an abrasive edge and stank faintly of diesel. I had always thought of this as a city which turned its back to the sea, but here each corner gave another angle from which to look down into the bay. I saw places where the bricks ran out, so that you could have climbed down to pebbles, bladderwrack and sea-wet sand. Beyond the grey water the factory chimneys were merging with the sky. The well-dressed pair continued ahead of me, passing bleak little bakeries and guesthouses, all shut, and I followed, hanging back until they were almost out of sight, hurrying forward to the next doorway in which I could conceal myself. Had they been paying much attention to their surroundings they would have noticed me, no doubt, but they were absorbed in their conversation.

We came to a cul-de-sac of terraced houses. I watched from the corner as they walked to the end of the row. They had run out of talk now; there was something sad, even hopeless, in the way she leant on his arm. The yard was overgrown in front of the last house and the upstairs windows were boarded over. She searched in her bag, produced the big, messy bunch of keys she always carried, and opened the front door. Leo placed a hand between her shoulders and followed her into the house.

I lingered a while at the end of the street, trying to work out what it was that I had seen. Then, automatically, I retraced my steps until I was home.

The image of that house, with its tangled yard and defaced exterior, lay on my mind like a sheet of glass for the rest of the day, suppressing other thoughts. When she arrived home I greeted her with a kiss, gave her dinner, listened to her day at work and spoke to her in reply, but I didn't have a clue what either of us was saying.

That night I lay awake until she was breathing regularly, then I got up and dressed in the dark. I went through her bag and took her keys. As softly as I could, I let myself out of the flat and set off into the city. It was well past midnight, quiet, few people around. All noises had retreated. The night seemed to have its own resonance. At that hour, the city's a gong that was struck at noon and is not yet quite still.

There were no signs of habitation when I reached the house. Half the streetlamps on the cul-de-sac were dead. Her key-ring held several keys I didn't recognise, but it didn't take me long to find the one that fitted the lock. Without knowing what I expected to find, I opened the door.

As soon as I stepped into the hallway, I was swamped by a sense of déjà vu so disorienting that I came to a halt on the threshold and had to force myself to carry on. I couldn't shake the illusion I had been here. I groped along the wall for a switch, and a bare bulb came feebly alight overhead. For a minute or two I forgot all about her and Leo.

The house was crammed from top to bottom with what looked like junk, or the debris of a lifetime's work on some questionable, arcane project. To enter the downstairs room you had to thread your way through a maze of wooden and cardboard crates, disordered bookshelves, chests of drawers and filing cabinets. Two large workbenches stood buried beneath stacks of manila folders and loose papers, antiquated computer equipment and boxes of tools. One of the benches was strewn with retort stands, stained, odd-shaped glassware and microscopes of various sizes. A fat reference book was held open by a tool-roll of black cloth, weighted with slender steel instruments: scissors, forceps, scalpels. I picked up a brass baton with a small glass eye at one end. It all reminded me of something, but I couldn't think what. I paused and listened. Nothing was moving in the house. The night murmured away outside.

Upstairs, the smaller of the two rooms was completely empty. It had no window, only blind bulging plaster, featureless except for an iron ring bolted at waist-height into one wall. The dark-blotched floorboards had not been swept for a long time. There was nothing remarkable about the room, but just like the bookshelves and the equipment downstairs, like the damp smell of the hall, the looseness of the stair carpet and the sticky-greasy feel of the bannister, the empty room produced a peculiar mixture of emotions in me. It felt like the time I had left my songwriting notebook lying open on the kitchen table, and had come back to find one of her flatmates idly turning the pages. As I closed the door again, I noticed the heavy bolt on the outside.

The last room showed signs of more recent use. It was a chaos of papers, but the workbench was clear except for a cuboid metal filing box, and a monitor hooked up to an obsolete-looking electronic console. A spot lamp craned over the desktop and an office chair stood as though it had just been vacated. Three of the walls were lined with shelves filled with more metal boxes, all of them identical, each one displaying a small handwritten label. But against the fourth wall stood an upright piano. A window in its front showed a spool of paper punctured with a complex pattern of holes: it was a pianola, I realised, a player piano. I tried pressing on one of the treadles, but nothing happened. Then I saw the bundle of wires that protruded from the lid and trailed across the floor into the console machine on the workbench.

At this, the feeling of déjà vu returned, redoubled. This room too was familiar, but as it would be familiar to hold your own polished skull in your hands. My eyes moved to the metal boxes on their shelves, and to the labels on their sides. Written on each label was a person's name. None that I recognised. They were in alphabetical order. I searched along the shelves . . . but the one I was looking for wasn't there. I broke the silence by laughing at myself. Why in the world would it be? Nothing but a gap on the shelf. I looked again at the box on the desk, and felt my face drain. Sinking into the chair, I leant closer to make sure. My name was on the label.

I glanced at the door behind me, undid the catches of the box and lifted the lid.

Most of the space inside was taken up by a thick, scuffed hardback binder with my name on the spine. I opened it and began to leaf through pages of closely printed text. It looked old – the pages, thin, low-grade computer printout, were faded, dog-eared and soft at the edges. As I tried to make sense of the contents, I became calm, giving myself up entirely to that sense of uncanny reiteration, because now I knew that I was dreaming or mad. It was an impossible book. I could not bring myself to read more than a few words at a time. '*Later I strummed my guitar* . . .' Wincing inwardly, I thumbed back and forth through the pages. '. . . *Without looking at her, I walked out* . . .' I felt dizzy with embarrassment. '*The first time we met, she was climbing into a rickshaw. It was a bitter night* . . .' I tore my eyes from the page. Of course, I had never written any kind of autobiography – I had never even kept a diary, never thought of it – but still I recognised the words right away. There was no accounting for it and no denying that they were mine. I slapped the binder shut, mortified.

At the bottom of the box was a bundle of data cartridges, labelled only with codes scrawled in soft pencil. Part of each number seemed to be a date, the earliest corresponding to last spring, the latest just over a month ago. I chose one at random; the old console on the desk had a slot the right size, so I clicked the cartridge into place and pressed the button. Then I nearly leapt out of my skin as the monitor and the player piano both came to life simultaneously.

It took me a minute to realise that the clonky old piano was playing one of my songs. It was exactly as I had written it, but it sounded oddly unfamiliar, perhaps because I had never heard it performed on anything other than the guitar. The monitor screen was split into several parts, one showing a horizontal line fuzzing out into jagged peaks and valleys in time with the sound from the piano, while a second showed staves full of black and white spots; I don't know how to read musical notation. In the third, my lyrics scrolled up the screen. I listened through to the end of the song, took out the cartridge, and tried another. The song that played was one of my very earliest attempts: I had never dared perform it to anyone, had all but forgotten it, but here it was, exactly written out and reproduced.

There weren't very many cartridges. One of them, I noticed, didn't have a code at all: the label was marked only with a circle, or perhaps a figure zero. I turned it over in my hands, wondering if I'd ever get rid of the feeling that all of this had happened already.

I was distantly aware, as I clicked the cartridge into the console, that the front door of the house had opened and feet were climbing the stairs, but by the time she burst into the room with Leo at her heels, the music was already playing.

The tune from the pianola consisted of several neatly overlapping, tinkling phrases – jaunty, sentimental and melancholy all at once. We stood facing each other as we listened. After half a minute it finished and immediately began over again. I knew the song well. It was the music that had always been pulsing through me, marked by each spasm of my heart, and all my other songs were only variations on the theme. I breathed in and out to the pulse of that tune, tapped my fingers to it in idle moments and dreamt it whenever I slept. I could hear it, now, in the ripple of my gut. Its harmonics were the vibrations of my blood pressing its way through the tissues of my brain. Its banal melody described the limits of my emotions, and its prosaic structure was the absolute framework for my thoughts. It had been jingling away inside my body, in my heart, ingrained so deeply that I had not been able to recognise it until it was played back to me by an automatic music-box. I had never before heard it: its cheapness, its small, comprehensible ingenuity, its limited charm.

Watching me carefully, she moved over to the console and pulled out the cartridge. The player piano ran down to silence, but the tune tinkled on inside me. For the first time I could hear it, and I knew I'd never stop hearing it now. Shivers ran through me; my fingers twitched. Neither of them had taken their eyes off me. I lifted my hand and she flinched. I clutched at my ribs as if I could keep the noise from spilling out. Leo edged forward with his palms raised in placation, but I was too ashamed even to try apologising for what I had done. I knew she couldn't excuse me this.

I understood that she was the single person I wanted and the only one I could ever want, the love of my life. Without looking at her, I walked out.

I remember all of this, and I remember how for the rest of the night I walked, not minding where I was going. For a while, my uppermost regret was that I hadn't taken my guitar when I left: I could have pawned it for breakfast and a place to stay and still had change left over. As it turned out I had enough in my pockets to rent a rickshaw for a few hours' work around dawn, and after that, life soon enough returned to the way it always was. The only difference is that I often think about the time we were together. Sometimes I remember it so deeply that I even forget the tune jingling away in my heart. This morning, I watched her disappear and then carried on just as before: but I was thinking of a certain time in our first few weeks, when I had returned to her flat dog-tired and aching after a long shift at work, wanting nothing so badly as to sleep, and she had helped me lie down, loosened my clothing and brushed strands of hair out of my face, tutting at the state of me. But as I began to sink with infinite gratitude into sleep, hands strayed over me, fluttering at my breastbone and throat, soft hair tickled my eyelids, fractional, insistent movements touched me, teeth grazed my skin, refusing to let me alone. And something happened that a moment before I had not been able to imagine. Strength ran into my limbs, my body was glad, my mind cleared, wide awake, and the taste of salts on my tongue opened into hot, liquid softness that plunged into me and drew me into itself, and at that very moment the first phrase of a new song dropped into my head. I caught her waist and rolled her over and drank until I had to gasp for breath. I tangled my hands in her hair and gazed into her face until we both breathed together. We moved together. A warm chord sounded. I filled my lungs. We were making a discovery, and it grew ever more remarkable, this disclosure of what each of us had at heart. All I needed to know was the way it unfolded, the song.

PART III

THE CITY ROOM

In from the street, through the hall and down, one palm making a squeak on the bannister, his feet pattering softly on the stairs, he can go at such a speed and still be so quiet. As he enters the dim corridor his eyes crowd with blocks of a colour that doesn't have a name, a colour that no one else has discovered.

He steals past the open kitchen door, as quiet and quick as he can, past his grandmother who is standing at the sink cleaning a chicken and listening to the radio news. In his cupped hands he hides what he has stolen. He wonders what the canal man will do. He would take it back if he could, but he knows he'll never be rid of it now.

The blocks of colour pulsate: they take their shapes from the doors and the walls, but get detached and drift free across his vision. The kitchen window is open, and in the distance the city murmurs its invitation. The autumn is laced with leftover summer. Without turning from the sink, his grandmother puts her sharp knife down on the counter. That is not a toy.

She has a straight back, a handsome nose bent

like a knuckle and hair dark as lead soldiers. She wears wool stockings and lace-up shoes. When they go out into the city, she haggles with market traders while he stands with his fingers twisted into her skirts. She knows all the people in the district. She chats to the greengrocer who sells them string bags filled with apples, and she jokes with the large, straw-haired woman who checks out books for them at the library. Whenever she takes him to the open-air swimming bath she greets the old ladies on the benches, and when they hear music from the bandstand in the park they can stop and listen for as long as they want. She rides the buses as though she owns them. She likes to press his face with her cool palm. Where she first came from, he has no way of imagining: he has never considered what she is like in herself.

He passes the kitchen and continues down the corridor, which runs the length of the basement flat. Her room faces him from the far end behind a door with a scrollworked brass handle. It is full of water-damaged books, boxes of ancient letters, clothes from long ago, significant jewellery. Once, late at night, he took himself down to wake her because he had stomach pains, and found her sitting upright in bed, awake. The green-shaded lamp on her bedside table shed light on the book open in her lap. The clock pronounced a slow nocturnal tutting. From this, he formed the impression that she does not sleep. She is always there in that room, upright in that bed, at all times of the night.

Halfway down the corridor another door stands ajar. Rather than move it on the hinge he eases through the narrow gap. This room holds things from his grandmother's past: insectile armchairs, a hard horsehair couch, a cherrywood rolltop desk owned by someone long gone. The windows look into slots of brick which are open at the top to let in the light.

The floor in here is covered with an elaborate model city, and he used to believe that the room was named accordingly: the City Room. He now knows that he misunderstood what his grandmother was saying, and that really the room is the Sitting Room. And yet, although he burns with shame to recall how often and how blithely he must have got it wrong – he imagines his own piping voice making the mistake over and over, and he can sense how it must have sounded to her, a lisping childish fault to be kindly overlooked – still he knows, deeper down, that this is the room's true and secret name. The City Room.

It has grown far beyond its origins, this city. He built the first crude settlement with small wooden blocks, originally the playthings of an earlier generation of children, some of them plain and some painted primary colours, but all stained and faded. Most were just bricks, but there were doric columns, too, and cornices and broken pediments to crown town halls and triumphal arches. Once these were complete, he glimpsed further possibilities, and a dusty cardboard box full of thin metal plates and girders that bolt together with the help of a spanner provided the city with rail tracks and fortifications.

The game must have lasted weeks – certainly as long as he can remember – but his grandmother has not objected. She doesn't understand the importance of the city, of course. He would try and explain if he could, but instinct tells him these things can't be communicated. He knows with absolute clarity that the model city is far more remarkable than anyone else can understand. It must in fact be more important than anything else in the world, but he can never admit it, because when his grandmother or someone else looks into the room and sees his creation spread across the floor, it makes him squirm. Only when he is alone can his mind move through the streets and buildings he's created, imagining the textures of their reality. This gives him a strange pleasure. He likes to perch on the floor, barely able to keep still, and hold it whole in his mind, letting the image deepen. What secrets. He floats in a warm capsule of possibility.

He has not grown; he is slight and tender, not like the boy from upstairs who has a greasy face and a forehead bristling with stiff fibres, and who would kick the city into rubble if he knew it was here.

He remembers a time in the upstairs boy's room. The window looked into the shared back garden, where the frame for a swing drowned in weeds and a tract of rough brown grass ran down to a decrepit fence. The light out there was failing. The bonfire had been smouldering all day, its gymnasts of smoke somersaulting upwards through the branches of the trees. In the room no one had turned the lights on. He could sense the upstairs boy's father moving around downstairs somewhere, but he did not know where his grandmother was. He had to pretend not to be disgusted at the meaty smell of the room. Meaningless objects, strange furniture. The bed was not like his bed, and the toys were fakes intended to deceive him, manufactured evidence of a world that didn't exist. There were comics as well but they were too strange to look at directly.

The upstairs boy, who had a large yellow spot in the back of his neck, collapsed on the floor, then got up again to kick over a chair, and came close, making gluey clicking noises. Nonchalantly, an arm grappled around his neck, fingers thrust themselves into his hair and a leg hooked behind his knees to try and bring him down to the floor. He had to fight off these attempts while pretending not to have noticed them. Time was strange in here. He knew that the scene was in some way permanent, pinched out of sequence: it is still going on, somewhere, in the inturned landscape of houses, waste grounds and streets where memory begins. In that loop of unevent he stands in the room with the upstairs boy prowling and grabbing, and a presence moving around downstairs, and the muddy, darkening garden lying under the window.

The city has spread and mutated, using whatever materials it could find. Roads from strips of cardboard, expanded polystyrene packaging for brutalist architecture. Once, abandoned beside some bins, he found three beautiful bricks of weathered yellow clay. They looked soft enough to crumble, but they chimed when they touched. They were rough and solid in the hands and two together were almost too heavy to lift. His grandmother helped him carry them home and in the City Room they became great landmarks. The city moulded itself to the terrain. One quarter flourished beneath an armchair, always in shadow, while elsewhere bridges and stairways gave access to the massif of the couch, and outposts spread along the ridge of its arms and back. He divided the city into districts and gave each one a name.

Under a windowsill, his grandmother's plants trail down towards the floor in a strange perpendicular jungle. On the sill sits a heavy wooden box which she gave him. It has a sliding lid like an old-fashioned pencil case, and it contains a regiment of lead soldiers in chipped red coats, the grey showing through, jumbled in their mass grave. Perhaps she meant him to use them for the garrison of his city. Who knows what dead darling they first belonged to? When she gave the soldiers to him, he emptied them out on the floor – they were identical men with pigeon chests and white faces – and began to set them on their feet, but he could not pretend to care much. What he wanted at that time was a Captain Maximum figure.

For his birthday she took him to the toy shop on Bittergreen Street and they had a whole rack. There must have been twenty. When he saw that, he was bereft, because he knew he could only have one. Captain Maximum led the goodies. The baddies were led by Caesar Skull. He wanted a goody but he did not know which were which: they looked at one and his grandmother said it must be a goody because a baddy would not have such a sad expression on his face. He agreed. One figure was a girl, the only girl allowed in Captain Maximum's team. He did not look at her in case his grandmother noticed. He got the man with the sad expression, and carried him home hidden in a crackling white polythene bag, concealing his excitement.

But at home, when he freed the green man from his transparent plastic blister and studied the back of the packaging card, he realised he was a baddy after all. It was a ridiculous mistake to have made. This was a minion, a fish-man who lived under-water and could not do anything good. Any other Captain Maximum figure would have been better. He felt an awful pity for the fish-man, then wrenched both his arms from their sockets.

Overcome with remorse and terror, he hid the figure in the bottom of his toy box. If only he had got the leader of the goodies. But he knew he could never ask for another.

He has made a map of the city and its surroundings by taping four sheets of paper together, and whenever he thinks of something new he squeezes it in, making tight marks with a pencil-point. He keeps the map safe in the narrow space between the wall and the bookcase. Not long ago, his grandmother came into the room as he was working, and he crumpled the paper in his haste to hide it.

He touches the edge of the map for reassurance but does not draw it out. He looks again at the thing he has stolen. It sits so lightly in his hand that he can hardly feel it, but he has the curious sense that in truth it is much heavier. He has a few hiding places but none of them is good enough for this.

Earlier this afternoon, down in the garden, the upstairs boy led him to where several fence-planks had grown sodden and fallen away, leaving a gap. It was choked with brambles but they stamped these out of the way and went through into a forgotten space, an alley running between the back of the fence and a brick wall. These enormous weeds must always have been here, crowding together competitively, stiff and furry and tall as men: all this time, through his life, they had been

112

here. They sneaked along the alley past the backs of houses and past gates of peeling wood, corrugated iron and chain-link. A puddle ran in a channel down the centre of the track. There was something the boy wanted to show him. The upstairs boy is always pushing and pulling, he always wants to show you something.

Further down was another flaw in the fencing. They squeezed between the planks, and on the other side dragged themselves free from the bushes into the bottom of a garden edged with long box hedges. Netted raspberry bushes hunkered to the ground in a dark clump, hovering below the horizon of the long, bulged lawn, and far off he saw the heavy-lidded windows of a house. The upstairs boy prised apart the limbs of the hedge, and vanished.

Following, he found himself in a tunnel woven from twigs. It was a secret passage. If you knew the hedge was a corridor, then it became one, close, tangled, hidden, floored in mulch. They fought their way along past the trunks and through twigs that scratched at his face. The earth made his knees wet and his hands dirty. Maybe you could travel unseen for miles inside a network of hollow hedges.

When they finally broke out of the sticky branches they were beside the unfamiliar house. He heard indistinct voices inside: they were unaware of his presence, saying words not meant for him to hear, and he looked up fearfully at the window. But the upstairs boy, unconcerned, lifted the latch of a tall garden gate and led them out to the canal path.

He and his grandmother had often been along the canal, and he had been here by himself, as well, but he had not known you could reach it this way. The upstairs boy's hidden corridors wrenched the city, folding parts of it closer together than it was possible for them to be. They came at familiar places from different directions, making them hard to identify. But now, as he followed the upstairs boy under a low bridge and saw the long shape in the water at the canalside, he recognised where he was.

Once, he and his grandmother were walking home from the bus stop, and the road took them beside a tangle of wet trees held in by a green wire fence. His grandmother liked there to be trees around. Woods were necessary, she would tell him, and so was water, especially for children. The light was slanting and the leaves dripped. In a certain place, a gap in the fence meant that he could plunge under the trees and along a narrow track of earth in the gloom, under the low branches and down to the towpath. Then he only had to run a short distance, under a bridge and past an old canal boat, to wriggle through another fence-gap in easy time to meet his grandmother. And all that time she would have gone along only a simple stretch of road. He had done it before and she had been pleased by his adventure.

He told her to keep going, and climbed through the gap. It was already evening under the trees, and his feet hit the earth in silence. He had left the sound of cars and buses behind. He moved through his short cut, clasping the wet mossy fingers to slip under them where they hung low. He reached the canal and began to run along beside the silted water.

Then he skidded to a halt. The way ahead was blocked. He was too slow to do anything but gape, unable to tell what he was seeing.

The canal boat was the same as ever, with its round windows, its algae-streaked hull and the row of old tyres roped along its flank, but beside it somebody was sitting in the middle of the towpath: sitting in a folding canvas chair, like a man out in his own back garden, with his head tipped back, mouth open and eyes closed. The man wore oil-streaked jeans and a towelling dressing gown which, long ago, might have been white. It hung open to show the pot belly and the creased indentation of the chest. The boots were missing their laces.

The man appeared to be asleep. The face was half-hidden by lank hair which was coloured grubby yellow-white, like teeth. The hands rested in the man's lap. Perhaps he could slip past.

He took a step forward, but straight away the eyes opened.

'There you are,' said the man. 'You took your time.'

The voice was groggy, the flesh of the face

bloodless and stiff. The arms and legs had a jumbled look, as if this were a dummy slouching immobile in the chair.

'Joking.' The upper lip revealed the pale gumline. 'You're here now, though. There's reasons to these things, that's what I say.'

The man made as if to rise from his chair, but fell back again. The wooden joints creaked with exasperation.

'You can see I'm bad,' the man said, pressing a hand into his lap and wincing. 'It's worse now than before.'

On the ground beside the chair, among heaps of old newspapers and crumpled tins, lay a tubular metal crutch. The man's hand seemed to drift towards it, then to retreat again. He settled deeper into his chair.

'I have a story to tell you,' said the man. 'It's very important. It's a secret.'

The flat roof of the canal man's boat was piled with an assortment of things: broken crates, plastic buckets, oil cans, tarpaulins, planks. Crouched among them a small tabby cat watched with great vigilance.

'I've never told anyone else. But I need to tell you. I can't say it out loud, in case anyone hears. You'll have to come closer.'

He had no answer. Dimly he grasped that he was involved in a mistake. The man's hand was reaching for him, palm upwards, fingers curling and uncurling.

116

'You'll hear my story, won't you? I need you to listen.'

The cat watched carefully. He could not move. Time had closed around him like a membrane and he could not break out. The hand was beckoning with more agitation now.

'You're not scared, are you? To come closer? Look, I have something for you. A present.'

The man cast around. Showing his teeth, he stretched down beside the chair and snagged one of the newspapers. He flourished the front page with its big black capitals – RAW HEAD AND BLOODY BONES – and then collapsed it between his hands. His fingers twisted and folded the paper, moulding it into a shape. Soon on the man's open palm stood a small paper person, grey and smeared with newsprint but so cleverly made that it could stand up by itself.

'This fellow is special.' The man was holding it out towards him. 'He's for you. But only if you'll come and listen to my story.'

The figure's torso and limbs were just twists of newspaper, but they seemed ready to move. He could see the way it would walk, gracefully on its tiny pointed feet but unevenly because one leg was thinner than the other. As he looked at it he had a thought so private that it felt shameful: he imagined putting the figure in his city. Before now, the city had always stood empty and had not needed inhabitants, but the paper figure was exactly the right size to walk its streets.

'You want it, don't you?'

The man was quite wrong. He did not want to touch the paper figure, let alone accept it. The thought of adding it to the city was unwelcome, invasive, but he did not know how to refuse it now that it had been offered. There was a catch in time, here beside the canal, and there seemed no other way to move forward.

Then his head broke through the oily surface of the moment and he took a step backwards. The man's face grew ugly. The hand began to claw at the ground, the fingertips brushing the metal of the crutch.

'Why did you come, then, you little sneak? You big girl's blouse. Go on!'

Before he could explain himself, he found that he was retreating, running all the way back through the short cut, with the grey water below and the wet twigs flicking at his eyes. His shoulders crawled. He blurred his vision on purpose and urged himself towards the green wire fence, but the foliage sprung back, not letting him through. He pried the branches apart, pushed deeper and twisted his body through the gap in the fence. Seconds later he was back on the road, already forgetting how the vindictive trees had fixed their fingers in his clothes and tried to drag him backwards into a world of damp wood and foul water.

Springing from the towpath to the boat, the upstairs boy hooted with an invader's triumph.

This was what he had come for. He stood at the stern and jumped up and down, doing his best, without success, to make the boat rock in the water, then yanked on the unmoving tiller before scrambling up to the roof and kicking things into the canal. Empty cider cans and shards of plywood began to drift towards the opposite bank.

The upstairs boy motioned for him to jump across as well, and, when he failed to do so, shrugged and slid down into the cockpit, to rattle at the hatch leading into the cabin.

He looked at the boat and at the towpath. It was the same scene he remembered from that time, so long ago, but he was disoriented by having approached from the opposite direction: it was as if the upstairs boy had brought him through a back door to visit the vacant stage set of an old dream. The spot was deserted. The canvas chair stood just off the path, empty and cockeyed. The once-white dressing gown lay thrown across it. Even the paper figure was still there, lying flattened but intact on the ground.

What he did next would be a puzzle to him later, and already, as he reached out to take the paper man, he could not have explained why he wanted it so badly. He shrank from the memory of the man's blotched fingers folding the figure into existence, but he reached out. As he picked it up he noticed the tabby cat crouching in the long grass, watching the trespassers with flattened ears and bottle-glass eyes.

At the same moment the upstairs boy yelped and tumbled back to the bank. The hatch had been flung open from the inside and the man was clambering into view, supporting his weight on the frame and on the metal crutch. The upstairs boy was already crashing and giggling away into the distance, but he stood there, slow to react, with the stolen figure in his hands.

'You could have listened.' The man did not sound angry. 'I only wanted to tell you.'

He used the crutch to swing himself, clumsily but fast, to the bank. He took a step forward, moving with an unbalanced, three-legged gait, and there was nothing to do but run.

And now, with the theft complete, he has crept down the corridor and into the City Room.

Ramifications knit in his head as he examines the stolen figure. The limbs and the head move slightly as the screwed paper eases. The face has dents for its eyes and mouth, but he can't tell what the expression is.

He wishes there was some way to give it back, but he knows he can never confess what he has done. Discovery is unthinkable. He can only imagine the world would burst into flames and vanish like paper in the grate. He sees now how events have unfolded: how, unrecognised, the choice has been made and the action taken, and how all he can do now is follow the consequences through. Obeying the logic in which he has netted himself, he picks his way across the floor to the very heart of his city. In the central plaza, he stands the figure on its feet.

It is only now, as he places the figure and steps back to judge the effect, that he fathoms what he has done. He doesn't know how, but the presence of the tiny paper man has changed the whole meaning of the city, to the smallest house and the farthest street. All that secret joy has gone, and all that possible magic, gone in an instant and replaced by another kind of secret. It would be useless to remove the man: far too late for that. He may have made the city, but the laws that govern it are not his to alter.

In the corridor the doorbell rings. He hears his grandmother run the kitchen tap, then begin to climb the stairs. He lies down, presses his cheek into the carpet, shuts an eye and sights through one of the gates, along a boulevard towards the centre of the city. Glimpsed like this, the paper man seems to be on his way somewhere, absorbed in some errand of his own.

He can hear grown-up voices above. His grandmother and someone.

He notices, as he often does, the clumped, near-transparent strings that seem to float inside his eyeballs, tumbling and darting around when his attention shifts. He wonders why they are there and whether he can get rid of them one day. He knows he must not let himself be found like this. The time is coming soon when he'll take it all apart, knock over the walls, bulldoze the wooden bricks with his palm and heap handfuls back into the box, and his grandmother will come in to find a clear, spacious floor. But it's not that time yet.

He hears the feet descending the staircase and moving along the corridor. His grandmother's familiar tread, and another tread too, heavy and halting, which he can easily imagine as the sound of someone walking not on two legs but on three. But it is too early for him to be sure of that, and perhaps he sees already that it makes no difference. He lies there, looking with a narrowed eye into the city, until the door opens.

PART IV

GALLATHEA

Let's try this one more time, kid. Let's get this straight.

Why did you do it?

1. Breakfast with Violence

That day, the day the Cherub boys came looking for me, I was down at Meaney's. It was summer: hard summer. The city was chafing in its sweat and had been for weeks now. Nights, the poor devils of the Liberties slept on the roofs of their apartment blocks. Daytime, you ventured into the street, your necktie wilted and your shirt glued itself into your armpits. Walk as far as the corner and you were coated with grit. Dust hung in the air like it had no place else to go. Come mid-afternoon, heat thickened, fell in slabs out of a purplish sky. Shadows scored themselves into the pavements behind every lamp post and railing. The alleyways were heaped. They buzzed. No one had seen a refuse truck in a month. Down at the quays there was nothing but dried mud and the reek of hot rotting bladderwrack. You had the needful, you were out of town until things improved.

In Meaney's it could have been any afternoon, any joint. Overhead the fan stirred the air like a listless cook. The starch was oozing out of my collar. The bouncer, his belly straining his braces, studied a newspaper: some psycho was carving people up nightly down in Glory Part so we all had to have the details. The potboy, propped like an elderly broom, had no custom but a gaggle of doxies perched at the end of the bar. They were leaning in close, clucking, their heads together, passing round some secret recipe. As I came into the place they all went still for a moment, then broke up in giggles. Dolly leant away from the others and called over to me.

'Hey Hal,' she said, 'ain't you hot in that wrinkly old suit?'

The rest of them giggled again. I tweaked the knot of my tie, rapped on the bar to wake up the potboy, and slid into one of the curtained booths along the back wall. My hangover was the kind where your mouth's a bandolier of spent cartridges and your skull's filled full of dull lead. It wanted all my attention.

When the old fellow came over I told him to bring me the special and a hair of the pitbull. But a minute later the curtain scraped back and I found myself looking not at a nutritionally trivial breakfast but at the faces of the Cherub brothers. They grinned in unison.

'Wotcha, Hal.'

None too pleased to see them, I nodded back.

'Hello, Don. Dave,' I said. They pushed their way into the booth, their trouser-seats squealing on the leatherette. Don pasted me up against the wall. Ever had a refrigerator share your seat? Dave sat opposite, looking about as reassuring as a vending machine in a lift. The table complained.

I ignored the special as the potboy slapped it down in front of me. Don Cherub snagged the glass from the old man and tossed the spirit away in one pop-eyed swig. Dave sniggered at a high pitch.

The potboy withdrew. By the door the bouncer was perplexed over the small ads. Don twitched the curtain shut.

'You look well, Hal,' he said, pressing me flatter against the inside wall. 'Tie goes lovely with your shirt. It don't match that hanky in your top pocket though.'

'Yeah, well,' I said. 'You don't want to overdo it.'

Don's eyes slid over to his brother and back to me.

'Anyhow, Hal, we stopped by in hopes of finding you. And what do you know. First time lucky.'

'Hur hur,' said Dave, picking a mushy pea off my plate.

Don lit a cigarette. Dave pulled the plate over to his side of the table, doused the peas in ketchup and started forking them into him. Sweat was crawling down my chest and my arms were pinned to my sides. I waited for the Cherubs to get to the point.

Then Don said a single word. It was your name. That was the first time I heard it: it meant nothing to me then. I gave him a blank look and he repeated it, making the syllables careful and clear, his eyebrows hitching up.

'Don, you've lost me. Your diction's really come on, though.'

Dave's snigger started up again.

'I'm talking about the girl,' said Don, slowly, watching me. 'You telling me you don't know her?'

'Like I said. Can't help you.'

Dave licked the plate, his eyes above the white disc rolling from me to his brother and back again. Don sizzled his cigarette down to the filter in one draught. My ribs felt him inhale but were in no position to raise objections.

'Don't signify,' he said. 'Fing is, we know this certain brass is looking for you. Got a job she wants done. We come here to tell you you ain't doing it.'

As it happened, it was true what I'd said. I didn't know your name, back then, and I didn't know what the Cherubs were talking about. But of course that made no difference. There are rules in this business. There's decorum.

I hauled an arm free, fished out my own crushed cigarettes, knocked one from the pack and lit up.

I tugged the bitterness down into my chest, then, with the burning paper twist bobbing on my lip, I gave Don my coolest eyeball.

'You're wasting your time, boys.'

'Awful sorry to hear that, Hal.' Don's brows were kissing caterpillars. 'I always fought you was a sensible man.'

I shrugged as well as I could. Then, reckoning it couldn't hurt to try, I tipped my head so much as to indicate that the civilised move would be to let me out of the booth.

'You know it don't work like that,' Don said.

Dave reached across the table. Next thing I was on my way out of the joint, the fist of a Cherub brother clamped on each shoulder like it meant to separate ball from socket. On the up side, the journey cost me nothing in shoe leather. Those boys move fast when they want to. We were through Meaney's in a single lurch of mirrors and bottles, the bouncer's bored sweaty face and the powdered, surprised faces of the whores, then we were out in the frying-pan street, and down an alley where I was pinned against hot brick, my toecaps waving clear of the tarmac.

2. A Street Named Pain

I glanced down at my shirt-front, bunched in Don's fist. Laboriously, Dave unbuttoned his cuff and began to roll up his sleeve. I noticed a big

129

lizard, black with gold stripes, on the lip of a bin opposite, motionless and wilting in the heat. I'd never seen one like it in the city.

'This is the way it works,' Don was saying, 'as you well know. We give you a friendly warning. You got to say something clever. We end up out here.'

Dave's fist coasted at my face. Everything went haywire. My eyes were swingballing in opposite directions but I was aware of the fist, at the end of its trajectory and beginning to fall back, a wrecking ball on its return to the ragged gap in the masonry. He clocked me again. Either that or the alleyway turned a somersault all by itself. Beyond the silent splashes of black and blue, he was shaking out his fingers and rotating his shoulder.

I was still suspended against the bricks. Dave wound up one more time and opted for the solar plexus. I dropped off the wall, curled up and took some time to myself. Footsteps receded.

At length I rolled over and opened my eyes.

The alley walls were two cliffs of clay-red shadow, leaning towards a strip of acid bronze sky, burning and still, far and close all at once, hard-pencilled with the lines of fire escapes. Rubbish sizzled softly all around me. I drifted off. When I looked again the shadows had ticked a few degrees across the brickwork and Dolly was leaning over me, her lower lip bulging in the gap between her front teeth.

'Dammit, Moody,' she said. 'This is how you handle your problems?'

She made me sit up. My jaw didn't seem to fit together. Something began to flow freely in my nose.

She clicked her tongue. 'Looker this.' She rummaged about her person and pulled out a big piece of white cotton, which she folded up and pressed to my face. She tipped my head back. I meant to tell her to leave me alone but I couldn't seem to get around to it. She sat away on her haunches.

'Why'd you make trouble with the Cherubs, Hal? I don't know what business you got between you but I know it ain't worth it.'

She eased the sticky cotton off my face, and brushed damp strands of fringe out of my eyes. Her big features kinked sympathetically. The sweat had cut through her powder, leaving a runnel of dewed skin down the side of her neck.

I stared at her. Then I stumbled to my feet, lurched into the opposite wall, and blundered away through ripe milk cartons and a drift of deliquescing vegetables. As I turned the corner she was getting up, the heel of her shoe twisting under her.

3. Beauty with a Concealed Blade

I headed towards the quays. A couple of blocks that way, the stink of fish rose up like the neighbourhood was getting sick to its stomach.

On the opposite pavement, among the jumble of tenement fronts, I passed a white door just as two figures ducked out. They wore duster coats which dragged on the ground, close-fitting leather skullcaps and leather masks with elongated snouts. Their hands were gloved to the elbows. I sweated harder just looking at them. They rummaged in their kitbag and one of them did something to the door. When he moved, I saw he had painted a cross, two diagonal red streaks. *This house has been visited.* Next, he got to work on the door with a nail gun, while the other figure began to swing a hand bell up and down, shoulder to hip, up and down. I pulled my handkerchief from my breast pocket and held it to my nose and mouth as I went by.

All I wanted right now was to soothe that throbbing you only get from a week-old weapons-grade hangover followed by a meaningful discussion with the Cherub brothers. I wished to be where others were not and I knew just the place. A few doors further along I ducked off the street and down a constricted staircase into a cellar room.

The light was low enough it didn't thrust white lances down my optic strings. That made a change. It was even cool.

I stepped up to the bar and put down a coin. The barman put down a shot glass and filled it. I knocked it back.

The place was near empty. No Cherubs and no skirt. Only one shadowy customer propped at the other end of the bar studying a shot glass of his own. I raised my finger to the barman and, as he poured, I caught my eye in the mirror behind him. Not a pretty sight. The eye in question was purple and black, and closing up so fast I couldn't blame it for preferring not to watch. My reflection and I returned to our drinks, neither of us looking for any trouble.

My appearance. I'd give a wide berth to that ugly character. Now and then people tell me I have a resemblance to someone, a rasping musician who had a bit of success in the last century with deconstructed gothic blues and macabre chanson. I saw a picture of him once in a magazine. A gargoyle in a hunch hat and a postmortem suit, dustbowl stubble, set of teeth you'd find on a bar room floor. Is that what you saw when we met for the first time? You never said. I don't know.

I tipped the spirit into the back of my throat and choked appreciatively as it burned all the way down. The swell at the other end of the bar was taking a sidelong interest in me. He was a skinny kid, his oiled hair and snakeskin boots winking out of the shadow. The chalkstripe suit was cut boxy and expensive and his fedora lay upend on the bartop.

'Run into some trouble, Hal?'

The kind of question that recommends silence. The wise guy slid closer, put his elbows on the bar and revealed his face in the mirror. Fine down glowed on his cheek where it caught the light. I noticed the slenderness of the throat extending from the snowy-crisp collar, the rounding of the chin and the moulding of the mouth. My upper lip curled of its own accord and my fingernails scraped the bartop.

'This was a decent joint,' I muttered.

The person beside me grinned and fitted a boot to the footrail.

'What's the matter, Hal?' she asked, in a contralto I couldn't mistake. 'You ain't pleased to see me?'

'I'm not in the mood, Moll.'

'Ouch, let me guess. You ran into the Cherubs.'

'You heard what I said.'

She drew back, mock-offended, then unbuttoned her jacket and stuck her hands in her pockets, flashing the points of her braces. Moll Cutpurse, the Roaring Girl of the Liberties. I'd heard it said she'd been twice engaged to be married: once to a man who owned three factories out in Kinsayder Fields, once to an inexperienced heiress from Rosamunda. She booked both weddings for the same day, then left them standing at their respective altars and fenced the gifts for a tidy profit.

I made to leave but she stepped in front of me, blocking my way.

'What's the hurry?' she said. 'I got something to tell you. As a favour, like. Some frail's looking for you, you know that? Sparky little baggage. She's asking for you up and down the waterfront, spreading your name around. That'd make me uneasy. If it was my situation, I'd want to know why. But that's me. Maybe you're different.'

She caught her laughter at the corner of her mouth. I gathered the bitter stuff that had collected in my gullet and gave a little something back to the joint's sticky floor. Then I shoved past, swinging the Roaring Girl on her heel. I heard her throaty chuckle as I climbed back into the heat, and she called up after me: 'Quite the looker, too – quite the little looker, Hal!'

4. Fate Carries a Blackjack

My office was embedded high up in one of those great decaying blocks that lean out over the quays, ready any day to topple into the water. Black brick and flaked green paint outside, and, inside, a gentle purgatory of stairwell gloom, dead lift shafts and brown corridors with one electric light fluttering off and on. In my particular closet the filing cabinets held each other up like it had been a heavy night. The slatted blind hung splayed across the window. A defunct air conditioning unit lay in the corner, waiting for the end of the world.

When I first took the room I'd had my name stencilled on the frosted glass panel in the door, together with the two initial letters that stood for my profession. Seeing it, ghosted and inverted, used to hit me like hot coffee when I was working into the night amid stacks of case notes and coarse-grained photographs. These days I used the desk drawers for my collection of empty bottles. The city noises didn't get in here much. You could spend all afternoon watching the parallel lines of daylight creep across the cabinets and disappear before hitting the far corner. If I ever got around to making a will, this was where I wanted to be buried.

I toiled up six storeys and arrived breathing hard and in need of a restorative, but when I turned the corner of the landing something brought me to a stop. The corridor was still and silent, but was the dust stirring through the half-light? At the far end, was the door standing open just an inch?

The sweat had gone cold down my back. Automatically I patted the pockets of my suit but my hands found nothing to reassure them. I settled my hat and moved noiselessly along the corridor, took the last few feet at the pace of a paranoid gastropod and flattened myself beside the door. Yes: it was open a fraction. I'd shut it when I left, hadn't I? I'd locked it, too, I never forget, but there were no signs of forced entry. Through the crack all I could see was a dark slice of wall. There was no sound.

Then I caught the faintest creak, a creak I knew by heart. Someone shifting in my chair.

My jaw tightened till my fillings hurt. This joker planned to get the drop on me in my own office? Nothing doing. I knew the angles here. The window at the end of the corridor looked on the fire escape. So I'm no gymnast, but was I such a sack that I couldn't climb out, slip along the walkway and slap a nasty surprise on whoever was sitting in my damn chair taking aim at my door, waiting for the hapless silhouette to appear in the frosted panel? My office window swung open in just the right way to connect a clean smack with the back of a complacent skull, I reckoned.

I sank into a crouch and began to creep past the office door. You should see me creep when I want to. If I'd dropped a pin you'd have heard it.

Then I wasn't creeping any more. I'd caught the tip of my shoe in the hem of my trousers; the turn-up was trailing since my run-in with the Cherub brothers. Somehow I was flailing into a big stride and flinging my whole weight against the door. It flew all the way open, clattering against the cabinets. I just about bounded into the room and sprawled across the desk.

I'd have liked an hour or so to myself to come up with some really appropriate profanities for how I felt about this situation, but it wasn't to be. Because we were face to face.

5. Stick 'em Up, My Lovely

You know I'm not good at this kind of thing. What was odd, you seemed equally surprised. You sprang out of the chair like you'd been found out taking a liberty, then caught your poise like you calculated you could get away with it.

As I blinked up at you from a drift of the junk I hadn't got around to filing on a refuse heap, I knew there was only one way this scene was going to go and that was however you wanted. Not that I planned to make it easy on myself. I straightened up, screwed my hat into a ball and threw it at the hatstand. I bared my teeth like I thought the orangutans at the city zoo had perfected the art of conversation. Give me a break, I'd been punched in the jaw by my own desk.

You simply smiled. Anyone would have sworn you were pleased to see me. Then you looked shocked. Something I'd noticed about you already, expressions cross your face like ripples on water. Your thoughts astonish you all by themselves. It's a charming turn, I'll allow that. You do it so neat I could nearly buy it.

'I didn't know how else to find you,' you said. 'You never pick up the phone.'

My scowl sank deeper. I should have told you to get the hell out of my office but I said nothing. You were incongruous in the sedimented dinge of the room, reaching into your valise.

'Mind if I smoke?'

I grunted and lit up one of my own.

You raised your chin to me with the unlit cigarette balanced between your lips. Glowering, I tossed my matchbook into the desk debris between us. You wore a private face as you tore a match out and struck it.

'You don't change, do you . . . Hal.'

With your eyes slitted against the smoke, you dropped the matchbook into your valise. That valise, that brand of cigarettes, that gesture, that curl, I couldn't shake the sense I'd seen them before, and often. But not in this town. I gave up on my glower and tried stringing a sentence together instead.

'You don't know me, lady.'

You considered this.

'Maybe not. But I can imagine you.'

And with that, all at once, I was too tired. I was a body map of insults that no one needed to see.

'Look, miss. I don't know you and I got no interest in what you have to say about me. Now either you're here on business or you were just leaving.'

Against the window you were in silhouette, the daylight eating into your edges. You turned your head to me and smoke bloomed.

'I have a job for you, Hal Moody.' You reached without hesitation, without even looking, into the heaped desktop, and stubbed your half-smoked cigarette out in the chipped coffee cup that served me for an ashtray. 'I need you to search for a missing person.'

'That's more like it,' I said. 'Take a seat.'

Before I knew it, I'd gestured for you to sit back down in my chair, the big old bucket-seat creaker behind the desk. For all the world as if I was going to line myself up on the straight-backed broken-legged number I keep so clients won't stay any longer than they have to. But you didn't sit. You stayed dark against the bright pane and chuckled softly to yourself.

'Who are you looking for?' I blurted.

'I'm not the one searching, Mr Moody.'

You picked your way around the desk and looked up at me. You inspected my necktie, a no-nonsense job in navy silk with dark red diamonds. Then you turned your attention to my shoes, which, I was suddenly aware, needed to be polished, or possibly thrown in a skip. One of them had hairy brown parcel string instead of a lace.

Your finger traced my lapel, absent-minded. It was well done. It was as if you recognised my jacket from long ago, like maybe you'd known it well in your childhood, and it seemed for a moment this was the only reason you were here.

'Time is strange,' you said, almost too soft for me to catch. Then you came back to yourself, or you seemed to, and you twitched my lapels straight.

'You're not going to like it,' you said, 'but this is the story, so you'd better listen. The missing person – I can't tell you anything about her, nothing, no back story. I can't tell you where to start looking. All I can tell you is this. First, she isn't missing, not yet. And second, there's no way you're ever going to find her. But, Hal, I need you to search.'

This wasn't much better than talking to the Cherubs. 'Give me the facts,' I growled. 'Who is this frill?'

Your hand wavered. You hesitated like you

weren't sure which answer you wanted to give. Then you said:
  'It's me.'

6. *Blue Eyes and Greenbacks*

With that the whole thing became clear to me. Became quite routine. It's not like I get many clients, but when I get them, that's how it goes, these days, nine times in ten, more when it's a dame we're talking about. It's no mystery, nothing you could call a case. It's some private investigation of her own, a tale or fantasy with herself at the centre and who knows what shadows and worries webbing out in all directions to make up the rest of the thing. Not that it could make sense to anyone else, not that it's the expression of anything rational, but at some point the moist finds what she really needs is a schlub to join in and play along. So she comes to me and I charge her eighty a day plus expenses. I ask the right questions and look like I'm listening to the answers, she gets what she needs, I get what I need, everybody's happy.

  So with zero surprise I heard out what you had to say. You yourself were the missing person in your story, it was you I was supposed to find. I gave a practised professional nod. Sure, sure, you were here now, but there was no doubt you'd soon be spirited away. No, you couldn't tell me why or how you expected to vanish, who it was you were afraid of. My job was simple: meet you first thing tomorrow morning. You picked a scrap of paper off my desk, scribbled an address, folded it and passed it over between two fingertips.

'Seven a.m. sharp,' you said.

'And what am I doing at seven a.m. at –' I glanced at the paper '– eleven-seventy-four Lorenz? I gotta know if I'm walking into something here.'

'You'll be fine. Just be there. I need you watching closely.'

The way you made it sound, you were liable to evaporate right into the overbaked air. Not that you seemed too concerned.

'Once I'm gone, Hal, you have to keep looking for me. Promise.'

You dropped your chin and gazed up at me so your eyes were a pair of wells sunk into limpid darkness. I teetered over them, heels on the brink.

'Wait just a minute,' I said. And I said the word Don Cherub had spoken in Meaney's – said it as a question. 'That's you, isn't it?'

You said nothing, kept your eyes raised to me.

'I thought so,' I said. I shook my head and strode the length of the office, by which I mean I took a single reckless step before barking my shin. 'You've already given me plenty of grief today. You're the kind makes as much trouble as the nearest sucker lets her. And I can't think of one good reason why I should get involved.'

You raised an eyebrow. Then the other.

'Yeah, okay, I got a reason,' I said. 'Ninety a day

plus expenses, that's what. Call it a hundred if I'm getting up in the middle of the goddamn night. First week's payable in advance.'

You shrugged. Then, casually, you swept half the junk off my desk to the floor. From your valise you brought out a fistful of something like specie, but it was no currency I recognised: they looked like small gold coins from two thousand years ago, rubbed into smooth soft-edged ovals, worn as thin as seashell shards in the bed of a river. You heaped a handful on the desk, then another, then more. I lifted one of the discs; it had a buttery gleam, and a density to it in spite of being so delicate.

'I take cash,' I said.

'This is better, the way things are.'

I couldn't disagree. I held the disc up to the light. No markings were legible. The fine-veined tracery across the surface had no pattern or direction I could make out. I tried it between my teeth. I looked at the pile on the desk. There was a lot.

'Do we have an agreement, Mr Moody?'

I'd have liked to pause for an internal struggle, but what was the use? It wasn't much to do with the gold. The answer to the question had been out of doubt since the moment you walked through the door of my office and set yourself to wait in my chair.

You smiled like you knew that too. But along with the triumph you looked to be genuinely pleased for me. You came close again and your hand strayed up to brush something off my lapel. You leaned in, your lips not quite touching my ear.

'Take care of yourself,' you murmured, as if you were passing on a secret. You walked out of my office, and, just before you shut the door, I'd swear you granted a slow glimpse of one marble-smooth, masterly turned ankle, bound in its narrow black strap. And then you were gone.

I stood in the centre of the stifling box for a minute, then two, then five. Every scrap of the precious metal you'd given me I loaded into my pockets, and the weight settled into me like something of my own, some burden I'd been missing. Then I wrenched the old nine-iron from where it was holding up one end of the window blind, and beat up my chair and my clients' chair. I smashed my desk lamp, hacked divots from the plaster, slashed the fins off the ceiling fan and bludgeoned in the fronts of the filing cabinets. I cleared the glass out of the window frame and the frosted pane out of the door, and I didn't stop until there was nothing unbroken and the muscles across my shoulders ached with heat like the tarmac in the streets outside.

7. *The Heart is a Crime Scene*

Eleven-seventy-four Lorenz Drive was out in the hills beyond the city limits, one of the winding high-banked avenues that ran for miles with now and then a big villa set far back above the road. The final scrap of dawn-time cool was cooking out of the air as I steered my coughing, bucking jalopy round the curves. Most of the gates were chained and padlocked. In spite of the splendid seclusion, the folks who lived out here found it too close to the sickness stewing down in the city. Same as always they'd cleared out to their country retreats until the heat was off.

The last of the dawn evaporated, the sun flicked itself clear of the hills and got straight into burning, and the curves went rolling past, the gatepost numbers rising at a crawl. The aspect began to change. Soon the gates were rusted and broken in, and the paths beyond them choked with dark greenery. Then nothing for a stretch. I drove on.

When I found it, the place turned out to be only half there. Some time back they'd begun construction of the last in the necklace of hillside villas, but work had stopped at the bare structure, leaving an abstraction of a house in concrete and brick, which had since been crumbling. The doors and windows were bare rectangular gaps.

I zigzagged up the steep driveway and braked to a stop in the dish of dust out front of the house. What did you want to bring me here for? I clumped the jalopy's door shut, settled my hat on my head and shot my cuffs. I didn't like it. It was seven-oh-two a.m. precisely. Why had I agreed to come? There was no sign of you. There were no other vehicles. I squatted and eyed the dust fruitlessly.

Inside, the house was an undivided space, still wide open at the back. A stack of breeze blocks had partly fallen over in the uncompleted aperture. An approximation of a staircase led nowhere. All at once I was on the point of calling your name out loud.

Then I heard an engine snarl and tyres in grit.

Anyone could tell it was time to disappear out the back and wait to see how things unfolded. But I paused an unforgivable moment, there in the open of the half-made house. Doesn't that tell you everything, kid? Doesn't that tell you how much trouble I was in? More than anything else, what I wanted was to see a certain shape outlined in that doorless doorway, so I bought into the sudden lift of excitement in my chest, and I paused.

And the light was blocked out. Don Cherub shouldered into the room, followed by his brother.

'Hal. Seems you ain't given up.'

'Where is she?' My head felt as hard, angular and hollow as the heaped blocks. 'Where is she?'

'That,' said Don, 'is what you ain't going to find out.'

'Tell me where she is.'

'You should have listened in the first place, Hal, and turned down the case. But you ain't a man to take friendly advice. So here we are again.'

Don was holding something close to his leg, something blunt and leaden. Brass glinted at Dave's fist. I lifted my chin. No one quite seemed to know what to say next.

'Come on, then,' I offered at last, and, shyly, the brothers moved towards me.

★   ★   ★

. . . mid-morning sunlight angled through the holes and tracked across unfinished floor. Dust moved in small whorls, the motes buddying up and falling out again. I stirred. I was spread on the ground all ready for outlining in white tape. I moved a hand to find out what shape my head was, then sat up, full of regrets. From the precipice of the staircase you'd have seen me feeling my skull, surrounded by scattered gold bits. They had burst from my pockets and the Cherubs had left them where they fell. Those boys and their professional ethics.

You hadn't been here. I gave it to myself straight: she wasn't here, it was them instead. I was in no state not to despair. There were no leads, there was no way forward. I knew nothing about you except what wouldn't help.

With my thoughts cramped tight as my jaw I gathered up the thin coins, restoring every last one to my pockets. I knew their weight, now, to the penny. I thought I'd head back into the city then inter myself at the back of Meaney's and see how many whiskies I could swap them for. Then I noticed something else in the dust. I picked it up. A business card: a name, unknown to me, was printed on the front, and the name of a trade, and an address. But when I flipped it over, the pale-pencilled handwriting there nearly floored me again. The characters were already fixed in my mind. Four words. *Take care of yourself.*

147

8. Tough Guys Bruise Easy

I pounded the streets. I'd have driven but the Cherubs had cut my tyres, so the jalopy was beached up on Lorenz Drive and I'd slogged it back into the city on foot, parched, earning blisters. The cheap business card was in my pocket, its edges already rubbed soft by my fidgeting thumb. My thinking was, you'd slipped it into my pocket back in the office. I didn't like that but it was something to go on. It took me all afternoon to find the address. It wasn't a district I knew, and I kept having to turn back, making detours with my handkerchief clutched to my nose and mouth, because the red sigils clustered ever thicker and just out of sight the bells were ringing. Plenty of streets were too far gone for containment. The doors hung open and bodies lay half in and half out, kinked across doorsteps and kerbstones, able to crawl so far and no further, or perhaps in some confused attempt to cool down. In these murky trenches the air lay like piping hot asparagus soup. They moaned to each other, lifting mottled limbs, the ones that could. Here and there daring entrepreneurs, their bodies robed and their heads swaddled in herb-stuffed bandages, slung the still and the still-twitching alike on their carts before hauling them off to collect a few pence a head at the burial pits. I hurried past, monitored by the rats that laced themselves in and out of the mounds blocking the alleys to the first-floor windowsills.

The address on the card turned out to be a sullen door a couple of steps below pavement level. I had to shove to reach it because the street was obstructed by a crowd of young boys and old women clustered around a pair of dogs fighting over some raggedly round, bloodied object. The spectators slashed at the frantic animals with sticks and shoes, and called out bets to each other.

I consulted the card again –

DOCTOR S. DOGG
MYSTERIES OF SCIENCE
97 DAPPER STREET, GLORY PART

– and was none the wiser. So I tightened my greasy half-windsor, rasped a palm across my jaw, and battered the wood with the heel of my fist. At once, locks tumbled and bolts shot on the other side. I was all ready to go in hard and force some answers out of there. But when the door opened I was struck stony.

She folded her arms tight under her bust. It didn't look so friendly as sometimes. She spiked me with that challenging look she had, kohl-ringed for emphasis. The tough guy act is all very well for scaring up information from the unsuspecting, but what are you meant to do faced with a flimsy who's looking at you like she's seen all your tricks before? Worse, she had, and I knew it. The angle of her chin was saying she'd been more impressed by her puppy the last time it left a damp patch on the floor. I spluttered and found my tongue.

'What are you doing here?'

'Believe it or not, Hal, you don't know everything about me. A better question is what are *you* doing here?'

'I'm on a case,' I said.

'Oh, I'll bet you are. Listen –' she glanced back into the dark house '– this ain't a good place for you. Turn around and go home, all right?'

'I'm on a case.'

She leant closer, and I caught the bready flavour of her breath. She spoke in a hurried undertone.

'Dammit, Hal, I'm getting sick of looking out for you all the time.' Her brown hair brushed my stubble, and her eyes softened, but only for a moment. 'Do you even notice? You shouldn't have come here. Go away!'

As she flared, she shoved me in the chest. I caught her wrist and we tussled on the threshold. I saw the gap in her strong teeth and tested the sturdy softness of her arms. But then a voice flowed out of the house's interior, and a presence slid forward to encompass us. He was hard to see. He came over as a tidy group of impressions, a frictionless smile and hair parted with a ruler, a gust of cologne, a linen jacket crisply immune to the heat, a pair of pointed patent tiptoes that seemed to slip along on hidden rails, an arm that curled across Dolly's shoulders and mine all at once to guide us together into the house. Above all he was a voice, a pleasant, continuous hum of a voice. The man was hard to see straight because the voice never stopped describing itself so smoothly.

'Well,' it said, 'well well well, and who have you found for us today, Royal Doll, incomparable lady, can it be that you have brought us the well-known Mr Hal Moody? Ah, yes yes, very striking, most characterful, and so very much exactly as one would have expected, ha ha – we are honoured indeed though we flatter ourselves it was inevitable you should find your way here in due course – oh, allow me, yes, this way please, might I relieve you of your hat, ah, no, I perceive you prefer to retain that cephalic accoutrement, by all means, but may I introduce myself, I am known to one and all as the Captain, and may I express, Mr Moody, if I might, my admiration for, how shall I phrase it, your *straightforwardness* in coming here, no no, a particular species of courage without a doubt and I am quite confident we shall be more than able, and, needless to add, willing to ease you in actualising your desires given certain reciprocal considerations into which it would diminish us both to go further at this juncture. Yes, I can assure you it is merely a matter of procedures which though startling to the layman are for the initiated routine, and on that point I beg leave to introduce to you our learned colleague and I would go so far as to say the genius of our little republic – see how he appears from his potently befugged laboratory in the back – this is Dr Dogg himself, blinking behind the pebbly lenses of his erudition. Permit me to apologise in advance for the lapses in manners that are certain to ensue in the course of his conduct but we must take into account that he is a man of brilliance such as must not be yoked by the guidelines of quotidian social concord if we are to reap the bounty of his virtue – here, doctor, you see, our valued client himself, yes!'

This guy didn't draw breath. He only smiled, smooth as Vaseline. He'd ushered us into a room in the heart of the house. In here there were no windows in the stained brick, and the only light was from a bulb dangling bare from the ceiling. The cement floor was tracked with oily marks. Even so, the Captain hovered in the middle of the den like it was the set of a game show.

The short, undernourished figure stumping from the back room, with his multicoloured fingers and the scorchmarks down the front of his smock, was more in keeping. He peered up at me and pursed his lips so that against his yellow pallor his sparse moustaches wriggled in their own grease. Blackheads stuck out of his nose like peppercorns. He began to quiver silently.

The room was furnished like a bankruptcy in a rag-and-bone shop. There was a sofa that looked to have spent some considerable time on a landfill; there was an incongruous full-length mirror, a selection of packing crates, and a three-panelled screen whose printed cotton had been ripped out, leaving only the wooden skeleton. Against one wall stood a glass tank, murky with waterweed, in which I saw a grey-green shape moving with flicks of a flattened leaf tail.

'I observe that you share our esteemed doctor's passion for natural history,' said the Captain. 'Here we find yet another one of creation's young creatures which he has, with all the compassion and rigour of his vocation, nursed from sickness into health and now nurtures towards the fullness of its potential. It is, as you will of course immediately have recognised, an immature salamander, in the larval stage. Once it has undergone its metamorphosis and entered into its adult form, the doctor, evincing the hatred of all forms of bondage that is native to his constitution, is determined to set it free to live in the wider world with its many risks and fulfil-ments. Think of that, Mr Moody, and consider then whether Dr Dogg is not one into whose hands you are confident to entrust your hopes. If he would do so much for a dumb beast, then how much for you?'

The Captain's gaze tick-tocked between me and the thing in the tank. It was a bug-eyed blighter with a fringe of fleshy lobes around its neck, frantically pulsing its gills and waving its clubbed legs in the water. Dogg seemed to be suppressing a coughing fit.

While he creased himself up, Dolly Common hung back, hard-lipped, and the Captain bobbed around, his large, flawless hands flicking and stroking the air as if conducting our interactions. It was time to show these clowns what was what.

'What you're selling, buddy, I ain't buying,' I told him, acting like the diminutive sniggerer wasn't even there. 'I'm asking the questions here and you're going to spill, see?'

Dolly rolled her eyes and Dogg was still locked into his soundless convulsions, but the Captain dipped and swayed. 'But *natürlich*, but anything we can do, we are at your service entire –'

I cut across him with your name, clipped and curt. 'What do you know about her?'

'Ah, ha ha, yes, but of course, we know her of whom you speak, we share even if I may say so a certain intimacy, and who could know her without holding her in a deep regard? Not yourself, certainly, no, not you. He is a seeker, is he not, poor darling Doll? A pilgrim, we might say, don't you think, my dear doctor?'

His voice wavered as though he was having trouble controlling himself. But he went on: 'You have tracked a happy trail, Mr Moody, because my colleagues and I are in a position to help you. Oh yes – I see the salmon hope flash in the torrent of your heart, though your manly outer form strives to conceal it – yes, very much so, we can help. More! My friend the doctor here has a power in his receipts to bring you to her direct and immediate. Think of it, sir, you have succeeded against all expectation by the shortest way and now, very now, she will be yours, impossible though it may have seemed, and all you must do is place yourself entirely – in – our – hands.'

He wafted closer like a sheet flapping on a line.

'What's he talking about?' I asked Dolly.

She just shook her head.

'The lady is not, precisely, here,' the Captain was saying. 'But the important thing to bear in mind is that we can, if you will, convey you to her. The process, be assured, is quite painless and requires only that you place in us a modicum of the trust to which, as your well-wishers, if I may say so, we are surely entitled. Doctor, if you would. The, ha ha, solution to your dissatisfactions resides altogether here, in this rarest of the doctor's preparations, which I am happy to say is administered . . . orally.'

Dogg had produced a finger-sized glass phial filled with black stuff. But Dolly laid her hand on top of his.

'Put it away,' she said, 'and you: can the flim flam.'

The Captain's smile didn't flicker but very softly he snarled between his premolars: 'Enough, woman.'

'You don't need this, Hal,' said Dolly. 'Forget it and get out of here.'

'Aha, ha ha. You must pardon our fair friend, what she means –'

'Hold it.' I turned on her. 'Are you telling me there's something in this? These jokers can help me find her?'

Dolly's eyes pleaded.

'You're telling me I drink that stuff and I find her?'

She sagged. 'I ain't saying nothing, Hal.'

'Most credible, don't you think? Very convincing indeed,' the Captain's voice hummed in the background. Dogg snorted in response. Maybe the three of them were all nuts together in their own special fruitcake, but part of me was insisting it didn't matter. If this could be a chance, who cared whether it made sense?

I motioned to Dogg.

'What is that stuff?'

His face twitched. 'What you need to understand, Mr Moody,' he said, in a voice that threatened to dissolve into reedy giggles, 'is that time is strange in certain rooms.'

Before I could ask him what that was supposed to mean, he held the phial towards me and pulled the cork. It ponged like it should have been trickling in the pestilent gutters. The odour coiled out of the tube and fixed its claws in my sinuses. I gagged. Dogg's lips began to writhe again. Drink it? I've been clobbered in the homburg department my share of times, but what did they take me for? The smell flushed through my head and in the ensuing instant I saw the meanness of the low cellar, the streaked bricks, the drained faces. There was no help in this room, just two half-starved charlatans and a raddled hissy having fun at the expense of an old gumshoe.

Blackness crept into the edges of my vision and I lashed out at the so-called doctor, colliding with him awkwardly shoulder-first and knocking him aside. Hunched against the wall, shaking, he cradled his phial. His face contorted and tears pressed from the corners of his eyes. I spun around and swung my fists at the Captain, but he danced easily away, his hands billowing. He quivered with the effort of restraining himself. He couldn't even speak any more.

I shoved past Dolly and stormed up the corridor, fighting off insubstantial enemies. Behind me, they gave up their composure, and the howls of laughter propelled me back to the street. I couldn't tell if any were hers.

9. *City of Regretful Lights*

What was it that happened next? Tell me what, kid – because if you won't, then who will in the world? Whatever it was, it didn't unfold in ordinary time, moment linking to moment, beat to beat. I lost my grip on that like a drunk missing the handrail at the top of a staircase. I arced through a glutinous descent of unmeasured duration, days, weeks or months, clonking off every third step. I plunged, in fact, into the finest and most sustained period of investigative work I'd ever accomplished.

Let me tell you how it goes. It's nothing to do with observation or deduction. It's like running at an oblique angle into a brick wall and dragging your head along as far as you can take it. It means you have no trail to follow but you pound the pavements until in your lunacy everything's part of the trail. You never stop, think of nothing else, batter the world like if you go at it hard enough it's going to spill its guts. If none of it makes sense then why not call every last thing a clue? Why not think by sheer lead-skulled persistence you're going to turn bewilderment into an answer? It could happen.

I stopped going back to my office. That would have taken time from the search. Brittle, I crumbled myself into the stews, where I dissolved. I slept in snatches of minutes at diner counters, in tram shelters, in the porchways of derelict apartment buildings. Days and nights were the swinging of a bare light bulb, the rattle of a tram across a lattice of girders. I pounded. My beard filled out and my suit grew stiff and malodorous, I tugged at my necktie until the knot was unpickable, but I kept searching. Salt Park, Shambles Heath, Sludd's Liberty, Moebius Wall. Bloodstone Cross, Bittergreen, Gorgonstown, Low Glinder. Lawntown, Twistgate, Serelight, Glory Part. I went where I went. I was working on nothing better than an inkling that if I kept moving I might glimpse you. I did my best to follow the only advice you'd ever given me. But the longer I spent walking up and down those corridors and staircases, under those arches, along the interstices of dust and through the sweat-stale nowheres of the twenty-four-hour supermarkets, the more convinced I became that any guesses were useless. I might have been born yesterday. The news-stands were all disease and murder. I didn't know these streets. What I'd always thought of as the city was just an idea I'd been inventing without realising it for longer than I could tell.

Want to know the weird thing? It didn't even hit me that hard. I mean the moment that had to come: which came one overcooked evening on the Strangers' Market, no one around but me and this one big johnny mooching under a lamp post like he'd lost something. I reached up and touched his shoulder, asking the only question I had left to ask, the question I couldn't stop asking. But the johnny – he was one of your big slow armour-plated sorts, right up there with the Cherub brothers – he gave me a look like I was head-to-foot buboes, and scarpered. Couldn't get away fast enough. That did it. That was the moment that yanked my perception out of my skull and snagged it dangling from the lamp post so I saw myself like another person, a wrecked and bruised figure panhandling for a hallucination, approaching strangers and saying the name, just your name, over and over, as a question. None of that was strange when I saw it. Instead, in that lucid moment, all I thought was: yes. Now we're getting somewhere.

What did I want from you anyway? Did I believe I was earning the fee that I still carried crammed into every pocket of my suit? I hadn't lost or traded a scrap. But what did I want from you? It scared me what I might do if we ever found each other. You could hardly answer my obsession, it had grown beyond that, it had broken the decorum of scale so that as I trailed the tall streets I might as well have been meandering in the maze of one of your fingerprints, lost in your open hand.

And as I wandered, a commentary came to me, a monologue in the voice of Dave Cherub. Why was it his voice, which in reality only grunted with dumb laughter? Whyever. Aw dese men, it said, echoing up from some basement dive of my mind. Aw dese men chasin aw dese juicies, but for wot? Ve city's fulluvem. We follerem dahn ve streets, we cun taker ize offem. Bu'if we addem, fuknoze wop weed oowivem, yiih, if grasp wuz reech, if curridge wuz eekwal wiv dizzire, if we ackshly addem ve same uz we wonnem. You wooden avver clue, boy, woodjer. Vey say when a John's chasin some cluck – yiih, n vat's you, innip – vey say it ain't really er e's chasin at aw. Vey say e's really chasin is ahn sohw. Vat's ripe, boy, yer sohw, she fits ver discripshin: you cun getter aht yer ed an you dun nah nuffin abahter. Frangly, ooda forp yer sohwd be so easy on ve i? Hur hur hur. Yiih – an woss vat sayabaht you, enway, if yer asslin vis pore chitty buh yer ain even in'rested in er fer erself? Wossit to er if sum wank'a zonna prufahnd inna quest fer compleshun wivvin is bein? Sheeza yung zafty wivver ahn prodlems, nop yore bleedin hannimer!

The admonitions rang ahead of me as I dragged

out the search. I shambled along the waterfront in the molten core of the afternoon, when the sun was a bucketful of liquid lead and space itself on the point of crisping up and shrivelling. Anyone with a functional sense of cause and effect was indoors with a cool flannel over his face. The boards clunked under my feet, a bone-dry xylophone. Tide-abandoned mud extended to the horizon, an infinite vacant lot of mud, every bit reeking. Behind me was the Part bridge and ahead lay the wreck of the west pier, its grand pavilion listing down to the mud like a crash-landed flying saucer, with the fishbones of decayed struts bowed underneath.

Two figures were approaching through the shimmer. I couldn't tell how far off. They got bigger in uneven jumps. My dried tongue fumbled, forming itself around your name, so I'd be ready with the question when they were close enough. Why were they so large but still so far away? Then something slipped, perception ratcheted, and they were with me: one before, one behind.

'It's a mystery,' Don Cherub said, 'why you refuse to see what's good for you.'

He checked up and down the waterfront. No one else was in sight. He pushed me up against Dave, who pinioned my arms.

'My dog learns faster that certain acts have certain consequences. My geraniums learn faster.'

His fist jabbed out. I coughed, then cursed. Dave held me upright.

'I got nuffin against you, Hal,' Don was saying, 'but I got a job to do and you tire me out, see?'

Dave spun me around into the hardly-less-inescapable grip of his brother, who kept talking into my ear.

'I mean, you could've dropped your investigation at any point and spared everyone the inconvenience. But, all right, I can understand you got professional pride of yer own. You got standards.'

Dave rolled up his sleeve. I offered him a grimace, which he socked into the middle distance.

'What I don't get, Hal, is what kind of bleeding operation you think you're running. See, you're all over town, making a nuisance, getting on everyone's nerves, an' you keep running up against me and Dave here. But it ain't occurred to you to ask why *we* keep running up against *you*. You ain't asked yourself who's making it worth our while. We ain't doing it for our health.'

He spun me back into Dave's embrace. I spat colour on the boards.

'You got a point here, Don?'

'Yeh. I got one. Dave an' me, we view our work serious. We take a job, we do it, that's all. We was hired to warn you offuv searching for the broad. Fine. We done it. But we ain't patsies, yeh? We dunt like being in the middle of anyone's funny games. Each to his own, that's what I say, *day gutsy bus non dipso tandem*, but frankly you people turn my stomach. So that's it, we're finished. This is the last yer getting. If you find her, you can tell

162

her we done the job like we said we would, but we ain't doing it no more.'

I'd never seen Don Cherub look so forlorn. It was like watching a pneumatic drill come to terms with disappointment.

'And,' he said, 'you can give her a refund.'

From his pocket he brought a handful of delicate gold bits. He dropped them on the boards at my feet. Then Dave let me go, and the brothers continued along the boardwalk.

10. Perfidy in a Pencil Skirt

The boards had fixed their splintery teeth in my knees. The scattered coins, so familiar and so unexpected, filled my vision for what could have been any span of time at all, filled my clumsy hands; then that sight whirled away. Perhaps my legs were walking, perhaps I was hauling myself along the boardwalk railing like a man on an ocean liner in the kind of storm you don't survive. But I couldn't tell you for sure, because I was moving through a new set of dimensions, subtle dimensions of treachery, marked in increments of outrage. I discovered a whole new city, mapping streets of fury and avenues of humiliation and gridlocked intersections of desire.

Betrayal, kid. I'll grant you one thing, you were an education. Who knew one word contained such multitudes? Who knew that gaining a new fact about the world could make me understand it so much less?

You'd paid the Cherubs. You'd set me going one way and them going the other. Why had you come to me at all? Just what kind of ride were you taking me for? I tasted it over and over, now sipping delicately, now downing draughts, all the time finding new and more complex flavours of betrayal.

Meanwhile my legs freewheeled under me and the city spooled past. Maybe I could find my way to some high ground and from there I could get a good look at what you'd done, glimpse the masterpiece entire. I hadn't known you were an artist. But you must be the sort that has a special deal with the man downstairs. I contemplated what you'd done with a bitterness that you might as well call wonder, and a joy you can call rage if you like.

By evening I was moving through the streets with the ravaged assurance of a man who's seen it all and now knows everything. A pair of vulture physicians stalked past, their leather beaks ranging balefully towards me. I didn't bother to cover my mouth. Some bent-faced scrounger with a flower in his lapel came up to me with a story, putting an arm across my shoulders and prodding me in the chest with his forefinger, so I left him curling up in the gutter. A maquillaged damson clattered after me, yowling abuse, but I turned and snarled at her deep in my throat. She retreated, uncertain.

I veered into a bar and knocked back spirit until I caught sight of a ghastly face staring at me from somewhere in the mirror's shadows. I yelled for him to come out but there was no answer so I hurled my shot glass into the dark room at random. The bartender had his blackthorn out right away.

I picked myself off the stones outside with a vindictive spring that carried me into the next joint, where I swallowed more spirit till I noticed that the poppet serving needed to be told a thing or two about a thing or two. This decision bounced me right into the next place. I reckoned I was making good progress. But the old head was still too clear for comfort. I set myself at the end of the bar and got to work on that problem.

Over at one of the tables a couple of swells were making rowdy. They kept looking at the door. Their bravado faltered, then redoubled, as a sharp-suited chap swaggered in, shepherding a couple of gussied-up polonies, all long white throats and short fur coats. Himself, he was dressed to the nines with cane and crimson cravat –

No, wait. He wasn't a chap at all. It was Moll Cutpurse, playing her unfair tricks.

She slapped the two dudes on their backs. The painted consorts tripped along in her wake and sat themselves down at the table. Moll made introductions all round, chucked one of her dribs under the chin, and was on her way out again when she seemed to change her mind.

She crossed to the bar, signalled for a drink, and tilted her glass in my direction.

'Got to say it, Hal, you ain't looking great.'

I swivelled my eyeballs towards her under a brow like lead.

'I hear the job ain't going so well. Hard cheese, eh?' she said.

My teeth hurt. Moll grinned matily.

'Your trouble, Hal, if you don't mind me saying so, is you take things too serious by half. You make life hard for yourself. You should take a leaf out of my book.'

She drained her glass, nodded to the barman for another, and surveyed the room as if to affirm how swimmingly it was all going.

'But, see, you think you're something special. Like what you got to go through, no one else ever went through it. Like we don't all have these problems. We all meet ourselves coming back every now and then.'

'Just keep talking, Moll.'

'Settle down, now, Hal, we're all friends here. Let me tell you a true story. Happened only the other day. As I walked out of an evening to view the sights of Serelight Fair, I chanced on some poor unfortunate creature in the extremity of his human need. So, call me soft-hearted, I slipped him twenty and thought no more about it. But he wouldn't let me alone: started following me down the road. Said he had a secret to tell me, something of the utmost importance he had to get off his chest. Begged me to listen with tears in his bloodshot eyes. Said he could tell his story to no one else but me.'

Ignoring her as best I could, I ordered a double.

I thought it might do something about the ball-peen hammers working on my temples.

'So what do you think I did, hearing this plea? That's right. I told him once to scram. I told him twice. Then I tipped him amicably into a convenient refuse bin and continued on my way.'

I downed the glassful. It made no difference.

'What I'm saying, Hal, everyone has a hard luck story. You can listen to them and you can even buy what they're selling. But if you decide to make their hard luck into your own, then, soon enough . . .'

She looked me up and down.

'But then I'm old-fashioned,' she said. 'Straitlaced. Not like you.'

Blackness bubbled at the edges of my vision. I held on to the bar as Moll's grin slid in and out of alignment with itself.

'Listen, Hal. Could be the question you should ask yourself is this. How long have you even been in this joint tonight?'

She looked at me like she really wanted to know the answer.

'Because, Hal, it's true what they say. Time *is* strange in certain rooms.'

The blackness boiled in from the corners and this time it didn't stop. I was staring down a tunnel – at the guffawing foursome at the table, at Moll's cocky grin, at the shaking of my own hands.

I grabbed a bottle off the counter and swung it hard at her face.

She dodged backwards, evading me easy, beginning to chuckle. Spitting a blue streak, I halved the bottle on the bartop and lunged. She stepped out of the way and I cracked a kneecap on the fittings. A sharp blow to my wrist sent the brittle weapon spinning across the floor. My affronted hand sang with pain. She stuck out a boot, and next thing I knew I was down among the broken glass and the sawdust.

'Outside,' someone was saying. Hands felt my collar and I was back in the open air with a bloodied chin and a mouthful of grit. I clawed in the gutter for my hat. Some skinny kid with a violin case was gawping and I got ready to correct his manners, but then the Roaring Girl strolled out after me, her hands in her pockets, and sidestepped again as I grabbed for her throat. My knees were shredded and the whole front of my suit was soaked in something vile, but I wasn't giving up. I steadied myself against a lamp post and raised a quivering, accusatory finger at Moll.

She exposed a tooth. 'Sleep it off, Hal.'

Turning her back on me, she set off up the street. I wasn't going to be beaten so, not by her. A chunk of the kerbstone was loose at my feet: I scrabbled it free and, clutching it in one hand, I half-ran, half-staggered after her. I raised the stone, but my feet slipped on the cobbles and I lost my balance.

The stone clacked away and she caught me before I hit the ground. She set me back on my feet. Then she floored me with a right hook and left me there for the night.

11. *You May Kill the Bride*

'Welcome, welcome, do come in, excellent, aha, come in, no, please, let us not refer to any regrettable misunderstandings which may previously have crossed our purposes, to do so would be an irrelevance and a transgression of the principle that all is well which advantageously concludes, yes, welcome, it is quite usual and . . . and . . . and often indeed beneficial to all concerned for a gentleman to allow a period of reflection before taking as it were the plunge, but in my view for what that may be worth you have made a fine, a very sound judgement in returning to us so promptly, and if I may say so you are looking so very much *yourself* this morning . . .'

The Captain, his tall brow crimped in the middle, trembling with self-control, urged me down the corridor. Something had shifted in the weather this morning – there was more space in the open air, a breathable coolness, as though the heatwave might be releasing us at last – but in here it made no difference. As he followed me into the windowless room there was a scuffling, and I had the idea that someone else was being hustled out by another door. But all I saw was the same debris as last time: the skeletal screen, the fish tank, the long mirror set up to face me as I entered. The figure in the glass was crusted with foul stuff, and his hat was a tatter in his lacerated hands. Two black eyes were ripening in competition with the purple bloom on the cheekbone. The beard was clogged with dirt and dry blood.

Dolly Common bustled out of the back room, caught sight of me, searched her repertoire of dirty looks and came up with a real beaut. She disappeared again and returned with a bottle and a rag. I stood inert as she dabbed my face and hands with the stinging stuff.

For a while she worked silently. But she wasn't going to be able to keep that up. 'Okay, Hal,' she said as she sponged the gravel out of my chin. 'You choose to come back here, that's fine. You do what you're going to do. I ain't going to try and discuss it with you. I won't be doing that no more.'

She shoved the antiseptic into my hands and retreated into the back, leaving the job half-done. Alarming sounds of metallic clangour followed.

'Dolly?' I said muzzily. I didn't investigate what was happening in there, though, because, as if an actor had thrown off one guise for another, she was replaced by Dr Dogg. He was more composed than last time, but he kept darting amused disbelieving glances my way.

'She's gone now,' he said, pointing at the tank. 'She was a pretty thing after the change. Black as tar and yellow as gold. I let her go yesterday. Took her up into the street and off she went.'

He scuttled around me in a circle, examining

me from all angles, his fingers curled under his moustaches.

'Who knows where she'll get to,' he said. 'Time is strange. In certain rooms, you have to be careful how you leave, or you might meet yourself coming back.'

He peered up at me, standing very close, smirking more than ever.

'Certain rooms – and this is one of them. Have you thought about that, Mr Moody?'

I didn't like his tone. I'd have told him to get away from me, but now the Captain's voice was insinuating itself into my attention.

'. . . all quite painless,' it was saying, 'and any sensation of, what is the *moe juiced*, of *disorientation* will become, in time, second nature. All that is asked is that you place in us an absolute trust, that you do as we say. No small thing to ask, perhaps, of a man such as Mr Hal Moody, but, yes, yes, I see that it is possible, I see it in your demeanour, I perceive that you are at last prepared to countenance our services . . .'

The Captain cut himself off with a snort and turned to the wall, his fist jammed against his mouth. At length he got his breath back.

'Your pardon. There is, I cannot any longer delay to mention, one other matter, the matter of – well – naturally, a procedure such as this involves a not inconsiderable outlay and we do ask as a gesture of good faith in advance . . .'

He paused, balanced at an expectant lean towards

me. Catching his drift, I emptied my pockets. The gold pennies heaped up on the floor. The doctor hissed, scurried out and returned staggering under a cumbersome pair of scales. The Captain weighed the metal meticulously.

'It so happens that this will cover our fee exactly.' He made a courteous movement, as the doctor lifted the bowl from the scales and whisked the gold into the back room. 'No further reason to delay, my dear doctor,' the Captain said offhandedly as the man returned.

The doctor uncorked his phial of black grue and the smell filled the room. A stiletto rictus carved itself into his face as he passed me the potion.

I thought of you. Or I tried to. I realised with a clutch of dread that I couldn't picture you or hear your voice. I looked for Dolly, but there was no sign of her. I thought I might be running out of time. The stench was noxious, but it was nothing I wasn't used to. Only the city. I brought it to my lips, expecting to gag. The strange thing was it had no taste at all.

As I swallowed, the Captain and Dogg watched, appalled but intent, as they'd have watched a performer specialising in self-mutilation. At least I'd wiped their smirks. I took a step towards them, but I was hauling an anvil. I tried to drop the phial but sending orders to my hand was a long-distance call and no one was picking up.

'What's happening?'

They didn't reply. Maybe they hadn't heard. I

didn't want to see what was going on but my eyes were locked into the mirror. Cold was creeping in from the edges, terrible cold, and settling in my core like dread was a sensation of immovable weight.

So we come to this moment. I am fixed in place and my time approaches a vanishing point, slicing itself by thinner increments and thinner. What's gone before is a past-tense prologue funnelling into this crux. I'm sorry. I'm sorry I tried to hurt her. I wonder if, in whatever follows, I'll be able to throw down all these things I carry around with me, all these things I've done and wish I hadn't.

Then what's happening reaches my mind, and that too turns to metal.

Gallathea

To begin with, I was the world, which is another way of saying I did not exist, because when you're that way there's no need to mark lines between what's you and what isn't. Then the divisions came, and what was me began to find itself out. Everything I wasn't broke away, freeing the shape of myself that had waited implicit in the block of the possible. The extraneous matter came off in fine scales as if worked away by a sculptor or a process of erosion. I was aware of the surface, the plane of distinction, sinking in towards my skin, and soon I was able to watch it happening, since the first image that presented itself was, of course, a reflection. I saw the roughly defined figure, stocky and stooped, moulded all out of dull gold. It lost definition as the coin-sized shards loosened and fell. Soon they were a cascade, clicking and jingling as they hit the floor. As the gold encasement thinned it grew translucent and I began to recognise what was inside.

He fell so fast away from me, clothing and hair, skin and superfluous flesh, all translated into soft yellow metal and splitting and opening to let me out. My bare toes flexed in a nest of gold shavings, and I brushed the last fragments from my palms: a first gesture.

They were waiting at the far end of the room, the tall and the short one, turning bashfully away. I could see they weren't going to be much help, but still I cleared my throat and offered them my first hello. I couldn't think why they wanted to be the way they were. I gave another hello to this woman who was watching me so cautiously, and, because there was something about her I liked, to her I gave my first smile.

A sweet early feeling; it must be the start of the morning or the opening of a new season; I had all the world's time to do what I needed to, or what I wanted. With each exhalation and inspiration I was discovering more about what that might be.

The woman was wary, but eventually she gave me back part of my smile, and told me I looked well. While I stretched my waking muscles, she spoke sharply to the men so that they shuffled out of sight. She went away too and for the first time I experienced abandonment, piercing and inordinate while it lasted; but she came back right away with a bundle. She told me – I drank up her every word – that these ought to fit well enough.

I hardly needed her help as I dressed, and with every garment I put on I shed a layer of simplicity until I stood revealed in my sophistication in the glass, in pillbox hat, sharp blouse, pencil skirt and ankle-strapped tango heels. I thanked the woman as an equal as I accepted another gift, a smart rectangular valise; I asked if she had a cigarette to spare and she gave me the pack.

There wasn't much more to be said between us. We had no quarrel. I couldn't blame her if, in spite of her kindnesses, she was reluctant to meet my eyes, but I was glad that as I prepared to leave she wished that I would take care of myself.

The men faltered in again, and began to collect the scraps of gold from the floor. They insisted on heaping them into my new suitcase, telling me they were mine and it was only right I should take them.

Before leaving I asked the tall one with the grubby cuffs for a business card. He spilled a whole stack in his eagerness. I used his pencil to scribble on the back of one the advice that the woman had given me; I thought it might come in useful.

There wasn't much more to do before I left the

city, only a few appointments to keep and engagements to make.

As I stepped out into heat and stench, bristling faces turned in my direction and became avid. The maelstrom tracked me as I passed. I went by a stoop where they were sitting, sweltering, their chest-hair pushing out of their vests and their legs planted wide apart. Friendly voices called over to me, but they were too friendly, they were insisting on their friendliness, and they were asking questions that my friends would not have asked. So I straightened my back and walked on without giving a reply, my heels clicking on the pavement. The voices grew loud and disappointed, and followed me down the street, telling me exactly what I was.

As I crossed the city, others, young and old, well-heeled and scruffy, called out, or barked doglike, or they darted close and made muttered suggestions. Some simply stared angrily, as if I had given them personal offence. One of them, his pink face perspiring above a collar and tie, followed me at a distance for several blocks, so I kept to the middle of populated streets. After a while he gave up.

I stopped in at a café, where, standing up at the counter, I drank a miniature coffee and a glass of iced water. The waiter wouldn't let me pay. Instead I asked him for some local advice and he gave me directions to a certain establishment nearby. I smiled at him and his eyes grew hooded and secret.

At the place he'd told me about, I spoke to a stout, sad-faced man and his blushingly tongue-tied brother.

176

I explained what I needed them to do and paid them in advance. After thanking them and promising to take care in the contaminated streets, I went out again, having more business to attend to.

Later in the afternoon, near the docks, I stopped to watch two figures in huge coats and long leather masks going into a tenement. They were more witch doctors than medics, with their bell and their stink of garlic that drenched the street. After only a minute they came out again and opened up their bulky toolbag on the pavement. On the white door they painted a red diagonal cross.

As the bell beat I caught sight of a man approaching on the other side of the road, his face concealed by the brim of his hat and by the handkerchief he held over his nose and mouth. I stepped into an alleyway's shadow while he passed. It wasn't yet the moment to begin. I had many things in mind that were my concern alone, nothing to do with him; in my thoughts were futures he could never have hoped to imagine. Soon now I'd set out for other places and for the rest of what I planned. Let's try this one more time, kid . . . Before that, though, I'd find him, and give him what he needed never to cease from seeking.

PART V

PART

GOOD SLAUGHTER

Work stopped a heartbeat back. There's no hush like the hush when the machinery shuts off. It's an uproar of silence. We keep our thoughts private. The workers remove their goggles, hard hats and earplugs, peel off their spattered overalls, scrub their hands at the sanitary stations and file to the exits. The concrete gleams. Clear droplets form on steel points, swelling and falling, mechanical, slower and slower. They don't want to count away the time that's left.

Fischer is carrying out his inspection, now checking the overhead rails, the conveyor belts, the hooks, the chutes and the basins, now seeing that tools have been sterilised, drains cleared and work tables hosed down. It's the same at the end of each shift. If he finds something out of order then heaven help the culprit. Any moment now he'll see that one of the tools is unaccounted for. I watch for it. I've waited here, out of sight, watching, not moving: but now it's time to move.

Hello, Fischer. Here I am, dressed for work, carrying the implement of my trade. The last of the others has gone, you see. I thought in this

181

moment I'd find some words to say to you, to settle what's happened between us in these weeks. But look, we're here and I have no words to add. In my head it was easier. You must be pleased the things you've done to me have worked so well.

The flesh of his face looks heavy under the lights. As I stump towards him his lips twitch and he tilts his head a few degrees, letting me know that what's happening is well within his expectations. He's quite sure he has the upper hand. He tugs each fingertip in turn and draws off his gloves, then lays one on the other and bats them against his thigh. He'll take his time and decide what to do with me.

We all know Fischer's floor is run to the hardest standards. No second chances: you let him down and you're finished. He smiles that lazy, dangerous smile as the distance between us closes. But he fails to understand that I do not make mistakes here on the floor. I'm good at my job.

Now we're within arm's reach, I can see where the hairs are thinning on top of his head and how his pate glistens under the lights. There's a mark where the hard hat has been clamped into the skin. He looks up at me and his mouth shows the rough line of his teeth. He thinks I'm slow, but that's only because I never know how to answer him.

Puzzlement shows in his expression. Odd that so small a delay, just long enough for me to walk across a sloping cement floor, can add up to the error he now suspects. He should have acted differently, but now it's too late. His eyes are the colour of dry concrete. The pupils contract to pinpricks as they note the implement in my hand. I've sharpened it according to good working practices. All the others are hanging in the racks across the floor. I wonder what I'll do next, but the action I'm taking is all in one piece, impossible to dismantle. A sharp edge with a sharp point, that's the tool of the trade.

With my glove I cover his face, gripping hard with my fingertips on temples and orbits, forcing his chin up and his head back in a subduing hold no different from the hold I use a thousand times and more in every shift I work. With the edge at his throat, he comes to attention.

Wait now.

My hand is moving, but wait. Stop. Riffle backwards through nights and days, the glare of the abattoir and the dark of dawn in Glory Part. Find me, walking alone in a small hour of the morning, in the Market where I saw what I saw. I wish it wasn't so. The hand is moving, I can't take it back, but I need to explain. This is my account, slipped in before the stroke of the knife.

If I had taken another way back to my lodgings that sole time, all the rest would have been different. But my habit never varied. Each morning I walked home ahead of first light. I left the meatpacking district by the back streets, passing the canal, the dockland warehouses and the garment factories, then cutting down the length of the Strangers' Market. I liked that time of the day, the maritime atmosphere that filled the district for an hour and the sense of depletion before sleep. The air opened, the dew fell, and the decaying industrial hindquarter of the city showed another side: you saw that, beneath the wear and the work, it was pretty. The silhouettes of the chimneys and derricks were one shade darker than the sky.

Bread was baking, and I could hear birds in a strip of parkland two streets away. Work fell further behind as I walked. Weariness trickled through my limbs to settle in my hands and feet. A din of dying nightlife rose from the city centre, far away across the river, but around here the night was bleeding out undisturbed.

A gust of stale wind got up in the street, and the loose front page of a tabloid newspaper tried to stand upright: it was dragged a short way along the cobbles towards me, showing a headline about serial murders, before it was sucked into the backwash of a waste lorry that jolted across the intersection with men hanging off its tail.

Once I was outside I didn't remember much about what I'd been doing in the slaughterhouse. It was like sleeping and waking: each evening, I knew I'd surfaced from a region as complex as the city of waking life, but I could no more retrieve my dreams than I could tell you what I'd soon be doing in the abattoir. That made me very good at my job.

The Market was a broad, kinked half-mile of cobbled thoroughfare as old as the city. Soon it would be jammed with stalls and the daytime folk carrying on their transactions, but for now it was all desertion and stone. Sodium lamps at intervals blotted the dark. Shadows wriggled behind sheets of vapour. Try the wrong alley or underpass and you could meet the Flâneur.

The Flâneur of Glory Part. You had to know that name by now. There had been four victims, so far.

I was halfway along the Market when I saw figures approaching. Between one spill of light and the next they turned from imperfections of my eyesight into a pair of shapes, male and female, with their arms linked. He was wrapped in a long coat, but her legs were bare. I relaxed, and my heart, always slow to catch up, unclutched and flurried in its cage. A man and a woman strolling in the Market by night only wanted to be left to themselves. I would pass on the far side of the road, I decided, to reassure them. They hadn't seen me. She leant into him and whispered, then tugged at his arm, keen to get somewhere. He was dragging his feet in playful or real reluctance. I was hurt they hadn't taken any notice of me, but I kept my eyes fixed straight ahead and kept walking.

When I looked again, they had stopped, and the man was holding the woman, taking all her weight. She had wrapped her arms around his neck, but they slipped open as I watched and he lowered her to the ground. Her limbs began to quiver, and he released her, sinking to his knees to cradle her head and shoulders. He lifted a gleaming hand. I saw the glint of the edge and the stain blooming over them both, black in the artificial light. Even at this distance, I could tell it had been a proficient stroke and that the outcome was beyond doubt.

My boots were drifting a mile down. I missed my footing on the kerb, and would have fallen except that I caught myself against the wall, raking the palm of my hand. The woman seemed listless, groping at his arms as he kept her head off the pavement. She grew still, and the man rose to his feet.

For what seemed a long time we faced each other across the Market. I did not breathe. The lamplight outlined him from behind, and his face was invisible, a dark mask with a pale halo. He stood as though now he was his victim's protector. The knife was no longer in his hand. He did not move: he only watched and waited.

As I stood there, I felt future time crowding into the present moment. A kind of serenity came over me as I saw that by doing nothing I was agreeing to a burden of guilt that would not lessen for as long as I lived. It was all quite clear: how in this instant my sole chance to intervene was passing, and how bitterly, later, I would wish to turn time back and do it differently. One more breath and the city would sweep the waiting figure away from me. I was making a choice. Stale in the back of my throat, I could taste the self-condemnations to come over years and decades: why did you stand there? Why did you not do something good when you had the chance? I saw what a tiresome riddle it would become, why I had bowed my head in apology, turned and continued to my lodgings.

As I left, he raised a hand in salute.

In my coat pocket my own hand was stinging. Something sharp had been fixed in the wall where I stumbled, and I'd be picking rust-flecks out of the cut tomorrow. My boots struck the pavement and the Market slid by. Daybreak slipped a notch closer, and my guts twisted: I braced my hands on my knees and coughed a cupful of fluid on the cobblestones. When I raised my head there was movement a way off. Men in donkey jackets were unloading boxes from a van while others trundled handcarts across the stones. One was sorting through polystyrene trays wrapped in clingfilm. They worked without talking, their faces tense against the dawn chill. One of them came towards me, holding what looked like a shovel.

I was a craftsman when it came to my work, you see. I was good at the job. Not everyone can slaughter well. It may look like medieval warfare in here, but don't be fooled. I never blamed the others for their shortcomings. It wasn't easy work. They were sent by their agencies without choice in the matter, and lasted a month or two among the churning conveyor-belts and chains and the knives that sawed and squeaked inches apart. The plant was crammed everywhere with wet carcasses and labouring bodies, jammed up against each other and pouring off heat. When they slipped, it cost fingers. They were knocked off catwalks to the concrete by the half-carcasses swinging past. Sweat ran off them even in the refrigerated rooms: dozens squeezed bodily together, shin-deep in the flow sluicing ceaselessly down the gutters, fingers snatching past the blades, fighting wall-eyed through a double shift in the hope of keeping their jobs. They had been known to soil themselves at their posts because they dared not fall behind. Most spoke only the languages of their homelands. When they broke open the digestive tracts and polluted the meat, the line managers screamed in their faces.

Once a week they collected flimsy printouts with perforated edges which they tore open to be reminded what their labour was worth. Sometimes, though, the payslip was pink instead of white, and then you knew the worker would not be coming back tomorrow. There was no notice period, no explanation, no appeal against the printed sheet. Each week I watched to see who received a pink slip. I would avoid the ex-worker's eyes, not wanting to intrude, but at the same time a small warm feeling would melt luxuriously inside me. I didn't know why.

What could I do for them? Their existence had

two poles. In here, inferno under striplights. Outside, Glory Part waiting for them with open jaws: their rooms, their naggins of oily gin, some fighting and copulation, the cold stinking canals and, above all, our friend the Flâneur, preying on their thoughts because they knew well what he might do to each one of them if he chose.

Nothing I could do. In his own life, the good slaughterman cannot involve himself with the single principle by which the world proceeds. He hates how the workmen tear up the street for the new metro line; he is wounded by the sight of snails broken on wet pavements, and he doesn't like the way the children shriek by the padlocked park.

When the animals entered the slaughterhouse they came to us one by one along a concrete alleyway, and were guided into a rectangular pen as high as my waist and just large enough to hold one at a time. As it entered, the newcomer would pause, still wet from the spray, hiding its face beneath two big hairy leaves of flesh. It would be smiling to itself, a Chelsea grin, as the knocker pressed the captive bolt stunner to its brow. One side of the pen was a steel gate that would swing open under the weight of a body.

Every station had its own importance, but my job was the crux of it all. I say this without pride or bias. After being incapacitated by the bolt the animal was hoisted on the mechanised rail by its back legs and would begin to move down the processing line, struggling violently, more often than not, because the bolt stunner is a barbarous tool which leaps in the hand and inflicts unpredictable kinds of damage. My task came next: I used a sharp knife to sever the carotid and the jugular, resulting in exsanguination. With the proper expertise the animal was gone in three heartbeats, beyond unhappiness. I euthanised one every twenty seconds and it was an inflexible point with me that none suffered in its time on the killing floor.

I didn't mind working double shifts. I needed little money, but I did not like to abandon my responsibilities. It wasn't easy to get the stroke right every time. Most workers I had seen took several attempts to get the job done and let the pace of the production line overwhelm them so that, often, the beasts received the barest of flesh wounds and were sent dazed but awake into their turmoil. Not when I had the knife. I couldn't sleep if I knew someone else was trying to manage the kill.

What saddened me most was not the change itself, but that they never even consulted me. One evening I arrived at the slaughterhouse to an atmosphere of uneasy holiday and rules unseated: lorries we hadn't seen before were shunting in the loading bays and the forklifts were moving crates stamped with unfamiliar symbols. The older women, the ones who ruled the packaging rooms with their ribaldry and favouritism, had gathered to watch, dragging on cigarettes and passing comment, while this week's immigrants waited at a distance because no one had told them where to go.

My hand ached. It had knitted but not yet healed, and though I bound it hard for work, the cut itched. It was impossible to see how the shift was going to get started on time, but then the bell screamed, the old hands flung their fag ends at the ground and we trooped in to find that everything was different.

The new floor supervisor, Fischer, was a compact man with a sarcastic turn in his mouth and sparse blond hair scraped back into a greasy ponytail. As we entered, his stare searched us for resistances and weaknesses. I could see what he was and what he meant for the plant, and I was not surprised when he told us procedures had been reviewed and modified. We were being moved around for no good reason, but you can't argue. It doesn't matter if you're an artist with your tools and you have more experience than the rest of them put together. You go where the supervisor tells you, do the job you're given.

That night a lanky agency worker I'd never seen before was assigned to my rightful post. As for me, my task now was to drag the stunned animals along the trough from the knocking pen and hook them on the bleed rail. All my expertise and they wanted me hauling carcasses. But there's no arguing. The shift was about to start. In the holding pens the animals debated their suspicions.

191

Soon the floor would grow gluey, the drains would inhale without relent and the flow would leap across the insteps of steel-toed rubber boots. The air would choke with waste heat. All would do their tasks: the bleeders, the scalders, the dehairers, the eviscerators, the splitters, the washers, the deboners, the carvers and the sorters. The bolt gun would crack, the workers would gag and the new supervisor would stride back and forth behind the scarlet chorus-lines.

I settled my goggles and pulled my hard hat on so tight that the cartilage crackled in my ears. Strapped into my apron, belt and rubbers, I was a golem, crude but potent. The machinery groaned, strained and locked into action.

Before the shift was an hour old, the quality of my replacement's work began to degrade, and soon he was botching fully half his strokes, though he did not seem to notice. There was nothing I could do about it. I had work of my own, and the muscles in my back were already beginning to quiver.

Fischer stalked the floor all night, yelling instructions over the crashing of the machines. His barrel body seemed spring-loaded on its small legs, and the cords twitched in his neck and forearms. I could picture him lifting weights to make up for being shorter than he wished. The surprise was that he and I were the same in one way. He was a talented slaughterer who handled the knife beautifully whenever he was called upon to step in and correct a mistake. It pleased him when they lost the run of the work and, in panic, blew their air-horns to call him over. He would respond to the summons at a measured pace, shoulder the workers aside and make the necessary incision.

In the canteen, halfway through the shift, Fischer spoke to me. His gaze travelled all the way from my breastbone up to the top of my head, and he asked: 'What do they feed *you*?' But before I could answer he turned his attention to a couple of new arrivals, skinny young men with livid faces, and told them a story from another place he'd worked. A rookie slaughterman on his first day there had slipped in a puddle, cracked his head on a steel rail and fallen into the knocking pen. The other slaughterers were in such a hurry they grabbed him by the ankles, strung him up and sent him along the line. His lights were down the chute and his two flanks swinging in opposite directions before anyone knew what had happened.

The young men gazed at the tabletop, at the headlines telling us FLÂNEUR KILLS AGAIN. He was full of stories like that, I would discover, about slaughterers being knocked into scald tanks, or mistaking hands for trotters, or stepping outside in their work gear and sending grown men into hysterics. He didn't mind that half his audience couldn't understand him and the other half didn't want to know.

'One place,' he said, 'it was swine same as here, but we stunned them with carbon dioxide. They go through the well, get a lungful, don't feel a thing.

But that night there was something wrong with the mixture. They were halfway down the line, some of them, but they started waking up, and I promise you they sounded exactly like people when they screamed. Whole place echoing like a church. No one knew what to do. In the end I had to go round with a knife. It was an hour's work before the noise stopped. And when we took off our helmets you know what had happened? The hair of every person on that floor had turned pure white.' While he spoke I sat silent, slouched in my own thoughts of the night Market, stains spreading black in the lamplight and a white-haloed, featureless face. He ended his story with a laugh and turned to me as if I'd challenged him, but I had nothing to add. I didn't doubt that what he said was true.

The night after that, he strolled through the mayhem, took up a position a few feet away from where I was working and folded his arms. I glanced up at him, breathing hard, then stooped to the trough and hauled another half-dozen animals through. When I looked again he was still there, his safety goggles reflecting one of the striplights so that a glaring white bar hid the upper half of his face.

I knew what he was at. He'd seen that I was different from the rest, and he didn't like it. He knew that I was a craftsman, and that was unacceptable to him: he wanted nothing in this room but straining flesh and labouring blades. Very well, I thought. I didn't make mistakes on the killing floor, so he could watch as long as he liked. I could work hour after hour without a slip. I wouldn't be rattled. I knew the knocker would be gaping at this diversion and working even more sloppily than before, but I kept my head down. I don't make mistakes, but still, this wasn't fair: under Fischer's scrutiny my boots and gloves were heavy, and cramps rippled down my back, stiffening my hand. I clenched my fist and the wound stung as the newly mended tissues came apart. All I needed was half a minute's rest, but hooks were sliding past empty on the bleed rail and the animals were building up beyond the knocking pen.

The knocker fired the bolt and opened the gate, and I swung myself heavily around, but the timing must have been wrong because my heel shot out from under me and I found myself lying on my back beneath a suffocating weight. My hard hat had cracked on the concrete and purple rings were spreading across my field of vision. I couldn't catch my breath, or find enough purchase to free myself from the barrowload of hot wet flesh under which I was buried.

A moment later the inert animal was rolled off my chest, and as I gulped for air Fischer braced, heaved, and hooked the trotter on the rail. Then he strode off in search of his next intervention. Job done. There was nothing left to see over here but a few splatters up the walls.

★　　★　　★

After that I worked in a picture-show of revenges. Who would have guessed he had such a power to fascinate? Soon I was thinking of him all the time, his loose twist of a smile, his arrogant technique with the knife. I knew when he stepped on to the floor because my flesh tightened and prickled from scalp to fingertips. I had not spoken a syllable in his presence but I spent nights denouncing him in the private courtroom of my skull. I knew every detail of his face, with its pitted cheeks and its nose that might have been squeezed out of a tube. When he humiliated an underling I could taste his satisfaction. I studied the torsion of his wrist: I could have sworn I'd known it always, that flick of the knife.

Afterwards, I could not tell when the idea was born: the most important idea I have ever had. There was no flash, no revelation. Instead, as I was dragging on my street clothes at the end of another shift, I became aware of a notion lying hidden in a fold of my mind, waiting to be noticed. It was frail and incomplete, no more than a seed, but I could tell that if I took care of it it would grow. The idea offered itself in two images. First, Fischer supervising the shift, goggles unblinking, hands by his sides, feet planted wide on the killing floor as the production line thrashed all around him. Second, that faceless figure in the Strangers' Market, watching across the body of his victim to see what I would do. Two images, and a question. What is the difference?

The good slaughterer belongs only on the killing floor. At dawn, when he crosses the threshold of the abattoir, he must disappear. He must forget the version of himself which knows how simple it is to end the lives of warm-blooded animals, because that is not a person we want walking around the city.

And yet, in the city, the Flâneur.

SICK SLAUGHTER. The papers loved him. CARNAGE IN STONE LANES. When I found the canteen empty I opened the pages out on the Formica and caught up with developments. LAMBS TO THE SHAMBLES. They said that he must be skilled either in surgery or in butchery. COPS BAFFLED. The television that gesticulated away to itself on the counter had a fixation with him too, but I never dared turn up the sound. DON'T GO OUT AT NIGHT. I kept a eye on the images of police jerkins loitering near ambiguous sections of brickwork. RAW HEAD AND BLOODY BONES.

Why did we want to know? The screen showed graphics of a figure with a question mark for a face, and on the radio in my lodgings, when I could coax voices out of the fuzz, they described his tools and his psychopathology. The papers had a photograph of the latest one to cross his path: it showed her young self in sunny times, her eyes slitted, the light intense. She thought she was in one kind of story until he proved to her that she was in another. And what is she now? A few facts, craning out like struts in the wreck of a burnt house. If I understood anything about the Flâneur, it was that his actions held no interest. He had nothing to tell us.

The Flâneur of Glory Part. A stagy figure, with his straight blade and his risible air of Victoriana. Some crass newspaperman had awarded him the nickname because, if we knew nothing else, we knew that each of his victims had encountered him walking in the streets of the city. He was around every corner in the fogs which the season brought. When I set off for work with night fanning out across Glory Part, I knew I was entering his jurisdiction, and when I fell asleep in the early morning – so finished by the night's work that oblivion came in the time it took my body to pass through a quarter circle, face first, into my bed – it was like falling into his arms.

But it was pitiable, the way he scrawled his marks on the walls as though he expected us to look there for what he had to tell us. As though his clever clues would be puzzled over and then pursued along the alleyways by brilliant detectives and assiduous constables. There was no great mystery about him. Anyone can become what he was. Nothing. A mask stuffed with straw. A bad thing that happens.

I lost my balance, teetered on a high catwalk for one long gasp, and fell. The stained concrete flung itself at my eyes, and I woke, the springs of the mattress clanking. Red figures on the clock told me I had slept longer than usual. Each dawn now I returned to my lodgings worn out by the lurid show in my skull: the bloody man striding up and down the killing floor and the shadowed figure walking the streets. Continually, now, the two of them met and merged and changed faces until they were one and the same. I turned the idea over and over, finding no flaws and no way to tell whether it was true.

I sat on the edge of the bed, bewildered in the glare from outside, and put on my boots.

Most evenings I went to the Rose Tree for a breakfast of fried bread, baked beans and dark red tea. I always sat in the same booth at the back of the restaurant, far away from the grease-clouded plate-glass window. I felt inconspicuous there. I could rely on most of the customers to ignore me; but sometimes, as I came in, Bill would turn from his usual place at the counter and greet me with a nod.

Bill was an older man with an air of chronic ill health and outmoded bohemianism. His long hair and pointed beard were steel-grey, shot with white, and his face was netted with fine wrinkles. When he climbed off his stool and slid into the booth to talk to me, he moved painfully, pressing one hand into his belly. He wore faded floral shirts and always the same elderly corduroy jacket: I had seen him more than once in the Strangers' Market buying a flower to thread through the buttonhole of the lapel. And yet he carried himself with the air of a man who had knocked around the city for long enough to know how things work. His pale lips pressed often into a sardonic line, and his china-blue eyes were steady and disbelieving. In our conversations he had dropped enough hints for me to understand that Bill was not his real name, and that in the past he had been a malcontent and a political radical. He implied that he had been suspected of involvement with the activities of the Cynics a score of years ago, and that, even now, he had to exercise caution because the authorities were not yet tired of persecuting him. But the clues he gave about his past all came with a teasing twinkle.

He knew what I did for a living, and although I could not have said how, I felt that our occasional talks had helped me to see what it meant to be a good slaughterman. If I were to confess to anyone it would be to Bill; and now, as he slid into the booth, I knew that I could not remain silent.

'You can't go to the police,' he said, as soon as I had blurted out my secret. He stared across the table for a long time, his eyes narrowed into an unreal distance, like a man performing a calculation in his head. Then he seemed to reach an answer that satisfied him.

'Someone like you can never go to the police. You realise how it'll look to them, if you go in saying you're not sure, but you think you might have guessed the Flâneur's identity? That you don't have any evidence? That you think it's your boss, but you can't prove anything?'

The crows' feet deepened at the corners of his eyes.

'I'll tell you what happens. At best, you're sent away with a clip round the ear for wasting their time. More likely, they decide you're sick in the head and arrest you on suspicion of being the killer yourself.'

He studied me thoughtfully until I looked away.

'You're on your own here, my friend,' he said. 'They can't help you any more than I can. You can't hand this on, and there's no one else for you to persuade. You're going about it the wrong way. You're looking outside for a solution: but this isn't happening outside.'

I must have looked startled, because he checked himself and spoke more softly.

'We're talking about your conscience,' he said. 'It doesn't matter how: find whatever proof you need, search your memory, watch for clues. But you have to tell yourself a story you can believe. You have to make an account. Then, only then, you'll be able to do it.'

I didn't understand, I told him. Do what?

He paused, choosing his words. Eventually, he said:

'Something good.'

Glory Part was a tangle of alleys, wynds and lanes, all built of sooted bricks, the surfaces opened by oblique evening light. In places the walls pressed so close together that they brushed your shoulders on both sides. The foundations were uneven, so that the pebbled lanes rose and fell in steep and unexpected ways and kept breaking into flights of steps. The houses, built up high because there was nowhere else for them to go, leaned together overhead and often enough they joined, turning streets into tunnels.

I walked, led by Bill's advice, and kept walking until I found myself standing beneath a lamp post on the Strangers' Market. It did not look out of the ordinary. If there were signs that anything had happened here, I couldn't see them. When I looked up, the glass held a searing green squiggle on my retina and the rest of the world was shuttered out. Still, this must be the place to find what I needed. I squatted to examine the cobblestones. The surface of each stone was a mountainscape, and the cracks between contained ecosystems of muck, moss and grit. The closer I looked, the more the simple stones of the Market broke down to a chaos of detail. I crossed to the far wall and, after some minutes, found an iron nail sticking out. It was low down, at my knees. I couldn't tell what adhered to the rust.

Then a jolt of panic straightened me up with my heart churning. A hand had closed on my shoulder. I turned around, expecting handcuffs, a lynch mob, a knife: but instead a stranger stared up at me, haggard and unshaven, his red-rimmed eyes filled with accusation. In the evening shadows and the low red light his face looked to have been hacked from the same bricks as the walls of the Market. For an instant I felt certain that I was confronting a personification – an envoy of all Glory Part, come to insist that I explain myself. What is your business, his eyes demanded, in the empty Market at sundown? How can you prove that you're not guilty? My throat tightened, and as he began to speak I fell back from him, away from the lamp post, the nail and the stones, and fled.

As I left the Market, rubbing my head in agitation, I found that nothing had changed inside. The same pictures looped over and over, the two figures swapping places and swapping back again. I had learned nothing: or I had learned that scratching at the surface of the city would not answer my questions. Going back to my lodgings I knew less than before.

I MET THE FLÂNEUR AND LIVED REVENGE HAVOC FEARED WHO LET HIM IN

I stood in the shadows at the edge of the loading bay, waiting for Fischer to finish up whatever it was he did in the supervisor's office at the end of the night. In the dark my pulse was slow. He stepped into the prism of the security lights and locked up the exit behind him. He was wrapped in his overcoat with his face muffled to the cheekbones. I waited until he reached the far side of the tarmac, then followed.

I did not like what I was doing. I could not have justified it if anyone had asked me, and, worse, I suspected that I was violating the principle of the good slaughterman: that when the shift is over he must cease to exist, must pass through the streets as an absence, without intention or desire. But I had to take the risk. It was a decision I had made.

Most of the workers used the shuttle bus into the city centre, where they could catch the early trams home. But not Fischer, who preferred like me to go on foot through Glory Part. We passed through the gate in the plant's chain-link perimeter. I followed him as if I were tethered to a weight and falling through dark waters. Up ahead his form tremored on the edge of visibility, but I kept pace and did not let him out of my sight. I did not know how sudden or how subtle it would be when it came, the transformation of one figure into the other.

He paused under a lamp for no reason I could see. A column of drizzle drifted above his head. He flinched and moved on. We passed through lanes where, for all I could tell, they had pulled down the route back to my lodgings and used the pieces to mock up Fischer's way home instead. A patch of cobbles, an archipelagic puddle, a low overhead arch, a triangular storm drain, a tree in an iron cage, a peeling green door. I could have sworn these featured, differently arranged, in the journey I walked each morning.

Pre-dawn light was up by the time he turned on to a steep residential street with identical front doors set close together, each one stone step higher than the pavement. Each would open directly into the downstairs room, in the way that had been thought best for the factory workers of an earlier generation. He dug around in his coat pocket. Those were his keys, two linked strips of metal, clinking once. As he addressed his latch he peered back the way he had come, doubting something in the corner dark.

Once he was inside, I withdrew to the mouth of a pedestrian tunnel on the far side of the road. I could just make out his door. The cold clamped inside my boots and gloves didn't trouble me, nor the smell of urine. There wasn't much difference between his lodgings and mine. It hardly mattered whether we'd come this way or that through the district. In there, I thought, he probably had the same bed frame and table and chair as me, arranged another way on the same worn carpet. I watched the door as if it might still prove something one way or the other.

I WILL KILL AGAIN
VIGILANTE ATTACKS RISE
WHO IS SHELTERING THIS DEVIL

Halfway through the night an animal slipped from its shackle and fell eight feet from the bleed rail, striking two of the workers. All three sprawled on the concrete, but it was the pig that got up first. It spasmed, its whole body a single muscle, and sprang to its feet, its head bobbing. It was bigger than any of us: its belly alone, strung quivering in its frame, was bigger. Coarse blond fur bristled along its back. A glancing wound had creased its skull. From its mouth projected a jumble of bloody tusks.

Rolling crimson eyeballs, the creature lifted its head into the side of a fallen worker and scooped him clear of the floor. It shook him free and charged off, scattering the onlookers and demolishing a rack of tools. It headbutted a safety rail, then clamped its teeth into a steel sink which with a shake of its head it wrenched loose and dropped. White strings of froth eased from its jaws. Urine poured rearwards from its bright pink funnel and began to crawl through puddled blood. The workers had retreated to the edges of the room.

Fischer watched without surprise. After a minute's chaos he had stopped the conveyors so that the machine din lifted and only the clamour of beasts and workers remained. He folded his arms, and for an instant he caught my eye.

One of the fallen workers was curled on the floor, cradling something fragile in his side, his face turning grey. The pig approached him, champing as if the knocker's work had stripped away a layer of its evolutionary history. The worker was taking quick, shallow breaths, with one hand pressed under his ribs and the other searching for a finger-hold in the texture of the concrete. The pig's breath streamed into his face. Heaps of muscle mounted across its shoulders as it lowered its head.

Then Fischer was straddling its back with his heels deep in its sides. It thrashed and raked its tusks across the floor, trying to strike sparks. It crashed into another section of conveyor belt, but he hung on, hooking his fingers into its nostrils. Steel blurred and he stepped away from the creature as it exhaled and collapsed.

Workers came forward, pulling off their gloves and removing their earplugs. Throwing glances at the pig, they gathered around the fallen man. The floor looked like the nest of a carnivorous machine. Fischer cursed softly. He was drenched. As the workers carried their comrade towards the exit he caught my eye again, and for once I did not look away. I was reading the message there and piecing together what it meant, adding it to the account along with everything else I had seen: the way he had grappled the animal, the nuance of his technique with the knife.

Others were fixing chains to the pig's front legs, hauling it upright to expose the taut, blond-furred length of its belly. They didn't wait for the machinery to start. This was more pressing. Someone accepted a knife from his fellows and moved in close.

In the booth at the back of the Rose Tree, Bill leafed through today's paper. It was the Flâneur again. Just when they had been losing interest in the story, he had fed them fresh material. It was a young man this time: no more than a child, out with his friends in one of the back streets near the Market, far too late at night.

Finally Bill looked up at me.

'What kind of city is it,' he asked, 'where we sit here and gobble up this stuff, then shake our heads and do nothing? And tomorrow we buy the paper again for more. How do we explain it to ourselves? Tell ourselves we're not responsible? Doing nothing has its own cost.'

There was no patience in his face, no indulgence.

'But you know that,' he said.

I wanted to explain myself to him. I wanted to tell him how much I cared for the welfare of the people of Glory Part. I felt that at birth I'd been given the duty of protecting them. I didn't ask for anything in return. This morning, as I walked by the laundrette, the women leaning in the doorway had fallen silent to watch me out of earshot. I had crossed to the other side of the street where men were blocking the pavement, joshing each other, slapping hands and bumping fists. I had passed by like a duke in disguise as a beggar. I couldn't imagine how life went for them. What we had in common was this cold day. Its failed light. The rain throwing itself away on the tenements.

'Have you heard the story of the Sibyl?' Bill asked, speaking more to himself than to me. He drank the last of his coffee and turned his face to the window. The daylight seemed to be filtered through the yellow-grey newspapers the Market's fishmongers used to wrap their wares. We were not quite alone in the restaurant, but Dilks was keeping to the kitchen and the fat man sitting at the corner table looked away when he caught my eye. Without warning I was gripped by the conviction that I had forgotten to do something terribly important.

'She wished never to die, and that was granted. But she neglected to ask for eternal youth to accompany her immortality. Her body grew old and more than old, but she lived on until she was a shrivelled, unrecognisable thing. In the end, she vanished from sight, turned to dust; but still her voice could be heard. Think of what it must be saying by now.'

A few raindrops began to crawl across the window. I wanted to ask him what he meant, but he was examining the paper again, scowling and kneading his belly under the table. I looked up at the big electric clock that hung above the counter, but as always the hands were stopped at a quarter past five.

'These kids,' he said, 'these kids were out in the Market every night. They didn't have anywhere else to go. For all they knew, this city was the whole world.'

I had to go, I told him. I knew it wasn't true, but I could not shake the idea that I must leave at once. Bill didn't respond. He only went on talking to himself.

'I can't imagine the boy was surprised, when it

happened,' he said. 'Poor child. He never doubted the city went on forever. And now he knows.'

Printed on a slip of pink paper, formed in faint grey dots, was my name, and a few numbers, and the information that my employment had ceased as of today's date. I should remove any personal items because after vacating the premises I would not be permitted to return. My responses are slow at the end of a shift, and I stood there until the locker room had emptied around me and the implications had soaked into my brain. So this, I thought, is how it feels to reach a decision. This is how it feels to enter into an action: to become a person who, very soon, will do something good. It feels like receiving a slip of paper informing you of a change in your situation.

The good slaughterer can't live in two places. He has to choose between the city and the abattoir. He has no story of his own: that's something he has to do without, because he has no place in the world outside. I had been resisting the choice, I saw now, but I couldn't do it any longer. The moment comes to say goodbye. I stood for a long time with the paper in my hands and my eyes unfocused, and allowed myself a last farewell. I let myself remember an afternoon, not long ago, when I had walked down to the Strangers' Market. I remembered the polyvinyl awnings with their broad blue and yellow stripes growing hot, the crowd thinning and thickening and the sun moving in and out behind a trailing curtain the colour of zinc. Everywhere hands felt in pockets, rubbed notes and coins, and strayed towards dark green melons, second-hand pots and saucepans, racks of leather coats, cheap clocks and watches, jewellery, sweets, medicines, bath salts, chestnuts in scalding paper bags. The avenues between the stalls were solid with browsers. I imagined the Flâneur here, moving through the crowd, patrolling the heart of his principality incognito.

I had loved the Market when I was younger. The women at the greengrocery stalls would look at this boy towering over them, his face implanted with sore lumps, and crow that I needed some meat on my bones. I used to browse the tables in the plaza, and had a compulsion for crumbling paperbacks. Later I gave it up, but for a time I would devour everything I could get, always in cheap, obsolete editions. I had a great need for all those stories. Once I bought an old novel for a few pence and for months came back to the stall to check for more by the same writer, feeling that if I searched through all she wrote I would discover something crucial. Thinking of those times, I was filled with the memory of mad excitement bottled secretly inside, the world succulent, rinsed and lit. Back then everything astonished me. I could be dumbstruck by the smell of rain and the slow gather of light on a green stone wall.

A viaduct cut across a corner of the marketplace, creating several deep arches in which stallholders had their pitches: vegetarian curry stands, coffee stalls, specialists in dyed silk scarves, purveyors of art posters. On the bricks above, a weatherbeaten sign spelled out the Market's name in circus lettering. Inside one blue and white kiosk, three handsome black-haired young men in striped aprons, winking at their customers, ducked around under the strings of cured sausages and the dangling plastic bags in which pale balls of mozzarella floated. They trimmed the meat into deft, bloodless pieces, weighed them out and wrapped them in waxed paper before handing them over in elegant rectangular bags.

I remembered the day, soon after I had started working at the slaughterhouse, when I visited that stall. On the white refrigerated slabs, the cuts were displayed in their shades of lavender, plum, pastel and candy-pink. Someone spoke to me. I looked up. The young man flicked his fringe out of his eyes and asked again how he could help. When I didn't answer, the crease in his brow deepened, but he pointed at sliced bacon of the palest coral.

'How about this, sir? It's rather special today.'

I nodded, and watched his gloves peel the floral tissues apart. I wanted to let him know who I was, so he would understand that we were both part of the single great scheme that linked my bleed rail and his blue striped canopy. He and I were brothers dedicated to the hunger of the city. But I couldn't work out how to tell him and in the end I said nothing. It was only as he rung up my purchase on the till that I found I hadn't brought my wallet.

You can go out among your fellow creatures but you can't stay out there forever. You have to come back in. It's not so easy to leave your account once you've begun it. It always wants you back. The pink slip is in your hands: rub the paper between finger and thumb. Think of Fischer. Think of the Flâneur.

One of his eyes is looking out between the first and second fingers of my gauntlet, and the eye is asking me a question. This won't take long. There will be no suffering. I've said what I can, I've given my account, and what happens afterwards is not my concern. The good slaughterer knows his skills have their place. He does the work.

PART VI

PART VI

THREE TRANSLATIONS

Dawn was walking home along the seafront when a voice called her name. As she looked around, a tall, fair-haired girl hefted a rucksack on her shoulder and started forward, shading her eyes against the hard sunlight, almost colliding with a cyclist as he zipped by. The tall girl, whose name was Andie, called out again. A man selling treats from an icebox slung across his chest was watching with interest.

Dawn returned the greeting with a small smile and a wave of the hand which, she felt at once, must look badly lacking in surprise or enthusiasm, or even as though she'd made an instant, calculated decision to be rude. She had been at school with Andie in another country and the last time they had spoken to each other they had been fourteen years old. For a while they had been well known to others and themselves as best friends. They had both stayed at the school until they were sixteen, when Andie had left. But after the last time, they hadn't spoken.

Andie had just arrived in the city, she'd literally walked here from the station, she hadn't even found a hostel yet or anything. What a coincidence that Dawn should be here and they'd met like this! She'd only been backpacking a fortnight so far, but she was having a great time. There were six weeks more on her ticket but she could see herself extending it further. She'd had no idea Dawn was in the city. How long? Two years so far. What doing? Teaching assistant at a language school. This was amazing. Andie wanted to know everything. She could hardly believe she'd found Dawn like this, it had to be more than a coincidence. She loved travelling but the only problem was not being able to read the signs or get people to understand you. But Dawn practically lived here! She could tell Andie everything. Andie had only been planning on a night and a day in the city, two days at most, but now she thought she might stay longer.

Dawn was already conscious of a desire to unfold the city. She wanted to claim the blinding ingot of the sea and the men hauling their nets up the wharf, and to present a city more true than the one mapped out in Andie's brand-new guide-book. At the same time she felt how little she knew, even now.

They continued along the seafront, picking their way through the preparations for a public event of some kind. Long trestle tables had been set up on the broadest stretch of the promenade, and young men were shinning up the lamp posts to hang bunting. Dawn explained that her apartment was not far from the Boulevard Mino, just a few minutes' walk away. Andie could easily come back there if she wanted, if she didn't have anywhere else to get to. She could freshen up, even leave her bag for a few hours. If she liked?

In the apartment, Dawn watched Andie unshoulder her rucksack and let its tail thump into the floor, then knit her fingers, stretch her arms and rotate on the balls of her feet to take in the apartment. Despite the fairness of her skin, the sun had not burnt her. Instead, it had given a healthy rose-and-gold varnish to her face, throat and arms, paled her blue eyes, and turned her thick fair hair silver. It suited her, and only heightened the Nordic look that, it was already obvious, made her conspicuous here. Dawn herself represented a more common physical type in this part of the world.

What a nice place, Andie said, so bright. (It was bright; a textbook lay on the windowsill, and the inpouring light kicked a spray of buttercup yellow from its cover across the white wall.) Did Dawn live by herself? Dawn explained that her flatmate, another assistant at the school, had given up her job a week ago and moved out without warning. It had left Dawn short for the month's rent.

Andie was shocked to hear this, but then delight broke across her face. What if, listen, she'd stay here. Not for long, just for now, for a while, the rest of the month at least. It was the perfect idea. She could change her ticket no problem. Dawn needed someone to help with the rent and Andie was sick of staying in hostels, she'd love to see what it was like to really live somewhere. They'd be flatmates.

Dawn didn't know what to say. But, well, why not?

Once Andie had changed into a white summer dress that, she said, she had not yet worn, they went back out. It was late afternoon, and the town was full of foreign backpackers and families on holiday. They walked down to Tall Quays, where Andie exclaimed appreciatively and held Dawn's arm as they looked over the parapet, then back up the seafront to where rollerskaters stitched around pedestrians and prams, occasionally pointing their toes in opposite directions to whirl to a stop. Dawn and Andie left the path and picked their way down the stony beach.

Tarry clutches of lobster pots lay here and there, and the reek of decaying fish rose everywhere from the water and the pebbles. Gusts of wind battered along the strand. Andie stopped to watch some men launching a boat, rattling it down the stones and splashing in after it, thigh-deep, roaring at each other. She laughed when the wind snatched at her dress and chucked sheaves of her hair across her face. Dawn observed the long central groove of Andie's abdomen appear under the thin wind-flattened fabric. Some youths with bicycles had stopped above to watch, too.

Andie barely looked any different now from her

long-necked, gracefully equine school self, except that she had become a fraction fuller in the upper arm and around the waist. Dawn was able to judge these changes because she had spent a lot of time over several years gazing at Andie. She knew the appearance of her arm crooked on an exercise book, and that of her neck bent forward, revealed by fallen hair, viewed sidelong from the next seat. She knew well the stances Andie adopted when viewed full-figure from a distance, long after they had ceased to speak. Today Andie was no longer quite so self-contained in her movements. When she was excited – when she expressed astonishment at a detail of the life of a language assistant, or as she tried to pick her way back up the pebbles while evading the wind – her eyes seemed to point askew for a moment.

They climbed back up to the promenade. Andie licked her upper lip and said she could taste the salt. Among the trestle tables and the bunting, the young men were now laying a series of small bonfires. Here the promenade was not marked off from the sea by any railing: instead the ground sloped straight down into a broad, shallow slipway. As they watched, one of the men chased another into the water, shouting, then pushed him so that he fell, and immediately dived headlong after him. They began to wrestle, coughing and hooting.

Dawn explained that these were the preparations for a festival they had every year. Tomorrow there'd be a kind of party. No, she wasn't intending to go, it wasn't like that. It was really just for the locals. An indigenous tradition. Andie noticed that the tables were arranged in a bulging semicircle, as if backing away from the city towards the sea. I wonder why that is, she said; but Dawn didn't know.

They walked on. Andie had been working as a receptionist in a solicitor's office until a few months ago, but she was going to apply to train as an actress when she got back home. She had always liked drama at school. Not that this was enough in itself, she knew, but what could you do except give it a good try? When it was a passion there was really no choice. But that was for next year. For now she was seeing where her travels took her. To begin with, she and a friend had been travelling together, but it hadn't worked out and they'd gone their separate ways. Don't look so worried, she told Dawn, it's not a problem! Anyway, she preferred travelling by herself. Really, that was the whole point.

Before they could say anything else, a body blocked Dawn's path. She tried to move past but he dodged to keep in front of her. He was doing it on purpose. The young man's arms were spread, his palms exposed. He was watching for her reaction. He wore a sag-necked T-shirt and threadbare, bleached-out cotton shorts; several other young men, identically dressed, were loitering on the far side of the street. One drawled out a comment either on the accostment or on something else entirely.

She tried again to walk on and again the youth prevented her. She ought to know better how to deal with this, she thought furiously. She was supposed to know her way around here. She couldn't guess what he wanted from them. She risked a look at his face. His lips were dark red, and narrow as a cut except for a central cherry; his eyebrows were dense bars, so regular and sharp that they might have been plucked. She realised that she knew him. She had seen him around the language school, and he'd been in one or two of her classes. She was nearly certain his name was Charles. They had never spoken, but now, seeing her recognition, he grinned, and spread his palms wider.

He pointed from Dawn to Andie and back, establishing the relationship between them. He introduced himself to Andie and, when she looked blank, Dawn translated for her. Andie gasped in happy comprehension and told him her name in return, separating the syllables with care.

But the conversation went no further, because a small young woman with dark, short hair appeared beside them and spoke sharply to Charles. Her voice was low-pitched and hoarse. The rhythm of her words matched the jabs of her forefinger in the air, but Charles didn't seem troubled at all. He gave a quick humorous bow to Andie and Dawn, then walked away with the girl. He caught her hand with a darting motion and twined his fingers into hers. For a moment she tried to resist.

*   *   *

In the streets, later that evening, several men made a show of admiration. Dawn had not had time to put in her contact lenses and once, as they walked, a man seated on a street-corner bollard made an obscene observation, in a loud, cordial voice, about girls in glasses. Andie asked what he had said, and then had to stop walking in order to laugh. The youths killing time on the streets, with their tar-streaked shins and stained cotton shorts and their body hair showing dark through their T-shirts, had a way of gaping, with heads forward and mouths hanging, that implied a violent, voluntary stupidity. Dawn could imagine them battering their skulls together like goats until their foreheads were dented enough for the lives they wanted.

Up ahead the preparations for the festival looked complete. Flags and banners fluttered from the lamp posts above the tables and the unlit bonfires. A group of men in cut-off trousers dumped an enormous tuna fish, bigger than a person, on the paving stones. Andie grabbed Dawn's arm at the sight of it. Once the men had laid it out, dappled and gleaming, they moved away, wiping their hands off on their thighs. They were replaced by five women with knives and buckets, who began to butcher the fish, wrapping lumps of its meat in paper and passing them to a school of small girls who darted around the carcass.

Dawn explained that, as far as she understood it, the festival was for the city's unmarried men. It was supposedly a celebration of some figure of archaic local folklore, some legendary personification of the city. But all it meant was that they had a barbecue, sang and danced, and took part in feats of strength and machismo: wrestling, drinking competitions, games of luck with painful forfeits. The meal was prepared by the city's unmarried women, who also waited on the revellers, but didn't themselves take part. It began in the afternoon and continued into the night.

Andie was highly amused to hear all this. That's how it used to be, said Dawn, or at least that's what I've read. It's probably changed nowadays.

The women did seem to be preparing for something, carrying heavy-looking cardboard boxes, covered tureens and sacks of fuel pellets. A few groups of young men lounged at the tables, watching them work and drinking beer from small brown bottles. There were other early signs of festivity. A carnival figure, wearing white grease-paint and a scarlet ringmaster's coat with a giant sunflower bobbing from the lapel, was prancing in between the passers-by, accosting the unwary with flourishes of a long-necked bottle. A fright wig protruded in stiff white tufts from beneath his bowler hat. He approached in a mincing waltz-step. Halting in front of Dawn, he poured clear fluid into a tin beaker, lifting his bottle up high to make a thin, bright stream in the air, and mimed an invitation to drink.

Dawn shook her head, and he transferred his invitation to Andie, mugging and winking madly.

She wavered, then – oh well! – she accepted the beaker and tried a cautious sip. As she screwed up her face, the clown squealed in grotesque pleasure. He pointed after her, cackling, as they walked on.

Andie was smiling sportingly. That was sea water!

Next Andie wanted to try a bistro she had spotted near the promenade. She ordered metal saucepans full of mussels for both of them. She'd pay, she wanted to. Then she told Dawn that since they last saw each other, she had been married. It had been a year or so after she left school. He was nine years older and very good-looking and charming, but dishonest, as it turned out. It had been a mistake: she preferred not to go into the details.

The mussels were large, green-tinged and watery, and contained minuscule specks of sand that squeaked against the teeth. Dawn picked them off her lip and arranged them along the edge of the plate. At the next table, two girls were unwrapping something that lay between them like a human hand, damp, white and curled. It belonged in the sea. The head was decorated with fleshy whiskers. Its mouth worked weakly. One of the girls turned it over and bit into its pallid belly. Her teeth seemed to sink in easily: translucent skin stretched and separated. Her chin shining, she swallowed, and passed it to her companion.

To escape was the hardest thing in the world, Andie said. It had taken her a long time to realise no one was going to help her. She didn't think it had made her less trusting, but it had made her a lot stronger. She had always known that he had a troubled past, but she had thought that investigating his history would mean she was too suspicious. She wouldn't make that mistake again.

Dawn wondered if she should reach across the table, but her fingers were covered in grease.

She wasn't working the next day, and they both slept late. They were not long up – Andie leaning against the kitchen counter with her coffee, Dawn sitting at the table getting ready to correct a stack of exercise books – when Charles appeared at the apartment.

He was dressed in the same clothes as yesterday. He carried himself like someone who knew the place well and had every right to be here. In the entrance hall behind him, three other young men waited, one sprawling on the sofa with his legs stretched out, the others shuffling their feet. Dawn couldn't imagine how he had found out the address. But before she could find the right words to challenge him, he walked straight past her into the apartment, bowing in a small parody of civility.

As he entered the kitchen Andie gave him an uncomplicated grin, and waved hello. She didn't seem surprised. He had apparently forgotten that Dawn was here. He took hold of Andie's hand, his eyes flickering around her face, and said something. Dawn hesitated, and then explained to Andie's look of eager inquiry that Charles and his friends had invited her to go with them to the feast at the seafront. Charles nodded in satisfaction, pulled over Dawn's chair and sat down. He folded his arms, looked up at Andie, and said something else. It was a special honour for her to be asked, he was saying, a special chance. Usually, no one from outside the city. But he would take her.

He settled back to watch her make up her mind.

Andie heard the voices; they didn't so much wake her as call her attention to the fact that she was awake. She felt fresh and clear-headed, as though she'd been asleep a long time, a sleep she had needed. The window was uncurtained and a searing placard of light hung awry on the opposite wall.

The voices were just outside the room. One of them, a man's, deep and lazy, spoke with a heavy emphasis, just a few words at a time. By the sound of it he wanted something and was not going to leave until it was given. Dawn was responding, rebuffing his demands, it sounded like, in a placatory tone. Andie couldn't really tell what it was about: they were speaking the local language. Well, it was nothing to do with her.

The door of her bedroom was half-open, and

it seemed to her that the apartment door must be open too, with the speakers standing on either side of the threshold: she could picture them standing like that, Dawn perhaps even blocking his way in. If she got out of bed and put her head out into the corridor, she'd see. But she only pushed herself further up in the bed, and listened.

She didn't know how to interpret the tones of voices here. She hated this city that made her seem so stupid. Last night had been a complete waste of time. She didn't know why she'd gone. Once it was over, she'd felt like an idiot for leaving Dawn, and all the more so because when she finally managed to get away she'd lost her bearings in the stupid city and had ended up walking around by herself until late, wandering long stone lanes for what seemed like forever. Finally she'd recognised Dawn's building. She'd tried not to make any noise when she came in.

The night felt, now, like a story she had heard, not a place she had been for herself. Everything about it was unconvincing. Charles had seemed nice enough, but as soon as they got down to the waterfront he'd dived, shouting, into a squad of his mates. The whole promenade had been filled with men sitting at the trestle tables, sharing bottles of wine and eating grilled fish off paper plates, or standing around in gangs which continually broke up and reformed in laughing discord. The sun had set half an hour before. Heat had gusted from the bonfires. What had she been expecting? To talk to new people, to hear some singing and maybe do some dancing. But none of them had seemed to want to talk to her or even look at her. In a funny way, she'd had the feeling they hadn't noticed she was there, even as they crowded around with excited chatter and much impatient gesturing. The city's words had cloyed the air, thick and meaningless, and no one had seemed willing to switch to a language she could understand. They hadn't offered her anything to eat.

Her bitterness began to drain away. She was bored thinking about their boring festival. There was nothing to look at in this room except the sun on the wall. It was like those times when she was six or seven years old and had stayed at home pretending to be more sick than she really was, for which her reward was a day that was genuinely endless, not in length but in breadth, in which she lay in her bedroom, not reading or sleeping or really doing anything, with afternoon light dusting through the blinds and the bedroom door and window half-open so the strange sounds of daytime were removed from her not by barriers, only by distance.

She couldn't tell, now, why she'd stayed out as long as she had. She didn't know why she hadn't just left as soon as she realised that it wasn't going to be a normal party at all but some weird old tradition. At a distance, she had spotted a few red-faced women watching her with disapproval, but the men had led her through the crowd and into the empty middle of the semicircle of tables.

They had drawn back and left her standing there in the centre of the space. The faces at the tables had turned towards her, and it had struck her as funny that all of them were looking away from the sea: it had been as if she was standing on a stage with the city as a backdrop behind her. The streets had been vacant, their brick mouths lamplit. Then something had changed in the men's faces and she had seen the figure walking towards her.

As she listened to the voices in the hall, she saw how things might have been if only she had behaved differently from the moment she had arrived here. She saw herself going to a language school or, better, learning in private from Dawn, or by herself from a book, learning another language properly for the first time, not to please anyone or to persuade them of anything, not even because she needed to, but just learning to speak the language. Just staying and not telling anyone, and perhaps, in good time, disclosing her new knowledge to her friends. Why shouldn't she?

The man who had appeared from inside the city, limping towards her where she stood on the promenade, had been very old: one of those frail, shrivelled old men you could easily mistake for an old lady, with the face so hollow and small and the sparse white hairs curling from the chin. He had pitched sideways every now and then as he came towards

231

her. She had seen worms of yellow matter in the corners of his eyes, and caught a smell of sickness. But it was important to be nice to elderly gentlemen, and she was good at it, so she had greeted him with a friendly smile and got ready to offer him her arm if he needed it. He must have come for the festival too. Touchingly, he had decorated his coat with a rather bedraggled carnation.

She had been about to offer to help him to a seat, but he had gripped her hand with fingers which were narrow and knobbled as twigs but stronger than they appeared, and would not let her move. She hadn't liked the intensity with which the clouded eyes looked up into her face. The men at the tables had watched as she had tried to draw away, but the old man had leant on her arm, threatening to fall, and tightened his grip so that, although he weighed very little, she couldn't bring herself to shake him off. Craning up towards her ear, he had begun to speak.

The strange thing was that, now, she could remember nothing at all about what he had said. At the time, she was sure, she had understood him – had even felt a swell of relief that someone was making the effort – but now it was gone, the old man's story, whatever he had wanted to tell her. She only remembered that it had made her very uncomfortable and that she had known that she did not want to hear it. The ruined eyes had been fixed on her so hungrily. Lifted by a wave of nausea, she had tugged her arm from his clinging grip, and, before he could get out more than a few words, she had left.

A ripple of outrage or disappointment had followed her from the trestle tables, but she hadn't cared. All right, yes, she had thought furiously, as she hastened away from the waterfront without looking back: yes, I've embarrassed myself again, I've come blundering in and shown myself up at your stupid festival that I don't see the point of, I've probably let everyone down and I don't even know how. Let me get away.

She felt tired. She wondered why she presented herself the way she did, why she could only wheedle her petulant demands of the world instead of being brave and humble and simple as she knew she could be. Why were all her actions forgeries and all her words lies, when the last thing she really was, was a liar? The one thing she wanted was to be honest with people. Why had she made such a fool of herself to Dawn with every single thing she had done and said? Dawn, who was never unbalanced, who had everything she needed and who never flailed around like a stupid marionette. Andie had tried her best, but there was a law that said wherever inside yourself you place what matters most, that's where you will fail. The voices came down the corridor into the room but they told her nothing and she was not trying to listen.

★   ★   ★

That evening, when Dawn arrived home from her afternoon's work at the school, Andie mentioned that her train left in forty-five minutes' time and it had been so kind of Dawn to have her to stay. Dawn wanted to ask what about the plan of staying for the rest of the month, but she could find no tactful way to do so when apparently it had been forgotten. As Andie collected up her things she chattered brightly about the next city she was going to see, sharing highlights from the guidebook.

Dawn walked with her towards the station, but only part of the way. Possibly she had eaten a bad mussel the other night, and she had certainly swallowed several bits of grit: all through today she'd thought she could feel tremblings of food poisoning, and she wanted to go back to her apartment and address them in private.

They paused on the promenade before separating. The remains of the feast had been cleared away, and an older woman was sluicing down the flag-stones with a bucket.

Andie shifted her feet, her legs braced against the weight of her rucksack. She looked down at the pavement and across at the sky which was growing deeper over the sea. Fine strands of hair at her temples were filled with the light. She said she would see Dawn back home. They should stay in touch. Dawn agreed, her attention drifting into the silver floss. Andie was saying something else, her voice low, and too late Dawn realised that she had not been listening. Andie's face was fretful as she waited for a reply.

'All right,' Dawn said, and she imagined that the pieces of grit were fragments of a precious material, specks of pearl. 'I'll let him know.'

PART VII

PART VII

THE SIGNIFICANT CITY
OF LAZARUS GLASS

Exquisite enigmas, mysteries sinister and bizarre: for Peregrine Fetch these were at once a vocation and the keenest happiness in life. As an archive of the gruesome and the perplexing his casebook is without peer and yet, even there, the details of his final adventure must strike the interpreter as anomalous. It may be that we have yet to grasp the whole pattern of the crimes. Which of us can hope to explain the events of the night on which the most gifted investigator of our time met his match? Peregrine Fetch was the man who solved the Theft of the Paper Orchid, and who exposed the trickeries at work in the affair of the Nightmare Gallery; it was he who brought to its denouement the sanguinary chronicle of the Revenge of the Trelawneys, and who won the horrified applause of every citizen by unravelling the case of the Riddle in Brass. Regardless of the outcome of the investigation whose narrative it is my task now to set down, I count myself privileged to have been his assistant, his apprentice and his friend.

In the small hours of one night in March last year, I was at work in the consulting rooms where, by day, Peregrine Fetch received his clients, heard their tales and meditated on their problems. I myself often puzzled late over the files of our ongoing investigations, doing my best to follow my mentor's ratiocinatory principles as far as they could lead – far enough, perhaps, to tease out whichever snarl of human evil lay before me on the desk. When on occasion I accomplished some small success in this regard, Peregrine's features would crinkle and his grey eyes would release the spark of warmth which at other times they hid so well.

All night I had worked alone amid columns of case notes, kept company by the raindrops that flung themselves at the windows, but now I heard hurried footsteps in the street below. Moments later I was joined by Inspector Nimrod of the City Watch.

The Inspector's greeting was gruff as usual, but he was evidently in a state of some agitation, short of breath and sweating in spite of the cold. Beads of moisture clung to his leather car-jacket. He looked around the clutter of the office.

'Dr Fetch not here? You don't know his whereabouts?'

He swallowed, the point of his throat leaping.

'Then I fear the worst.'

Having witnessed several investigations in which the constabulary, reaching the limit of their own wit, had begged Peregrine's assistance, I had learnt to set but modest store by Inspector Nimrod's deductions. But there was a grim note in his voice tonight which I did not find easy to dismiss.

'What do you mean, inspector?'

'I've never known a night like it,' he said. 'It's beyond me, I don't mind telling you, Ms Byrd. I thought I was losing my marbles back there and I'm still not sure I was wrong. Bleeding Lord, if they've got him too . . .'

But before he could continue, a soft voice wished us good morning and we turned to see, standing in the doorway, the slight figure of Peregrine Fetch. The inspector sagged with relief. Peregrine's hair, I noted, was disordered and dirtied, his left cheekbone and right knuckles sticky with fresh blood, and the sleeve of his raincoat torn, but he met us with a half-smile.

'They used to say that, in the city, as many deaths await you as there are windows open above your head.' His diction was light and precise. 'I can fairly claim that since you saw me last I have tried the truth of that proposition.'

'You were attacked?'

'Yes,' he said, sounding as if he had not quite thought of it in those terms. 'Certainly, I have been attacked.'

I began to ask him what had happened, but he raised a punctilious finger.

'Never fear: in due course I will unfold this further. But first, perhaps, the inspector has his own story to tell?'

241

Nimrod, who had been listening open-mouthed, found his tongue.

'I wish it wasn't so,' he said, and drew a deep breath. 'But yes. I'm certain of that, if of nothing else I've seen.'

It had been a punishing night for the inspector. He had been called from his bed to the scene of a murder. This in itself was not so unusual an occurrence; but no sooner had he laid eyes on the corpse than news arrived of another killing, a second ugly spectacle which he had barely surveyed when he was summoned away to the aftermath of yet a third homicide. Three murders. Death, it appeared to Nimrod, was opening its grisly blooms across the city as if its season had arrived. There was nothing in their manner or location to link the killings, but when he realised what they did have in common, the inspector, gripped by fresh dread, had turned on his heel and made all haste to the consulting rooms of Peregrine Fetch.

'The victims,' said the inspector, 'were all –'

'Please,' said Peregrine. 'Allow me. They were all of my profession. The murdered individuals were my fellow private consulting detectives.'

He said three names: the names of the three foremost investigators in the city, besides Peregrine himself. He gave Nimrod an inquiring look; the inspector's shake of the head was a gesture not of negation but of bafflement.

'Yes,' said the inspector. 'Hyperion Weill, Electra Cavendish-Peake, Brutus Thorne. Three of the

242

leading private detectives in the city have been murdered tonight. How did you know?'

Without removing his raincoat, Peregrine dropped on to the Chesterfield and stretched out full length, adopting the position in which, motionless, with eyes closed, ankles crossed and fingers laced on his sternum, he had solved many of his more arduous cases.

'It is as I anticipated,' he said. 'To begin with: you are both familiar, of course, with the name of Lazarus Glass.'

We were. For anyone concerned with the city's criminal element, Lazarus Glass moved in the mind like a shadow, never quite absent. Such was his reputation that he seemed not so much a man as a fable, a splendid monster: his infinite hunger for malfeasance, his genius for cruelty, his mastery of disguise and misdirection, the patience with which he executed his stratagems, all of these were recounted in whispers by common criminals and ordinary policemen alike – and they spoke, too, of the man's consuming hatred for his enemy, the detective who so often stood in his way, Peregrine Fetch.

No street or house was safe from Lazarus Glass, and not one citizen, bad or good, rich or poor. His tendrils linked the city's lowest robbery with its most grandiose jewel theft or political assassination. His name seldom appeared in the news, his face never, but Peregrine had many times assured me that Glass, through his manifold indirections, was behind the greater portion of the crimes it had fallen to my mentor to combat. And however often Peregrine thwarted the particular villainies which betrayed the presence of that hand on the strings, he had never come close to apprehending the puppeteer.

Never, until now. Lying on the sofa Peregrine resembled a recumbent statue on the tomb of a crusader. Without opening his eyes, he explained that, after months and years of hunting, of feint and counterfeint and invisible chessplay, he had at last found a route into the maze of defences with which Lazarus Glass surrounded himself, and had taken up the chase. He could not have hoped to succeed alone: he had joined forces with three other investigators, the bravest and most brilliant of the profession. Together they had closed the net around Glass by slow degrees, and tonight they had been on the point of drawing it fast. But the man was tenfold a devil when cornered, and it was no surprise that, in spite of all their precautions, he had struck against his pursuers with a violence testified by the sickly shade of the inspector's face.

'You're telling me it's Glass,' said Nimrod. 'In a single night he's wiped out three of the best private detectives in the city, and come close as dammit to doing the same to you too?'

'This would appear to be the reasonable inference,' said Peregrine. Only the soft voice showed that he was not asleep. 'Nor is there reason to suppose that the attempt is at an end, given that I remain –' he opened one eye '– active.'

'Then there's no time to waste. I'm placing you under police protection. We call for reinforcements.'

Peregrine sprang to his feet in a single movement.

'By no means, inspector. Do you think it is beyond the powers of Lazarus Glass to infiltrate the ranks of the law? Tonight I trust three people only and they are in this room. We will do well to move fast and inform no one of our plans. Cassandra, I must ask you to come with me. Nowhere is safe for any of us with Lazarus Glass so close behind, and I feel I may have need of your help in this affair.'

I rose.

'Besides,' he continued, 'three murders have been committed tonight. Our place is at the scenes of the crimes: there, if anywhere, we will find clues to the intention of our adversary.'

'It's against my better judgement,' said Nimrod, shaking his head in acquiescence.

'Think how many of our shared triumphs have been accomplished in just such a mode, inspector, and lead on.'

As we were leaving the consulting rooms, Peregrine moved to the mantelpiece and opened the old cigar box that stood there. Inside it, I knew, was a revolver. He stored it in the box as a matter of habit, keeping it cleaned and loaded but never taking it with him on investigations. I had never known him to use it, nor any other weapon. He kept the gun accessible, I believed, as a daily reminder that he had no need of it – that he chose to face the dangers of the city armed with reason alone. Now his hand lingered over the box, but he did not touch the weapon. Instead he closed the lid and turned to me. He seemed to search for words.

'When I am gone, Cassandra, it will be for you to carry on my work,' he said. 'We have a number of intriguing investigations in progress.'

He was looking at me strangely.

'It would be a matter for regret, for instance, if the case of the Apples of Madness were not brought to a satisfactory conclusion, or the affair of the Chanting Leopard.'

'But you'll solve those cases yourself, Dr Fetch,' I said, faltering. 'You'll outwit Lazarus Glass, I'm sure of it.'

'Well, perhaps I shall, at that,' he said. 'It is in any case a nice knot, this business with poor Lazarus, not without certain points of interest.'

As I followed him down the staircase to the street, he added:

'We were friends, once, long ago, Lazarus and I.'

In Professor Hyperion Weill's study, the gloom was relieved only by the glow from a tasselled lampshade which hung, askew, next to what was left of the wingback chair in which the professor had been seated in his final moments. Bookshelves lined the walls, the floor was thick with rugs, and around us crowded keepsakes enough to fill a museum of criminology: pistols, blowpipes, jezail rifles and blackened daggers, chinoiserie caskets, bottles of chemicals, specimen jars in which pale forms floated, a human skull wearing a tiara of paste diamonds. The inspector assured us that nothing had been moved since the discovery of the scene by a porter investigating reports of an isolated nocturnal shriek.

The curtains were open, and through the windows I made out the branches of oak trees printed black against the night sky. Hyperion Weill had been a tall old man, and his arms and legs, broomstick-thin inside their sheaths of tweed, overhung the sides of the chair. The book lying open in his lap was glistening and darkly sodden. Evidently, no attempt had been made to free the corpse from the position in which it had been left.

I felt a shiver of outrage at this ugly end to so honourable a career. Hyperion Weill had been peerless among the investigators of his generation, but in due course he had retired from full-time detection to take up a post as Professor of Ratiocination at the university. That should have meant well-deserved years of reflection, writing and passing on the fruits of his experience to the respectful young – not this night of butchery.

Peregrine gazed at the scene for a long time, his features neutral.

'Perhaps I should not have drawn him back into active investigation. But he knew our enemy well. He shaped both of us, Lazarus and me. We were so determined to impress him.'

As he scrutinised the object comprised of the remains of the professor and those of his favourite chair, Peregrine spoke in an undertone. Many years ago, he explained, he and Glass had studied together under the tuition of Hyperion Weill.

Callow as they had been in those days, young Peregrine Fetch and young Lazarus Glass were each intent, already, on surpassing even their teacher and becoming the single greatest detective the city had ever seen. In talent and ambition there had been little to distinguish the two youths, and for a time they had been as close as only devoted rivals can be. Only later had Lazarus chosen a different path.

Peregrine fell silent for a minute. I heard a droplet hit the floor beneath dangling fingertips.

'I remember one of the earliest tutorials we had with him,' he went on. 'Lazarus had written an essay proposing an entirely new interpretation of one of Professor Weill's own classic investigations: the case of the Nine Surgeons, if memory serves. The essay was a remarkable piece of work for an undergraduate, bold and original, and, as he read it aloud before the attentively bowed cranium of our tutor, Lazarus trembled with delight at the unfurling of his analytical faculties, at the excitement of elucidating through sheer deductive prowess aspects of the case which even the great detective himself had not previously understood.

'Unfortunately, the argument was flawed. It was a small oversight, but crucial: if you recall, the Nine Surgeons affair involved a number of deadly weapons, and Lazarus's interpretation was founded on a failure to distinguish between the types of wound that may be inflicted by a duelling rapier, a *tachi* sword and a cavalry sabre.'

Inspector Nimrod, standing back in the shadows of the study, muttered a heartfelt oath.

'When Lazarus's essay had reached its ringing conclusion, Professor Weill pointed out this simple error and methodically dismantled the entire deductive edifice constructed upon it. Lazarus received the lesson badly. I believed at the time that it took him an entire term to shake off his mortification.'

Peregrine, who was now squatting very close to the object of his inspection, looked up at me.

'It appears, however, that he may have nursed the resentment for longer.'

He indicated the three dissimilar sword-hilts protruding from the chest of the corpse of Hyperion Weill, their steel blades crossed at the point where they emerged through the back of the chair.

'These are, I notice, the very implements which formed the crux of Lazarus's early academic misstep. Our killer entered Professor Weill's study and perhaps engaged him in conversation. Then he snatched the first of these weapons from where it hung on the wall among the mementos of the professor's long career – note the three sword-shaped patches of unfaded wallpaper – and, with it, struck the first blow. The others followed, rapier and *tachi*, as if in excess of revenge for that distant humbling. As if to impart his own lesson in the varieties of possible harm.'

Peregrine looked into his old tutor's face, which was not peaceful.

'We begin to perceive the contours of a dreadful logic. Those who have thwarted Lazarus Glass would do well to beware tonight.'

The gothic apartment blocks of Juno Square showed a handful of lit windows, but the streets were empty as we followed Inspector Nimrod through Belltown. Few had business in the university district at this time of night. Black reflections slicked ahead of us in the pavements and great weeping globes clung about the head of each lamp post.

Of those who had studied the arts of detection under Hyperion Weill, the most promising of all had been Electra Cavendish-Peake. She was a few years older than Peregrine and Lazarus, and the two friends had in their early days regarded her with envy and awe. She appeared far closer to the mastery they desired, with her sharp scholarly manners and hermetic turn of mind, her knowledge of esoteric casebooks and the furthest reaches of ratiocinatory theory, and the chilly style

250

in which, while still a graduate student, she had solved the case of the Liars' League: it had been as if she fixed that conspiracy in a block of ice which, with one smart tap of the intellect, she shattered, breaching all its secrets.

But she had shown small inclination to pursue the life of investigative adventure which beckoned. She preferred more regular habits, haunting the reading rooms of the university and city libraries, spending part of each afternoon at her club, and dining each evening at the same bistro, alone, with a book of abstruse criminology propped open before her. She devoted herself to research and correspondence, very occasionally publishing a monograph putting forward some revision to the fundamental theoretical postulates of detection, or an article resolving beyond question a cold case which had stumped the best minds of a century ago. The previous year, when after months of inquiry Peregrine had been all but ready to admit defeat in the matter of the Doubting Child, Electra had provided the key to the problem in a two-minute telephone conversation.

Peregrine had recounted this much by the time we arrived at a restaurant with a handwritten menu tacked inside its grubby window. A pair of police uniforms moved aside to admit us, and we found ourselves among a jumble of tables on which suppers lay half-finished. Wine from overturned carafes had stained the checked tablecloths deep red. In the far corner of the room, the body of Electra

Cavendish-Peake leant across the table at which she had begun, but not concluded, her last meal.

'Cassandra,' said Peregrine, 'perhaps you would care to reconstruct what has taken place?'

I nodded, and for some minutes I studied the scene in silence. At last I straightened and exhaled.

'The sequence of events is apparent,' I said. 'Dr Cavendish-Peake was dining by herself, as we know was her practice. Her demise was sudden and dramatic. The restaurant was full and the other diners vacated the room rapidly, as we can see from these overturned chairs. Coats hang abandoned on the hooks beside the exit.

'How did she die? The puncture mark near the victim's mouth, and the colour and contortion of the face, give evidence enough of the cause. But if we wish for more, we have it. Note, first, the book which lies closed on her left hand, as if she wishes even now to keep her place: a new academic hardback from Bloodstone Press. Looking closer, we can identify it as a recently issued collection of essays by various contributors, offering new interpretations of the case of the Double Sun – a case in which, as it happens, Dr Cavendish-Peake herself played a part some dozen years ago. In solving it, by the way, she sank a blackmail operation as profitable as it was cruel, and behind which the influence of Lazarus Glass was, if not demonstrable, perceptible.'

Peregrine lowered his head a few affirmative degrees.

'Beside the book lies a padded envelope addressed to Dr Cavendish-Peake. We can hypothesise that, having received the package earlier in the day, she in all probability delayed opening it and examining the book until she was sitting at the table. Perhaps she was not paying attention as she opened the seal since, for a theoretician of her distinction, deliveries from academic publishers were surely a common occurrence. Closer examination, however, reveals that this was no gift sent in hopes of a favourable review. Peering into the book's interior where it is held open by her stiffened hand, we notice that a cuboid section has been excised from the central pages with a razor or sharp knife, creating a hollow cell within. When she opened the book, she released what had been imprisoned in this space.'

'Fiendish,' said Inspector Nimrod to himself.

'It sprang at her face, inflicting the injury we see here. She would have begun to feel the effects of the venom at once, and, given her quick perceptions and full acquaintance with the relevant arachnological data, she must have understood the severity of her situation. But she remained alert, and, observing that the instrument of her decease was now scuttling across the floor towards the restaurant's panicking patrons, she picked up a piece of cutlery and flung it with the necessary force and accuracy to impale the creature that we see here.'

I indicated the point, some distance away, where

a pale brown tropical spider the size of my hand was fixed to the floorboards by a obliquely angled steel fork.

'Alongside her more sedentary accomplishments she was always superb with a throwing-knife,' said Peregrine.

'*Phoneutria mortifera*,' I said. 'Commonly known as the poison pen spider. Its neurotoxin takes effect with atrocious speed and potency. She would have known that her own case was hopeless, and that protecting the other diners was to be her final action.'

'This is sound work, Cassandra.'

'But incomplete. I see what has happened but I cannot tell why.'

'True. And there I must assist you, because to uncover the *why* of this scene we must plunge further into those lost times when Electra, like Lazarus and myself, was a precocious neophyte.'

He plunged his hands into his raincoat pockets and contemplated the disarrayed restaurant as he spoke.

'I have indicated that the nature of Electra's gifts led her into the abstract and obscure reaches of our discipline. What you must also know is how profoundly Lazarus Glass, at that moment in his development as a young investigator, was influenced by her, this exceptional deductive intellect whom he saw as being always one step ahead on the path to mastery.

'He would follow her from lecture hall to library,

clutching the work of whichever theorist he had discovered most recently, pouring out his latest ideas, always wanting an argument – wanting, too, new ways to gain the advantage in his rivalry with me. Electra, for her part, found in Lazarus a keen interlocutor, and soon realised that while he shared her taste for arcana, in his case this mingled with an impatient pragmatism. He loved strange notions not for themselves but for what they might enable him to accomplish.'

Electra Cavendish-Peake had been developing an unusual theory of detection, Peregrine explained. Instead of the standard casebooks, she was spending days and nights in neglected reading rooms deep in the library, surrounded by heavy, crumbling volumes: Anacratus, Raymond Lully, Giulio Camillo, Giordano Bruno, Johannes Döhl, Robert Fludd. It was clear to Lazarus that she was pursuing some curious line of research, but he had to importune her for some time before she consented to share her ideas; perhaps she intuited, even then, that not she but Lazarus was the person to bring her theory to fruition. She told him that she was exploring what had once been known as the Art of Memory.

At that time, Lazarus had no more than a layman's understanding of the principles of *memoria artificialis*: the secret, well known to the ancients, that the human memory could be understood as a physical place, a spatial structure. The long-ago practitioners of the Art had discovered that it was possible to build, in the mind, houses of memory – temples and palaces of memory.

So, for instance, Electra explained, she had already succeeded in constructing a complete mental replica of the Green Stairs townhouse where she had spent her early childhood, recreated in such detail that, although the original building had been destroyed in a fire a decade ago, she could now close her eyes and walk its rooms and corridors just as if she were there once more: and inside her memory house she could store what she wished to remember. She had framed a certain afternoon on the riverbank seven summers past, and hung it in the hallway to be admired whenever she liked. In the garden behind this house of the mind, she had laid out in formal flowerbeds her plans for her career, some of them strong and bright, others no more than frail shoots. Before the sitting-room fireplace lay a Turkish carpet whose pattern she knew by heart, and into its symmetrical figures she had encoded the names of all her personal and professional acquaintances, so that, as she traced the relationships between them, their faces winked up at her from the nodes and buds of the design. And in the glass-fronted bookcases of her father's study she had arranged every book she had read in her time at the university. She demonstrated this to Lazarus, reeling off the authors' names alphabetically, then the titles in reverse alphabetical order. She pulled down one or two volumes and read from their opening pages as fluently as if she actually held them in her hands.

Which was a nice trick, said Lazarus, and useful enough as a tool for the busy scholar. But he failed to see how any of this was likely to advance the science of detection. He was missing the point, Electra replied; and, with that, he found he had to persuade her all over again to take him into her confidence. She had no patience with those who did not keep up. She refused to discuss the matter further until he had, at the very least, ameliorated his ignorance of mnemotechnics by reading the essential modern treatises by Yates, Hawksquill and Carruthers.

When he had done so, she relented. To convey to him what she had in mind, she read aloud the passage from the *Confessions* in which Augustine speaks of the 'spacious palaces of memory where countless images are hoarded, brought in from all the diverse objects perceived by the senses', and adds: 'There too are hidden the altered images we create in our minds by enlarging or diminishing or otherwise transforming the things we perceive.'

That was the crux of it, Electra said: altered images. It was true that, with long and gruelling study, a practitioner of the Art could learn to retrieve all the lost junk and treasure hidden away in the attics of the mind, and to arrange every-thing in order: each image in its place, tidy and accessible. But it was also true that surprising things could happen in memory houses. To embody ideas

257

in such a fashion was to imbue them with unpredictable life. They might move around when you were not there; they might change and grow in ways you had not expected.

She had noticed this already in her own small experiment. Further down the garden of her memory house, beyond the formal beds of ambition, she had one day been taken aback to discover another bed, in which grew a thorny tangle of grudges and resentments which she had not intended to plant. On closer examination she had been still more startled to recognise the forgotten wrongs that some of the older plants represented.

Later, too, when she looked at the Turkish rug in which she had patterned the network of her acquaintances, she found that the curls and interleavings suggested unexpected links between them. Guided by these hints, further investigation had revealed that, yes, those graduate students were working together on a furtive conference paper which came close to impinging on Electra's own research; that, yes, those two members of the Senior Common Room enjoyed a relationship which was not purely professional. She had not been conscious of these useful facts until her memory house had brought them to her attention.

Such discoveries were mere toys, of course, and nothing that would rebuild the foundations of detection. But the larger possibility she had glimpsed held precisely such a promise. Consider the nature of detection, she said to Lazarus, this art to which we have dedicated ourselves. Is it not also an art of memory, in which we must retain every insignificant detail which might prove to be the key to a case? And does our discipline not have a special affinity with the ancient practice of the memory house, for where does the detective live, if not in a *memory city*, a city that is less a physical place than a world of codes and symbols? Does she not, in her mind, walk the streets at all times, in search of the meanings concealed there?

Lazarus saw what Electra was driving at, now, and he realised immediately that although it would require phenomenal work to accomplish, the rewards could be commensurate. If a detective could build, in his mind, a memory city which replicated the real city in every detail, then every mystery contained in that city would lie open to him: he would have mastered his discipline with a perfection otherwise unthinkable.

They talked through the night, growing bright-eyed as they developed the theme. Supposing it were possible, using the techniques of *memoria artificialis*, to construct an entire memory city, how would such a system of investigation work? The detective would become a perpetual flâneur within his own mind, forever wandering the pavements of memory to read the symbols and to encounter the shifting images through which the city would give up its secrets. To walk endlessly in imaginary streets would be a price to pay, no doubt, but in return one would gain powers of deduction nothing short of uncanny. Such a detective would foresee crimes before they took place, and would know criminals' motives and hiding places before they knew themselves.

As the discussion became more excited, even fanciful, Lazarus kept one thought to himself. It was this: he was already some way towards the creation of the hallucinatory city that Electra posited. For all the hours he laboured over his books, Lazarus spent still more time walking the city, learning the mazes of its alleyways and slums, for he had always known that this was the only book that mattered to him. When he won fame, it would be for his readings of blood on brick, not ink on paper. He told himself that, in a way, the idea had belonged to him long before Electra had come to it. With her ancient codices and hermetic schemata, she had merely given him the tools to make it possible.

'For Electra,' Peregrine said, 'that night of feverish student talk was the apex of the project. She delved some way further into her inquiry, but before long her rationalism prevailed. She concluded that the obstacles were too enormous and the rewards too uncertain to make the idea worth pursuing, and she diverted her energies to more productive lines of research. When she mentioned this to Lazarus, he agreed, and assured her that he, too, had dropped the notion of the memory city.

'Years later, I learned that he had been lying.'

* * *

Steady drizzle fell as we left Belltown and hastened across the Old Quarter, trailing Inspector Nimrod through Twistgate to emerge into the stately public spaces of the Esplanade. In front of us, the facades of the Autumn Palace seemed to hang weightless, picked out by the floodlights. As we crossed the Parade we passed only a few night-owls on their way for a late stroll down the Mile, towards the cafés of Impasto Street or across the river to visit the headier attractions of Serelight.

Before us, overlooked by the Palace, lay the metro plaza. By day it would have been filled with stopping and starting trams, travellers embarking and disembarking, tourists poring over maps and locals pressing irritably through the crowd, but tonight the plaza was deserted except for a single tram, standing empty with its doors open and its interior lights making it a jointed yellow prism in the dark. And gathered around it, the familiar array: the saloon cars stopped at slewed angles, the slow-pulsing beacons, the bobbing torch beams, the reflective tape, the conferrals, the faces mingling nausea and boredom, the uniforms.

We approached the tram, and Inspector Nimrod paused to collect himself. Then, motioning his subordinates aside, he showed us the remains of Brutus Thorne, and the manner of the third murder.

'One headache is where we're going to place the scene of the crime,' said the inspector. His laugh was a single thump on a rusty drum. He kept his eyes averted from what lay between the tracks at the rear of the tram. Peregrine, by contrast, was all attention: a critic formulating his first response to a challenging new piece.

At last he turned away.

'Brutus was a fearless comrade,' he said. 'No two investigators could have differed further in style and temperament than Peregrine Fetch and Brutus Thorne; but many times we reached the same ends by discrepant means.'

Peregrine's voice was steady, his face calm and unlined. I could not exactly name my thoughts as I observed this. I admired my mentor's power to remain detached in the face of horrors, but as he confronted the grisly decease of an old friend for the third time in a single night, his composure untroubled, I experienced a fleeting chill.

Brutus Thorne had not subscribed to the principles of pure reason to which Peregrine was committed. He was a detective in another tradition. While Peregrine preferred to solve his clients' puzzles through mentation alone, and took the deepest satisfaction in those cases which he was able to conclude without once rising from the Chesterfield in his consulting rooms, for Brutus the tools of investigation were muscle and grit. He got results by using his ears in the dive bars of the Liberties, and his fists in the alleyways outside; by means of coffee-fuelled stakeouts and rooftop chases. Peregrine, an expert at impersonation, could mingle in disguise with the city's criminal element and never be detected, but Brutus Thorne needed no disguise at all, because he lived there.

In spite of their differing approaches to their work, the paths of the two men had crossed frequently in their shared campaign against the villainies of Lazarus Glass. Peregrine, for instance, had once devoted five months of archival research to the case of the Ship in the Mirror, and had been on the cusp of a solution when he read in the newspaper that Brutus Thorne had broken the case with a single well-placed hidden microphone. On the other hand, Brutus had once worked himself into the ground over the affair of the Green December, shaking down informants, tailing suspects and running phone-taps, only to discover that Peregrine Fetch had, weeks earlier, foreseen the whole sequence of events, and had simply been waiting for the would-be kidnappers to incriminate themselves before he informed the police of their intentions and whereabouts. And then again, the case of the Demolitionist's Song would have remained a mystery to this day had Peregrine and Brutus not joined forces to expose the conspiracy. Thanks to Lazarus Glass, the felonious genius of the city, the rival detectives had become allies over the years.

'What we do know,' the inspector said, 'is that Brutus Thorne was last seen alive in Shambles Heath, in the vicinity of Meaney's. That's one of the low drinking dens he was known to frequent, Ms Byrd.'

I had picked up several useful leads in Meaney's myself, in the past, but I just smiled.

'Witnesses confirm that when Thorne left this establishment he was deep in conversation with an unidentified companion, and that both individuals were seen to proceed in the direction of the Shambles Heath metropolitan tram station.'

That had been the last sighting of Brutus Thorne alive, the inspector told us. But there was no lack of testimony about what followed. The reports formed a long curving trail across the city, southwards from Shambles Heath through Serelight and into Glory Part, then across the Part bridge, up through Lawntown and Communion Town into the Esplanade: all the way along the line of the metro that this tram had travelled tonight.

At Shambles Heath station a person or persons unknown had lured Brutus Thorne into proximity with a particular tramcar. He would have had no time to offer resistance as a pair of self-locking cuffs were slapped around his ankles. The assault had been diligently prepared. Six-foot lengths of steel chain ran from the cuffs to the rear of the tram, where they had been attached in advance. The timing was precise. It was all too easy to imagine: as Thorne realises his predicament, he grabs for his assailant, tussles and perhaps lands a blow or two, but the villain struggles free and melts away, work done. Before the detective can call out, the tram begins to move and his feet are wrenched from under him. He scrabbles on the tarmac to regain his footing, but as the vehicle accelerates he is dragged along behind it, like . . . like . . .

The inspector stopped, lost for words.

'Like the fallen Hector,' suggested Peregrine.

'Like Hippolytus behind his chariot,' I offered.

'Like a sack of bloody potatoes,' said the inspector. 'Those things get up to fifty miles an hour, apparently, and it hauled him halfway round the city before winding up here. I don't want to think about that. We've got the driver over there: says he saw nothing and heard nothing. Had his paper spread out on the control panel all the way from Shambles to the Palace, and he wants to know how much compensation he's due for the distress. But I'm not bothered about him. It's this anonymous companion from Meaney's I want – and I can guess who you're going to tell me it was.'

Peregrine was kneeling close to the tram, touching the metal lumps where the chains had been welded to the undercarriage.

'Yes, inspector, no doubt you can,' he said as he got up. 'But the question, as always, is *why*. Why would Lazarus Glass choose this end, of all ends, for Brutus Thorne?'

I looked at the tram, still lit yellow in the failing darkness. It was newer and sleeker than the ungainly, graffiti-covered carriages which clattered around most lines of the metro.

'One thought occurs,' I said. 'The metro route that the inspector has described, the curve that

265

links Shambles Heath with the Old Quarter, terminating here at the Palace, is the most recently built line in the city. But, if I remember accurately, this is not the first time that it has been associated with criminal activity.'

'Correct and to the point, Cassandra,' said Peregrine. 'Once more we must unearth the past to make sense of the fate that has befallen our comrades tonight – and now I must tell you about the last time I encountered Lazarus Glass face to face.

'Six years ago,' he continued, 'the planned construction of the new metropolitan tramline had just been announced. Several organisations were in competition for the lucrative right to build it, and after negotiations the contract was awarded to an obscure group called the Lys Consortium. However, there were grounds to suspect that it had defeated its competitors through bribery, intimidation and violence, and soon Brutus and I found ourselves in a familiar contest, each of us working separately to uncover this wrongdoing.

'It did not take me long to establish that the Consortium was a front, and that somewhere behind it stood Lazarus Glass. But it was less easy to gather enough evidence to expose the misdeeds which had won the contract, and I set to work, spurred by the knowledge that Brutus would be doing all that he could, in his own way, to get there first. There was scant hope of demonstrating the complicity of Lazarus, who was as hedged and invulnerable as he always is in his schemes; but as I worked on the case I grew increasingly troubled by another question. The mystery, I felt, was not how Lazarus had won the corrupt contract, but why he should wish to do so. Certainly there was crude profit in it, but less than he might have gained through a thousand other illicit enterprises. No: I realised, as I analysed his plot, that the metro line held some other significance for him.

'It was at this point that I received an unexpected visitor in my consulting rooms.

'In person, of course, Lazarus Glass does not look like a devil. The air did not boil as he entered the room and the mirror did not crack. He looked underfed, or unconcerned with his body's needs. Since our student days he had lost his hair and grown a full beard, giving him a sober Aeschylean appearance. He wore a dark suit and tie. The only other change was in his eyes, which were as piercing as ever, but now there was a strange duality in his gaze: even as he studied me, he gave an impression of blindness, as if what he saw was not what lay in front of him.

'"Peregrine," he said. "You will forgive my calling on you without prior arrangement, under the circumstances. We need not waste time discussing all that has taken place since we last met in person – not when we have been continually in conversation through the medium of the city itself."

'"The medium of your crimes," I said sadly. "I wish it might have been otherwise, Lazarus."

'An expression of scorn crossed his face.

'"It will convenience you to know," he said, "that you may abandon your investigations into the matter of the Lys Consortium and the new metropolitan line. The thuggery of your associate Brutus Thorne has prevailed over your methodological elegancy, and he has beaten you to the proof. The Consortium will now fail, a scandal will ensue, and in due course another company instead will profit from the construction of the new line, while my name will, naturally, at no stage be mentioned in connection with the affair. At the proper time I will requite Thorne amply for the damage he has inflicted on my interests. Your own efforts in this case, meanwhile, have been wasted."

'"Not entirely wasted, Lazarus," I said. I thought I knew the true reason for his visit. "I have learned a good deal about you."

'"I am aware of what you have . . . surmised," he said, and for the first time he seemed amused. "I will allow that you have understood far more about my endeavours than any other detective – and although it will not help you, I am not unimpressed."

'"You are a puzzle, old friend," I said.

'This was the question that had nagged at me of late: why, all those years ago, when he stood on the threshold of a dazzling career in detection after graduating with a double first in Ratiocination and Criminology, had Lazarus turned aside and vanished into the city's underworld to become the inversion of all he had worked for? Perhaps the worm had always been there, curled in the bud of his brilliance. Perhaps he had concluded that he would never prevail in his rivalry with me, and, rather than accept second place, preferred the role of nemesis. But perhaps, too, I now suspected, his fall was connected with the Art of Memory.

'When I put this to him, Lazarus stared at me for a long time; then he gave me a cold-blooded smile, and I knew that my hypothesis was correct. He had never relinquished the idea of the memory city, despite what he had told Electra. After his disappearance, over the years in which I made my own reputation as a detective and could only wonder what had become of my friend, he had continued the research in secret, his obsession deepening as his expertise grew.

'"I have accomplished feats of mnemotechnics such as have not been seen for five hundred years," he told me, with a mixture of complacency and defiance. "I have equalled the greatest of the long-dead artificers of memory."

'"And what of the memory city you once imagined, Lazarus? What became of that wild notion?"

'"Oh, the memory city exists. It exists so completely, so truly, that I wonder sometimes whether anything else exists, anywhere in creation."

'"It exists in your mind?"

'"That is a tame way of expressing the reality, Peregrine. Say instead that my mind *is* the city. I have done nothing less than reconstruct my consciousness from the sewers to the slates, so that it matches in every detail the form of the city."

'My fancy about a doubleness in his gaze grew stronger; his eyes were fixed on my face, but they seemed not to see.

'"These districts and streets," he said, "from the fountains and brocaded sentries of the Palace Mile to the drab terraces of Salt Park, from the tower blocks of Sludd's Liberty to the canal walkways of Thin Gardens, from the acquisitive scrum of Clothmarket to the miniature wilderness of Whitethorn Common, from the desolated industrial estates of Kinsayder Fields to the derricks swinging over Greywater Quays, from the rows of unsold, new-built villas out in Gorgonstown to the introverted ancestral residences of Rosamunda and Lizavet: this is the landscape of my brain."

'"But why, Lazarus? What does it mean?"

'"What does it mean? It means that thoughts are no longer the vague, slippery things they once were. Memories, ideas and plans no longer drift and vanish like smoke, against my will; hopes, fantasies and dreads can no longer betray me. They are laid out in the city of my mind, in the form of houses and bridges, monuments and parks, as clear as a map and as solid as stone. You cannot imagine what richness it is for me to pursue the merest train of thought. I walk the appropriate route through the memory city, and, as I do so, every aspect of the matter I wish to consider unfolds around me: an explosion of instantaneous understanding, manifest in architecture. While the rest of you grope in darkness, a thought for me is space and light."

'Warming to the topic, he let me know that, moreover, he had discovered certain efficacious rituals. If he was preoccupied with some especially difficult question, he would make his way through his memory city to the statue of the Flâneur which stands incongruously in that small square off Grin Lane, behind the Strangers' Market, and would whisper his query into its ear. Then, he had only to wait and watch for how the memory city would reveal its answer: perhaps there would be a traffic accident at False Cross or a slow shipwreck of a sunset over Cento Hill, or perhaps a leaf would fall from a tree in the Autumn Park and brush his shoulder. Whatever it was, Lazarus would read the sign and know what his city was telling him.

'"When I sleep," he said, "in my dreams I walk only in the city's streets. There is nowhere else left."

'I knew that some of the more febrile memory-artists of ancient times had supposed that, if one could construct a perfect mental representation of the universe, sculpting the mind into a functional model of the whirling spheres and the mazelike earth at their centre, then by a form of sympathetic magic one would gain power over the universe itself, becoming not much less than a divinity. A mad fantasy, of course – but, if what he said was true, then no one in history had come closer to achieving it than Lazarus Glass.

'"The memory city gives you the power of insight that you imagined, then," I said. "But you have twisted it to a purpose far from what you first intended."

'"Oh yes," said Lazarus. "I was an ignorant youth in those days, and could envisage no greater use for the memory city than aiding a detective's chores. Indeed, soon after perfecting the system I tested its powers in that manner, by attempting to resolve the case of the Stolen Shadow. It had proved intractable for all the city's detectives – even for you, Peregrine, if you recall – but a glance into the memory city revealed to me every significant detail of the forgers' operation, from the location of their workshop in Low Glinder to the nature of the minuscule flaws that betrayed their creations as counterfeit. I saw, also, the fault lines of envy and mistrust among the criminals. Rather than report them to the authorities, I sent an anonymous note, a few words long and apparently quite innocuous, to one peripheral gang member, and watched as the repercussions of this intervention caused the entire scam to collapse in on itself. There was satisfaction in that."

'But, Lazarus explained to me, the capacities of the memory city went much further. Soon he found that he could manipulate events in the real city with impossible reach and prescience, so instinctively did he know its workings: and no

272

sooner had he realised the extent of his powers than he was beguiled by their potential for evil.

'"Spread before me," he said, "I saw all the offices and infrastructures of the city – bureaucracy, politicians, lawyers, police, industry, financiers, unions, news media, utility companies, organised criminals, all of it – no more difficult to control than my own fingertips. The skilled puppeteer needs to give only the slightest twitches on the strings to make his dummies dance. Was it any wonder that I ceased to trouble myself with the constraints of the law?"

'"No one can wield untrammelled power without paying some price," I said quietly.

'"You think so, Peregrine?" said Lazarus. "What an innocent you are. To whom should I pay a price, when nothing exists beyond my thoughts? Who in the city could compel me, when the city is my mind?"

'Hearing this, I knew what had happened to Lazarus. The city inside his head had fused with the city outside until they were indistinguishable. He could close his eyes and visit his memory city, but when he opened them again, what was the difference? Even when he walked the streets in actuality, he moved in the sealed world of his own thoughts.

'"My poor friend," I said, "I am sorry. You are quite insane."

'"You understand nothing," he replied. "True, I have gone beyond the flimsy pretence you call sanity, with its timid distinctions between what is real and what is imaginary. But never mistake me for some sad solipsist, locked up in my own skull. I am precisely the opposite: my mind is so distributed across the city that, for me, there is no difference between a thought and an action. Everything I do – murder and larceny, acquiring the building contract for the tramline, visiting you today, laying my hand on your mantelpiece like this – everything I do is a symbol soaked in significance, an adjustment to the pattern of the memory city."

'"Then this is why you wished to influence the development of the metro line?"

'Anger showed in Lazarus's eye.

'"Do you still fail to comprehend me when I tell you that the city and my mind are one and the same? If Thorne had not obstructed me, then by exerting direct control over the creation of a new part of the infrastructure I could have opened who knows what fresh conceptual possibilities.

'"Every action, however tiny, alters the meaning of the whole system. Why do you suppose the city quivers daily with my crimes? Any student of the *Rhetorica Ad Herennium* knows that we remember best if the images with which we populate our memory houses are vivid and violent, exceptionally beautiful or ugly, dressed in crowns and purples or disfigured and splashed with blood. Why do you suppose I keep you so well supplied with the bizarre mysteries and richly coloured atrocities to which you are addicted? None of you realise that when you walk through your crime-riddled city, you are moving among my thoughts."

'"And what of the citizens?" I asked. "Do you believe their lives have no value in themselves?"

'Lazarus shrugged as though the question did not interest him. "They, too, are part of the pattern. All things are symbols, all have their place in the web of relations. What meaning would the city's detectives have if there were no criminals for them to chase? Or take you and me. We were like twin brothers: we still are. Is our ancient rivalry not the axis of our lives? And does the life of the city, too, not turn on that axis, as I commit my crimes and you solve them, as you pursue me and I escape? You are the image by which I remember myself, Peregrine. Without you I would not be Lazarus Glass."

'He was silent for a time, standing there in my consulting room.

'"My responsibilities weigh heavily," he said. "But there is no other course for me now."

'As he left, neither of us offered a handshake. We exchanged only an ambiguous glance: an unspoken recollection of the past. That was the last time I saw him.'

Peregrine stood without moving, his head bowed to the shadow between the tramlines. The drizzle had stopped and the floodlights on the Palace were growing fainter as the rest of the scene came into view.

'Revenge, then,' said the inspector eventually. 'Thorne stopped Glass from doing what he wanted with the metro, so Glass used the metro to murder him. The same as Professor Weill and Dr Cavendish-Peake: Lazarus Glass held a grudge against each of them because they'd got the better of him in the past, and so he killed them in some way that seemed appropriate to his sick mind. Revenge. That's all there is to it?'

'On the contrary,' Peregrine said. 'Tonight's crimes amount to far more than revenge.'

For a long moment, he pressed his fingertips to his brows. When he raised his head again, towards the river and the plumes of dawn light leaking into the sky behind the roofline, he looked more tired than I had ever seen him.

'It is time we returned to where we began.'

No enemy accosted us as we made our way back to the mews in Syme Gardens where Peregrine had his consulting rooms. The twilit streets and brightening sky might have been ours alone. Peregrine tolerated the inspector's wish to climb the stairs first, and to ease his way into the rooms with his sidearm drawn; but all was undisturbed.

'The full evidence is now at our disposal,' said Peregrine as he settled himself on the Chesterfield. 'It only remains to assimilate the meaning of what we have seen tonight, and draw our conclusions. Cassandra, here I turn to you. Your apprenticeship with me is approaching its close, and I find myself hoping very much that you will make this present conundrum into the first success of your own crime-solving career.'

'I'll try my best,' I said, unsettled again by the peculiar cadence in Peregrine's voice. 'And I think I start to see a way of understanding what has taken place.'

'I'm glad one of us does,' said the inspector.

'We have visited the scenes of three murders tonight,' I began, 'and we know the link between them. These fallen detectives were close on the trail of Lazarus Glass, and so we may fairly suppose that he wished to strike them down. But in the manner of the killings – each grotesque and excessive in its way – we find other reasons too. Each murder vengefully recalled some incident in which the detective concerned had foiled the arch-criminal. Glass seems determined to load his killings with private symbolism.'

Peregrine, reclining with his eyes closed, looked serene.

'And in the history of Lazarus Glass's intellectual development, we have found an explanation for this, in turn,' I said. 'His criminal career, we now know, is directed by his conviction that the city and his mind are identical. In his memory city, events such as the deaths of detectives must be dense with significance, and the particular manner of those deaths, too, must be all-important for his deranged purposes.

'For Glass, the deaths of Hyperion Weill, Electra Cavendish-Peake and Brutus Thorne surely represent crucial changes in the pattern of the city that is his mind. One might say that, tonight, we have walked through the architecture of Lazarus Glass's brain, and witnessed the lingering presence of three of his more vivid and memorable thoughts.'

'This is a promising line of analysis,' said Peregrine.

'But what about you, Dr Fetch?' asked the inspector. 'If Glass wants to liquidate all the detectives hunting him, then he isn't finished yet, and you're not safe. You said yourself you were leading the chase. If I understand any of this, Glass is planning to kill you too, and we're still no closer to finding him.'

'It is true that the night's work is not finished,' said Peregrine. 'And true, too, that we do not know the whereabouts of Lazarus Glass. But that information is not necessary for us to defeat him. Cassandra: would you care to continue?'

'Lazarus's mental peculiarities, as you have described them, are extreme,' I said. 'And while they endow him with arcane capabilities, they would seem also to constrain him. For instance, if, as he said to you, he is convinced that detectives and criminals only have meaning by virtue of their interlocking struggle, then the massacre of his opponents tonight, while in one sense a victory, must in another way leave him greatly diminished: in a city lacking three such eminent investigators, the arch-criminal must himself be so much less significant.

'And if that is so, how much more true it must be of his relationship with you, Dr Fetch. In spite of the famous hatred he nurses for you, his old friend, his rival, his adversary, his nemesis – indeed, *because* of that hatred, I hypothesise that you need not fear assassination at the hand of your former comrade. He cannot eliminate you without also eliminating himself: for he said that he would not be Lazarus Glass without you.'

'You're not forgetting that the man's a lunatic, are you?' said Inspector Nimrod. 'You are bearing in mind that the city's actually a *city*, not the inside of this psychopath's head?'

'Your bluff sanity is refreshing, inspector,' said Peregrine, 'but, I fear, irrelevant. The reality that pertains in this case is that of Lazarus Glass's perceptions; the city we have explored tonight has indeed been the memory city of Lazarus Glass.'

'Which brings me to my last point,' I said. 'Glass boasted that his memory city enabled him to influence events in reality. But if the relationship between city and mind is as perfect as he claims, if every one of his thoughts is manifested in the city, then the reverse must also be the case: he must experience everything that happens in the city as an event in his mind. He saw the memory city as his great invention, but it seems to me that his plight is terrible to contemplate. He is unable to think without committing a crime to represent that thought; and, more than this, anyone can deliberately interfere with the constitution of his mind, by creating or destroying the symbols, out in the city, that embody his ideas.

'The theory then arises that Lazarus Glass was not in fact responsible for the murders tonight.'

I took a breath, and hesitated.

'Go on, Cassandra,' Peregrine said.

'It is possible that some other person contrived the killings of the detectives, in order to impose a significant change on Glass's consciousness. I have already suggested the nature of that change: he is diminished by the loss of his worthy enemies. As to the identity of this unknown killer, one possibility is compelling.'

I looked at my mentor where he lay with fingers laced and ankles crossed.

'The probable culprit, Dr Fetch, is you.'

'Good God,' said the inspector.

'Sound work, Cassandra,' said Peregrine. He rose from the sofa and came towards me, his grey eyes fixed on mine. He reached out with both hands and squeezed my shoulders gently, before turning to the inspector and grasping his hand. Then he moved past us both to stand by the mantelpiece.

'I have known for a long time now – ever since I understood the nature of the memory city – that the surest way to end the criminal career of Lazarus Glass would be to put an end to the detectives against whom he has always defined himself. For a number of years I hoped that it would be possible to find some other way around his defences; it has taken me until tonight to satisfy myself that no other way exists.

'The deaths of Hyperion, Electra and Brutus were

necessary to the negation of Lazarus. By usurping his role as killer, devising each quietus in a manner that belonged rightfully to him, I have robbed him forever of three potent symbols. He will feel their absence from his memory city as a numbing ablation of his powers. But he and I both know well that, so long as I hold my place as the city's greatest detective, he will remain as my diabolical opposite, dreaming our city's reality with his dreams of death and vice. For so long, and no longer.'

Peregrine opened the cigar box on the mantelpiece and took out the revolver.

'I have worked too long in this memory city of Lazarus's, with its maddening mesh of symbols. To leave it will be pleasant.'

He thumbed a catch on the weapon and checked its chambers.

'The night's work is nearly done. Thank you.'

He gestured towards the window.

'If you look out at the city, you will observe its transformation. You will witness the defeat of Lazarus Glass,' said Peregrine.

Beyond the window, the sky glowed in bands of pink and yellow, threaded with irregular silver ribbons. All across the rooftops, points of light gleamed off those tiles and slates that were angled towards the dawn. We heard the gunshot and the thump of a body falling, and then silence, but we did not turn around.

PART VIII

PART VIII

OUTSIDE THE DAYS

When Stephen's message came I had nearly forgotten him. Time passes, and on most days he never entered my thoughts, or if he did it was faintly and far off. But without warning now he wanted to see me again, and, although he didn't say why, I could find no way not to agree. I found myself walking along Impasto Street on a dark afternoon in mid-December when some influence had sent people out into the city in large numbers, jostling to spend money, zealous and hard-faced, shouldering each other aside.

He caught me unawares, laying his hand on my arm so that I flinched. I'm on edge in crowds. It took me several moments to recognise him, but he gave me as long as I needed, holding his gaze steady. Then he squeezed my shoulder and led me across Clarinet Street, back the way I'd come. We dived down a lane towards a bar which I only glimpsed as a blot of red and yellow before we were inside. He bought two pints and we sat down in a corner.

I kneaded the cold out of my hands. The message had made it sound as though we still saw each other all the time. I was surprised he'd picked me out again, but then our friendship had always been unexpected. I had known from our first meeting that we were not equals. He still had a way of making me – what's the word? Making me eager, perhaps. I was always too eager. After setting down my drink he didn't say anything. He sipped his beer, studied me slowly, smiled. It was time for me to ask why he had wanted to meet; why he had waited so long. Instead I began to babble, spouting clumsy trivia and asking about irrelevant things, where he lived, what he was doing for work. I could tell he was faintly amused in the old manner.

The bar was filling up with students and workers from city centre offices, all a few years younger than us. I took a sip which went down wrong, and struggled not to cough. Stephen watched with his lips parted and his head angled tolerantly. Just as ever, he was curious about my embarrassment, interested in the effects of his presence. An expression which might have been fondness passed across his face; but the pause grew longer, and I saw he was not going to reveal why he had contacted me. In the old days it had been his habit to withhold what I was waiting for him to tell. My face was hot in a familiar way.

To my surprise, however, Stephen himself now looked puzzled, as though his intention in asking me to meet him had temporarily slipped his mind, or he had forgotten I was with him at all. His eyes slid towards the snug on the far side of the bar, but as far as I could tell he was distracted by no more than an unoccupied table under a green glass lampshade. Weeks later, when he decided to tell me the real story, I would remember this moment. A group of students crowed with laughter and fell silent.

We contemplated the remains of our pints and in the hiatus I stole a look at him. He had changed more than I'd realised at first. The dark hair was thick but it didn't have its old shine, and his eyes were veined and watery from the cold. In his face I could discern the seams where the skin would slacken and fill. He had on the sort of scruffy old clothing he had always made effortlessly cool, but you might not immediately have known, now, that the untidiness was a matter of style. It struck me that his best time had been his youth.

Before I could find anything else to say, he rose from his seat, grabbing his jacket and leaving his drink unfinished. His eyes kept darting to the other side of the room. Not pausing to say goodbye, he disappeared up the stairs to the street, leaving me to gather up my belongings. I caught my train an hour earlier than I'd planned.

At university Stephen and I had read different subjects. We both had our first-year accommodation in the hall of residence on Juno Square, with rooms on the same corridor, but beyond this there had been no obvious reason for us to associate.

From the beginning you could guess at the career he was going to have here and the sort of people he would mix with. On the first day I saw him talking easily to groups of the older students. The beautiful, the fine-looking, the immaculate, assured ones whom I dared not gape at – they had gravitated to him. It was nothing easy to define, but they recognised his suitability. He exuded a natural right; his flirtatious, ingenuous manner worked with men and women just the same.

I was bewildered, meanwhile, in spite of the jollying welcome activities that had clogged up the whole of Belltown. Stephen didn't come to the clubs-and-societies fair, the pub crawls or the quizzes. While I was too timid to stray outside alone, he always had somewhere to be. When, carrying a mug and a slice of toast back to my room from the shared kitchen on the second or third night, I passed him on our staircase, he had combed his hair back and was wearing a dark suit which fitted him superbly. He twitched an eyebrow at me and disappeared out into the streets, and soft laughter moved past my door at six o'clock that morning.

And yet we became involved with each other. We became friends. Part of his trick was that he never calculated things, not consciously. It just happened that there was a sort of attractive chemistry between the two of us. He had an unsettling effect on me. When our hands brushed I got a jolt like a discharge of static. Once, in the union bar, he noticed it: he gasped stagily, fluttered his eyelashes, and breathed 'we touched!', mock-scandalised. I spent the rest of that evening angry with myself.

Does that get across the appeal we had for each other? It's not that he was unkind. On the contrary, he took a fond interest, and he teased as if he knew I had a touch more potential in me than I was managing to show. I really think he would have been pleased if I had, one unforeseen day, struggled free of myself.

I knew that by one view of things I was only there to provide contrast. I was the one to whom life did not happen, admitted to Stephen's world simply as audience to the spectacle of himself. I was the mark that measured the height of his ascent. Perhaps, but who's to say that's all there was to the story? I knew where I stood. Without the thrilling imbalance of unrequited admiration, it wouldn't have been interesting. There would have been none of the singular intimacy that was understood between us, no matter that we never spoke about it, no matter that I would not see him for days or weeks at a time, often, or that when we passed in public he might or might not choose to notice me.

That was all part of our silent agreement. Much of the world he occupied must remain mysterious because, though he conveyed to me what he could, so much was predicated on my absence. He stood out brightly against me, and it was needful I should lack the knowledge even of what I was excluded from. What did he murmur into her translucent ear to make her laugh as I observed them across the dining hall? Where did he disappear to on the pale nights of the summer term, while I stayed awake until dawn, watching the street under my window for the shadow that never came slipping into Juno Square? I did not know but I cooperated with a will. It was fascination enough that, whatever he did, he was doing it, so to speak, in relation to me. What unknown and private spheres of experience I glimpsed. Or, I mean, I glimpsed nothing; it was purer than that. His experience began where mine ended, that much I knew.

Some things were clear enough. He favoured sullen, grungy, extremely good-looking girls, often with dreadlocks or lip-rings, long-bodied and slender, exquisitely dishevelled and taller than himself. These came and went on our staircase, and he never introduced them. I think they understood that they were passing through.

More opaque, as well as more lasting, was the clique with which he became involved. Now and then he would mention them by name and allude to what they did together, as if to mock the idea that I too was one of the group. Very occasionally, I would catch sight of him in their company out in the city. At least that's what I thought I was seeing. I'd speculate about which names belonged to which of his associates, but I could never be sure, and of course I never approached. I was especially pleased with the time I spotted him lounging in the shadowy rear of a café along with a languid, scornful-looking, catlike young man and a near-identical girl. He had spoken about a pair of twins, Anna and Otto, and I was sure this must be them. For weeks afterwards I was plagued by the image of the three, leaning back together on the cushions, and often I thought I glimpsed the trio disappearing down a mews, or gaining admission at some unidentified entrance on the other side of a street; but always when the traffic cleared they were gone.

No doors were closed to him. If you were one of those who took him into the circle, if you saw yourself as an heir to the world, entitled by right of inheritance to the complex privileges, the sophisticated pleasures, the rich perversions reserved for the special children of this culture and its many centuries' decadence; if you were one of those, you would look at Stephen and know that here was the youth equal to your requirements, a born member of your caste who would enter into all privilege, all extremity, without a flicker of discomposure and would keep the secrets which, if revealed, would surely have the small people, scandalised and choking with envy, hurling themselves at the throats of the great.

Is this unlikely? Is it improbable that among my contemporaries, in the very same streets and lecture theatres, some moved in a rare and secretive world? That they were on their way to the highest places, and were already delectating the rewards that were their due? I don't know, but I'd be surprised if my imaginings have as much as rubbed the surface of what went on. I'd be more specific if I could. I can imagine more than I know how to put down in words, but what Stephen did when he was alone with his equals, what he saw and knew, I cannot begin to imagine.

We stopped seeing each other towards the end of our student days. I never understood quite why. With some people, shared experience drives you apart in the end; it teaches you that you don't have so much in common after all, and the things you've said and done together become an embarrassment you don't want to exacerbate. In any case, halfway through our final year he slipped out of focus for good. He became distracted and sour; he seemed disappointed. After our exams, we lost touch.

I stayed at the university and became a graduate student for a time, then found a job as an administrator in the department. Perhaps I stayed because I hadn't finished with the place, or even, in truth, started with it. I was always waiting for the way to open up so that I could enter. Even good old Belltown, with its libraries and playing fields, its coffee shops and vegetarian restaurants, was a riddle I couldn't quite solve. Crossing the park, I'd catch sight of the old bandstand as the rain was letting off. That was all it took to fill me with troubled desire. If I had been like Stephen I would have drained those years in a single draught, drained this whole city and skipped into the next escapade without a backward look, but instead I've stayed here at the edge of what I've never quite understood but which enthrals me the way it always did.

The city is a mystery when you notice it's full of sunken side streets falling away from you beside river and canal, by yellow and pink brick terraces, in September for instance, under castles of foliage, in deep light. Someone approaches and you're sure you recognise him, you've met just once, and not long ago, but he vanishes away down one of those streets and you miss him. You feel you owe an apology. And it only gets deeper, the riddle of it, as years go by and the special creatures stay exactly the same, just as they were when Stephen went with them. The modulation of names and faces makes no difference at all.

I didn't expect to hear from Stephen again after that evening. I put the encounter down as another of his less than readable gestures, partly satiric, partly flattering, and not in the end for me to grasp. But then, one evening in late January, he turned up at my door.

I invited him into the flat and tripped over my own furniture as I followed him through. With him there I didn't know where to stand. He waited for me to get around to offering him a cup of tea, then asked for coffee instead. He sat and watched while I got lost in my kitchen searching for the means to make it, and spilled the grounds across the counter.

But tonight there was an intermitted quality about him, a loose connection. One minute he was watching me, but the next he was gazing at his own linked hands on the kitchen table. I got the idea that he was ill at ease. I began to imagine that the surface of quick smiles and flirting glances had been hollowed out, and underneath was empty space, a vacuum tugging on his cheeks and eye-sockets. The lights were off in the living room next door, and the dark shapes of the furniture in there seemed to distract him. With this I noticed something else: it became clear that he had a reason for being here, as though we had agreed this meeting for some purpose so basic to us both that there was no need to go over it again. He hadn't come to pass the time. He looked like someone who had stumbled, bedraggled and uninvited, into a birthday party to dismay the revellers.

I sat down to hear what he was going to say. I remember how the kitchen counter's light lined the edge of his face, showing the softness of his jaw.

In telling over again the story he told me, I can't pretend to have the truth of it. I don't know how he would really have acted with the others, or how they would have been towards him. Maybe, with them, he wasn't the person I took him for. I can't feel the texture of his experience, whether he was the darling of the group or a diffident novice, whether he was unsure of his footing or eager to please or barely interested at all, whether he had doubts about what they were doing. Or was the whole experience something different again, something I can't begin to formulate? I can try and recount what he told me, but even that won't come clear: it'll change as I go, shifting out of true, because there's never a way back to the telling before. We build ourselves into a concentric nest, each shell smaller, each opaquing the last. I can't tell you what took place, I can only tell the story. So.

Every pleasure palls. In a short time Stephen had learnt to drink deep of experimental delights that would have frightened most of us if we understood them, but the richer the meal, the sooner the appetite wanes, and the epicurean longs for ever more esoteric flavours. He never saw himself as a sybarite; he thought of his explorations as light-hearted, even a kind of joke. But anyone can drift away from themselves when nothing is forbidden. Before he realised it the mask wouldn't come off: he was corrupt with luxury, famished with feasting. The society knew how to watch for its moment. His mind and body were precise instruments for their own indulgence, but his imagination was sickly with exhaustion. He had fallen into the lassitude of one who has gone too far in the secret regions of experience, achieved too much in the sphere of private ambitions; now the tawdriness of the world was making him ill. His exquisite appetites troubled him more than ever but there was nothing, it seemed, that could answer any more to his needs. He was bored.

He had never wanted to despair. Quite the reverse. He had come to long above all for the gleam in other eyes which said: together we are about to try what would appal the ordinary world; we might even, who knows, startle ourselves. In everything he had done, it now seemed to him, all he had really wanted was that glimmer of unspoken agreement. Even in the gravest acts, there had been something unspoilt about what they did. They had been finding their way back to the green heart of the hedge maze where everything tended to the condition of innocence and the deepest depravity revealed itself as happy mischief. This search, he had come melancholically to accept, was the project of his life, but he feared he'd never again find that bad, blameless joy.

And then they came to him. Later, he would ask himself whether they had been guiding him from the beginning. I imagine it was those twins who made the proposition, coiling themselves one on either side and mentioning casually that there was something else he might find amusing. Something he would not have seen before. Not the kind of experience, he must understand, that would suit more ordinary tastes, and not the kind that it would be desirable for anyone else to know about, but one which some of the more open-minded experimentalists had found diverting. This was how they framed it. They felt they were libertines. If Mephistopheles had come to offer them the world, they would have curled their lips and continued their conversation, or that was the impression they were at pains to convey. Stephen doubted their notions but he credited their sense of style, and he could not turn down the chance of relieving his ennui.

There was a – well, it was a kind of private club, they told him. A society, dedicated to investigating certain potentials, shall we say, certain possibilities usually overlooked; investigating, and, naturally, delectating. Its experiments had been under way for a number of centuries, carried forward with ever more refinement by a handful of like-minded individuals in each generation. From their arch suggestions, it was difficult to work out exactly what they were offering. But it would have been unseemly to press for details, and what difference did it make, for wasn't he capable of anything and desirous of every strange flavour the world could drop on his tongue?

Gradually he saw what, in their elaborately figurative way, they were hinting at. As it began to take on a shape, his instinct was to laugh: one of those soft, unassenting laughs, to dismiss the fun they were making of him. After teasing their story together by insinuation and omission, they left. He shook his head at the waste of his time, but the idea lingered and deepened, its impossibilities taking on subtlety and shading, so that he could not quite expel it. When we want, we give credence to unlikely tales.

And so Stephen was inducted. He travelled across the city at a specified hour of the night to an address far from his usual haunts, all the way out in Moebius Wall. He watched dubiously as the low streets of Glory Part and Three Liberties crawled past the taxi window; when he arrived he thought the driver must have mistaken the address. The house, a large suburban villa standing on a corner, was to all appearances derelict, surrounded by ramparts of weed and bramble, half-throttled by ivy and propped up on one side by scaffolding. A painted wooden board hung from the railings, warning that the building was unsafe. To Stephen the house appeared not only run-down but incomplete, as though it had fallen into long neglect before it had been finished. The night sky showed through the holes of the upper windows.

The iron gate, which was taller than he was and had layers of green paint cracking off like dead skin, had rusted into place on its hinges, half-open. He edged his way around it and pushed through the overgrowth. The house had no front door, only an aperture into which tendrils of ivy had wrapped themselves to reach along the ceiling. The hallway was defined by unhealthy orange light spilling through the house from the street behind.

Here it becomes difficult to keep hold of what happened to Stephen. What can I say that will bring us any closer to his experience in that house, that experience we are never going to grasp, but of which we can say that it was something, that *something* happened and he tried later to pass it on? It was the end of his association with the twins and their set. They avoided him after that night, evidently feeling he had let himself down rather badly. Perhaps he was not quite the right sort of person after all. His connections with that upper world seemed to go dead, but it made no difference to him now.

Stephen sat hollow-faced in my kitchen, his gaze flickering continually into the darkness of the living room. He asked for more coffee, emptied the fresh cup without waiting for it to cool and tried again to tell me. It was nothing, what had happened to him in that room, he said. It was all a fraud, a prank, that was obvious, but for some reason he couldn't seem to shake off the effects.

Something had been waiting for him in the derelict house. He didn't want to describe it, but it had been waiting in the front room, as dusty and motionless as if it had been standing there as long as the house itself. He might have mistaken it for some peculiar item of furniture except that it turned its head and stepped forward to greet him: it was very glad that he had come. It began to tell him a story. A minute later he was clawing himself away through syrupy space with his feet sliding on the boards as in a slow nightmare, and stumbling out into the streets of

Moebius Wall feeling its fingernails catch on his sleeve.

Since that night he'd had no peace. It had taken him weeks to admit it to himself, but there was no doubt that it was following him. He saw it everywhere. It would be sitting along from him in the metro carriage, or would pass him on the November Bridge; or, when he paused by a flower stall on Vere Street, one of the customers would turn to him, and he would have to flee before it could open its mouth. When he walked home late he would hear the dragging footsteps behind him, drawing closer if he slackened his pace, never falling away.

He hated knowing that his equanimity could be shaken so easily, but how was he supposed to get anything done when he was always watching for the next glimpse of that unnatural figure? It was a frail thing, polite and even gentle in its manners, but insistent. It wanted to finish its story. At first it had only been on the streets, but before long it was following him indoors, into restaurants, into the office and eventually into his apartment. One morning he'd found it standing in the alcove in his hallway, dragging its white-nailed fingers down the wallpaper as if to say, If you did not want my story then you should not have listened. He felt the pressure of its need at all times. It wanted him to finish what he had started in the derelict house, but he was damned if he was going to do that. Something had been stripped away as he had listened to its voice: since that night he understood less about his own life. The tale it had half-told him had pared him to the quick so that if he let it say another word there would be nothing left of him at all. But it was his steadfast companion now, and it wanted acknowledgement.

He eyed the dark of the living room and then, with an effort, returned his attention to me. There was no getting away from it. He could only repeat how that depraved gang had torn from his eyes the blindfold which most of us wear to the end, and had shown him what waited there, beyond our rooms, after all the streets and houses, behind the world, outside the days. He believed he would have sought them out and murdered them one by one in judicious revenge if not for the apathy that had settled in his bones.

I haven't seen Stephen since he told me his story. He left without making arrangements to meet again. Before he went, though, he did say one thing. He rose to go and as I prepared to say my goodbyes an afterthought appeared to strike him. He dipped his head from side to side, and gave me just the sort of smile I remembered from the old days. With the air of an indulgent elder brother, he said: Oh, all right, then. Yes. He knew what I was after and he would satisfy my curiosity. If I promised to listen carefully, he would tell me what he knew I wanted to hear. He would pass on the story that he had been told that night.

The corner of his mouth twitched as he waited for my response. I was touched. Both of us knew how much it meant, that offer. He had made it so casually you would have thought it hardly mattered to him at all, but I knew as well as he did that we had never before spoken so sincerely as we had tonight. For the first time in the years we'd known each other, he had confessed a need, offered to tell me a secret. He was finally willing to let me into the heart of the story.

Strip everything away, and that teaser's smile would be the last piece of Stephen to go. I didn't grudge him the attempt, but, as I gently turned down his offer, I didn't feel too sorry for him either. No; as I guided him to the door, closed it behind him and watched from my window until his pale, unsteady figure had disappeared along the street, I preserved my envy and admiration exactly as they had always been. I preferred it like that, and besides, there was nothing else for me to do. How could I know enough to pity him?

PART IX

PAROTA.

THE ROSE TREE

A few of us were in the café that night. On this side of town there aren't many places to go, so when we feel the need of a drink or some quiet company through the hours of darkness, we come here, where Dilks keeps serving till dawn. For as long as the season lasts, everyone knows that once dark has fallen you don't go out again before morning.

The café must once have been a comfortable retreat. Dilks runs the place by himself, and he's always there behind the counter, never misses a night. Behind him, the wall is lined with mirrors which must have been intended, once, to multiply gleaming ranks of bottles and scenes of busy communal life. But the glass is dulled over with black rust, and no reflections are visible: just a shadowy depth loitering.

He sells only rough spirit, served in scuffed water tumblers to the three or four of us you can usually find in here. We're steady customers. We cluster in faint light which does not reach the farthest corners of the room. Orbs of creamy glass dangle on chains from the ceiling, but they're cracked and cobweb-clogged, and only a few of them work at the best of times. When the electrics fail, we huddle closer still, and drink by the light of the storm lantern that Dilks hangs from a nail above the bar. We've got to know each other over time, and now and then we tell cautious stories about whatever it is has us living this way. The night yawns and we grow sluggish while the empty district waits out there with fog rolling down its walls.

I was in with Briggs and Baggott tonight. Dilks had set the electric fire beside our table, and we held our palms out to the glow. He stood watching us from behind his counter but we knew better than to invite him to join us for a drink. If you suggested anything like that, he'd roll his head to one side, abashed on your behalf, then scratch his beard and lumber off to rub at an old stain on the bartop. So we sat and sipped the neat spirit, making it last.

It was getting dark outside when we were roused by the hinge of the street door, and three men walked in. We didn't know them. They looked with distaste at the wrecked fittings: at the upholstered seats that had rotted long ago in the side booths, the few warped tables and chairs that were left, and the cold inglenook fireplace which waited like a tunnel-mouth at the far end of the room, with its grate full of damp sticks of furniture and the mummified bodies of birds. Then they sat down and called for Dilks to bring them a bottle of whiskey. He was nonplussed for a minute, and I thought the novelty of the situation might have defeated him, but then he did as he was told, labouring his way around the counter with a bottle in one hand and three tumblers in the other. He even poured out a slug of spirit for each of the men.

Soon they were talking loudly among themselves and drinking fast. They seemed some way drunk already, but not in the way that we got drunk, bewildered and tired and sentimental. They drained their glasses and clicked them down on the table. They laughed often and hit each other in the shoulder for punctuation. Their hands and faces were well-kept and their manners of speech were not from around here. The one doing most of the talking couldn't have been more than twenty-five or twenty-six years old. He was well-built, long-limbed, and dressed in good-quality gear: stout leather boots, navy jeans and a black reefer jacket. Once he pulled a leather-covered notebook from his bulky canvas satchel and consulted it, as if to remind himself of some point of fact. Brown curls framed his face, which was handsome in a boyish, rather delicate mode.

None of us regulars had much to say for ourselves this evening. We studied the tabletop. The great pale maps of mildew on the wallpaper glowed towards us through the room's dusk. Rain came on outside, and water began to trickle from several points on the ceiling into the black ditches in the carpet, but Dilks didn't seem to notice.

When it had been dark out there for an hour or

so, the curly-haired young man emptied his glass and pushed his chair back.

'Gentlemen,' he said, addressing the room in general, 'I have heard tales.'

Most of the bottle of whiskey was gone, but his speech was crisp.

'They tell me that in this season, in your city, no one dares go out after dark.'

He tapped his notebook against the edge of the table.

'Well, I'm going out. What's there to see, I intend to see it with my own eyes. Whatever I meet out there, I'm going to shake it by the hand and listen carefully to what it has to say. I have a few questions to ask it.'

He looked pleased with this statement. We blinked and swallowed, and examined our empty glasses. One of the man's friends murmured something. Another said, 'Henry,' and laid a hand on his arm, but he shook it off.

'It's nothing to be afraid of,' he said.

We looked at each other, Briggs, Baggott and me. Eventually I cleared my throat and spoke up. 'You can't be going out there,' I said.

The man stared at me, hard-eyed, then strode over, caught my hand and squeezed it.

'My friend, your kind concern is noted. What I'm going to do is this. I'm going to walk out of that door and take a brisk stroll. Then at dawn my associates here will take me out for a slap-up breakfast, and I will regale them with the story of

308

a pleasant night's walk in the city and, I fully expect, an unusual adventure and an illuminating conversation.'

I would have tried again, but I had heard a feeble note in my voice, and I faltered. Baggott took over, sounding irritated with the whole lot of us. 'You go out there, it'll find you,' he said, as if this were too plain to need saying.

'With respect, friends,' the young man said, 'and much as I appreciate your advice, I prefer to see for myself.' He stifled a belch. 'Besides, haven't I given my word to these gentlemen?'

His friends seemed to cast around for an answer. They didn't find it, although one of them gave a dry laugh.

The curly-haired man pulled on a woollen watch cap, nodded to us, and opened the street door. Outside, it seemed to me, a congregation of disused premises leaned inwards in anticipation, leering down with their broken and boarded windows. He paused, turning up the collar of his jacket, and looked back at us.

'Fine night,' he said. 'No one join me? No?'

He stepped out and the door moaned shut behind him. Through the window we saw him turn the corner of Halfmoon Street, heading towards the front of the station, his figure bobbing into the hem of a huge brown darkness.

It was time to get our glasses filled, but Dilks was busy scrubbing at something in his sink. The breath of cold air that had entered by the door dissipated, and the café grew tolerably warm again. We grew silent. The men at the other table had run out of conversation, too. Eventually one of them leant over to us.

'We tried to talk him out of it,' he said. His plump face was blotched pink and white. 'We never encouraged him. But once he gets an idea in his head he won't listen to anyone. We thought it was better than letting him go alone.'

We had no answer to that, but it was clear that now the newcomers wanted a parley. Baggott grumbled under his breath, but the pink-cheeked man grabbed the whiskey bottle and emptied the last of it into our glasses as he and his friend drew their chairs in closer.

'I would have gone with him,' he said, and paused uncomfortably. His eyes darted around, wanting our help. Then he shrugged and trailed off.

The electric fire glowed orange in the brown gloom, and with the whiskey in my gut it felt warm in here tonight. The wet smell of the carpet was in my nostrils. Baggott picked at his thumbnail. Briggs hawked and spat into his handkerchief. Dilks now stood with his gaze fixed on a curl of wallpaper that had, at some period in the past, peeled down to rest on the bartop.

The five of us were sitting in a circle around the table, our faces and hands hanging at the grubby edges of the pool of light. The rain had stopped, but rainwater still pattered into the floor. Above our heads the rest of the building was vacant.

Briggs touched his pockets, then got up and crossed the dim space to the counter. He returned to his seat with two cigarettes, laid one on the table in front of him, and lit up the other. There was a silence. He sucked on his cigarette, held the smoke in his chest, then allowed it to overflow gently and roll in a bib down his front.

'You want to know what happens when you stay out after dark?' he asked. He leant forward and indicated Dilks with a guarded tilt of his head. The barman, who was ponderously counting pennies into his money box, showed no sign of interest in our talk.

'He did it, once,' Briggs said. 'He never meant to, but he did. I'll tell you what happened.

'At the time, the café was nearly ready for its grand opening. The outside was freshly scrubbed and painted, very pretty. No one had seen the likes of it around here before, but Dilks was convinced this side of town was on the up and his establishment was going to be at the heart of it. To begin with I'd thought it was a foolish notion that would never work, but he was such a persuasive man in those days, such a man of energy and ideas, that I'd started to think he was going to prove me wrong. Whenever you spoke to him you felt you were living in exciting times, at the heart of it all, with good days to come. You came away wanting to work hard at some worthy project.

'Of course, around here people kept to themselves, and they didn't stay out after dark on those nights.

311

But Dilks didn't have any truck with that. He said it was nonsense. He said the district needed a place where we could all go for food and drink and warmth and fellowship. It'd be an inn where travellers could rest safely, he said, and a friendly hostel for tourists, it'd be a salon for talk and singing, and a tavern where locals would gather at the end of the working day; a feasting-hall, even, where every citizen would be welcome. When he talked about it like that, you believed him. You believed he and Poppy could make it happen.

'They'd married that summer, Dilks and Poppy, and since then they'd been juggling the thousand tasks that come with starting a business – but, he used to say with a rueful grin, they hadn't murdered each other yet. It had seemed impossible at first, conjuring a going concern out of a run-down building on this side of town, but each day they worked their plans nearer to realisation. They were up before dawn every morning. He was full of ideas, but she was the one with a head for figures. Together they'd done the research, put their plan together and got the investments they needed. Most nights they stayed up into the small hours working on the numbers at their kitchen table.

'They were renting an attic room over in Three Liberties, a cramped, tiny place, with their bed in one corner and laundry strung up all around, chimney pots and slates right outside the window and the milk standing out on the sill. When I visited once, she joked about how she wasn't going to fit in here for much longer. The child was just starting to show. Still, they'd only be there until the business got under way. I'm not one for family life, but when I visited the pair of them together I thought I could see the point.

'And now the opening was in sight. Sometimes they felt the whole undertaking was like a ship held together by willpower alone, hurtling down the slipway while it was still full of leaks to be plugged, but now they glimpsed the day, not too far off, when it would float on even waters and they could navigate into the future. They'd cleared the planning permissions, bought licences for liquor and music and every kind of insurance, met all the regulations on safety and environmental health. The refurbishments were coming along nicely. Soon it'd be time to hire staff. Only the day before, Dilks had put up the sign with the name they'd chosen: The Rose Tree Café.

'That night, he was working late on the premises, finishing off the paint job in the saloon. He'd intended to be home hours ago, but he and Poppy were used to these long days and late nights by now. They kept promising each other it wouldn't be for much longer. He cleared up his night's work, and briefly considered sleeping on one of the brand-new sofas in the lobby. The last metro had gone hours ago and he knew this was not the season to wander after dark. But he'd told Poppy he'd be home, and after all, he decided, it was only a half-hour's walk across town. So he locked up the café and set out.

'Much later I learnt what took place on that walk home.

'The desertion gave a kind of intimacy to the streets, as if the city were one huge interior through which he alone had access. Strong moonlight painted everything with a grey-green pallor: the wet pavements, the trees branching like lungs and carrying the malignancies of birds' nests, the high walls of the old houses, the frosted ceiling of cloud.

'He first caught sight of the figure as he passed an abandoned warehouse. It was some distance away, picking its way across the weeds and concrete of an empty lot. It moved with a curious, broken gait, stooped over as if it might be in distress, and Dilks paused. He almost called out to ask whether he could help; but he hesitated, and said nothing. The figure's face was blank with shadow, but it gave the impression of gazing directly at him. He walked on.

'A few minutes later he knew that it was following. When he stopped to listen, he could hear an irregular footfall, like someone waltzing drunkenly and alone through the alleys. He redoubled his pace, but when he glanced over his shoulder a slender pale shape was moving in the ashy-green darkness. There could be no doubt now of what was close behind him. But what could he do except keep walking, hoping that he would find himself suddenly at home and that this walk, which seemed as though it might last forever, would dissolve as

314

though it had never happened in the brightness of their room?

'He didn't glance back a second time. But the odd, slow footsteps, somehow more suggestive of three legs than of two, kept drawing nearer, and soon he knew that it was treading on his heels. He knew that, if it liked, it could have laid its fingers on his shoulder. At the idea his legs weakened and he staggered into a doorway for support.

'Turning, he found himself facing it. He was never able afterwards to describe what it looked like. He could only say that he pitied it a great deal. It stood there for a long moment, as if it needed help but couldn't bring itself to ask. Then it leant up to him, closer, until it was only inches from his averted face, and, softly, it began to speak.

'It told him a secret. A story about itself, that was what it told him. Later, the details of what had been said escaped him completely. All he could remember was wishing desperately not to hear, and knowing that nevertheless the words were slipping into his ears, soaking down deep, never to be recovered.

'At last it drifted glumly away. He thought that, before it went, it reached out and brushed his shoulder affectionately, or plucked away something small – a loose thread from his coat. The encounter had lasted minutes at most.

'He was shaken, but he pulled himself together and made it home. As he climbed the stairs he found that he was bright-eyed, light on his feet, fingers twitching. That story had trickled down like rainwater, out of reach. He had already forgotten what it was he had heard. He was ready for a strong restorative. He was excited, if the truth be told. Certainly it had been a peculiar incident, but he couldn't wait to tell Poppy. Once he talked it over with her, he knew, that meeting would become the well-shaped tale of a night's minor misadventure, seriocomic, perhaps mock-heroic: telling it over between them, they'd settle what it meant. It would become an amusing demonstration of how even the most hard-headed of us were prey to strange frights when out late in lonely places, and of how all those stories about this side of town were laughably exaggerated. She'd be asleep by now. He wondered if he should wake her, so that he could tell her tonight.

'He put his key to the latch. It didn't seem to fit. He tried again, but it refused to go in. He examined the key, but it didn't appear to be damaged, and the lock, too, looked the same as ever. Eventually he knocked on the door, and, as it opened to Poppy's sleep-fuddled face, he stepped forward, offering an apologetic embrace.

'But Poppy didn't move into his outstretched arms. Instead, her sleepy eyes snapped wide and she shrank away in sudden panic. She tried to force the door shut on him, but he was already inside the flat, and seeing that he was now halted with confusion and was not to be expelled, she retreated to the far side of the cramped attic with one hand pressed to her belly and the other feeling blind across the countertop of their tiny kitchen. She stared at him with no trace of recognition in her face. Her voice shook as she asked what he was doing in her home.

'It seemed to Dilks that he had missed a step between sleeping and waking, and had slipped into a bad dream. He had never seen such expressions on her face before. He tried to speak calmly in spite of the hysteria that all at once had a hold of his innards. She was backed hard against the counter, edging along towards the cutlery drawer. She thought he was an intruder. He wanted to shout till his lungs were ragged that she was wrong – that, if this city were a thousand cities, there would still be none in which the two of them were strangers.

'He reminded her who he was and where they were, and took a cautious step towards her. She kept still, but her eyes danced, mad to get out. He took another step towards her and she shrieked, clawed the drawer open and snatched out a carving knife. He raised his hands carefully, but when she shrieked a second time and slashed at him, he found himself grabbing one of their cheap wooden chairs by the back and swinging it to keep her off. She screamed at him to get out, get out, get out of her home.

'Well, they went at each other for a long while,

that night, screaming and yelling all round the room with the carving knife and the smashed-up chair. The neighbours must have had to bury their heads under their pillows. There wasn't much left of the flat by the time they'd finished. But at last he tottered out to the street in the first shade of dawn. There was nothing more to say, no argument left to have with this woman who claimed that he was a lunatic and that she'd never seen him before he forced himself through her front door. So he made his way back to his unfinished café, let himself in, and poured himself a drink with a jumping hand. And he's been here ever since.'

The five of us shifted in our seats. Dilks, slumped in his usual position, watching a puddle of rainwater quiver sluggishly larger on the bartop, didn't seem to have heard anything of what had been said. Briggs lit his second cigarette, took a drag, and rested his hand on the table. A scribble of bluish smoke climbed from his fingers. I looked over at the windows, which by now were streaked with condensation.

'But they say it takes everyone differently,' Briggs said. 'Who knows. Perhaps your friend will have no trouble.'

Something hit the window. We saw the flattened palm of a hand. It lifted away, then slapped the glass again. We all sat uselessly for a moment. Then one of the newcomers leapt up and wrenched the street door open. There was a red mark on the windowpane.

We were all on our feet. The young man came in unsteadily, with his jacket hanging open, confused. His mouth worked dumbly. Then his legs gave way and he fell against the wall, one of his arms twitching. The two young men caught him before he could collapse, and led him to a chair. One arm of his jacket was ripped and the blood was sticky on his hand, but examination revealed only a dirty, shallow graze on his palm and forearm, as if he had fallen on tarmac. We couldn't work out where all the blood had come from.

His lips trembled and great shivers went through his limbs. He didn't seem to know where he was. Something had changed about his eyes, leaving them incredulous and emptied-out. He looked to me like someone who had lived a century in a single night, or travelled impossible distances without meeting another living soul.

But we held whiskey to his lips and by degrees his breathing steadied. It took us a long time to calm him down and get him to focus on his surroundings instead of some awful imaginary prospect, but after a while he was able to clasp the tumbler in his hands. One of his friends said his name and, tongue-tied, with downcast eyes, he nodded. Eventually he raised his head. He drew a long, uneven breath, like a man recovering from a fit of sobbing, and we gathered around him, close, as if we wanted to keep inside the circumference of the light, weak as it was.

And then someone asked: 'What happened to you?'

Slowly at first, in broken words and phrases, he began to tell.

PART X

PART X.

A WAY TO LEAVE

Simon knelt with his body locked from groin to throat until the muscles opened and he succeeded in pouring out a caustic mixture of liquid and gas. When he could breathe again he flushed away the waste, rinsed his mouth and stood in front of the mirror, trying to decide whether the pain had lessened. The left side of his head throbbed from the eye-socket to the roots of the teeth. His migraines had been getting worse, forcing him to spend whole days lying half-awake in the darkened bedroom. In his dream Florence had murdered him but everyone had agreed that he was to blame. He scooped more water into his mouth and spat. From the silence downstairs he could tell that she was sitting in the parlour, listening out, waiting for him to appear. He studied his thin arms and the hollow of his chest. Isolated raindrops broke on the bathroom window and wet light came and went with the sway of the branches outside. It was the Flâneur's season now, without a doubt: tonight, no one with a choice would be found in the streets after dark. But Simon was not going to waver. The reflection granted a nod of approval. The migraine didn't matter; nor did Florence. By tomorrow none of these things would remain to trouble him. He believed that all of this would be changed.

He held his breath as he left the bathroom, but in the corridor a floorboard squealed underfoot. It made no difference. Florence would not let him escape the house unremarked. She had been in good form all summer, going out in the afternoons to visit galleries or see films, then coming home to fuss over her cats, but now that the season had turned she was showing indications of a decline. Her transitional moods were difficult for him: she stopped going out – neglecting even the short daily walks on the heath which she claimed were so crucial – and took to watching his every move around the house as if she knew he was plotting a betrayal.

Along the corridor he passed junk-crammed rooms with their curtains sagging half open. The sheets draped over the furniture made it seem that the upper floors were being colonised by giant mushrooms, but Florence continually put off sorting things out. She worried that she couldn't afford to keep the house, or alternatively to get rid of it, but she could never seem to gather the energy to discover which was the case. Ectarine Walk was one of those placid avenues which recede into the heart of Lizavet, lined with iron railings and elm trees reaching higher than the rooftops. Well-fed tabbies watched from behind bay windows. 'Salubrious' was how she liked to describe the street, in a tone of dry scorn that made Simon feel she had learned the word from some disagreeable ancestor. The townhouses seemed so solid and flush, so complacent in their presence, that he wanted to insult them with some glaring unreality, and he often fantasised that by walking on past Florence's house and turning a corner or two, you might discover the knotted navel of the world, with paving stone and tree trunk and space itself twisting impossibly and plunging out of sight. Such a thing, he felt, must be required as compensation.

In the bedroom he put on the first T-shirt he found in the bottom of the wardrobe and took his jacket from the bedpost. The vigilant silence continued downstairs. She could hear him getting ready but she sat tight-lipped in the parlour. The old grey cat yowled pitifully at him as he crossed to the head of the stairs. It did this all the time now, as though it needed to communicate some appalling realisation. The vet had said more than once that it was feeling its age and could only decline, but Florence, refusing to understand what she was told, really seemed to believe that with the right pills it would stop making that distressing noise and be again the contented kitten she had grown up with. It limped after Simon for a couple of steps before drawing back to its place by the bannisters.

*   *   *

He had first seen Florence at the city library, the one and only time he had been there. He should have known better, even then, but he had gone in the hope that the place might supply the kind of information he needed. The security guard at the turnstile eyed him and made him leave his bag in a locker by the front desk, and after that he didn't dare approach the librarians behind their beechwood counters: he could picture their faces as he tried to explain what he wanted to know. Instead, he wandered the open shelves without finding anything, and toiled up and down the gloomy cylinder of the main stairwell while rain surged across the circular skylight far above. Later he sat at one of the catalogue terminals and tapped the keyboard, but a panel flashed up on the screen requiring him to identify himself. As he pushed the chair back its rubber heels screeched, causing students to look up from their books and old men to lower their newspapers.

He was trying angrily to get the locker open so that he could go when a woman came in, fumbling with a flower-patterned umbrella, shedding droplets and pushing hair out of her face. Her pastel raincoat was so outmoded that she looked at first glance like an elderly lady, but he saw that she was around his own age. He watched with interest as she tried to hold her umbrella under one arm and search in her bag, while at the same time unsticking the soaked hem of her cotton dress from her legs. Then, as she crossed the entrance hall, the string of her necklace somehow snapped and tiny beads poured across the flagstones – it was the same sound he had heard that morning when rain began to fall into the park. She grabbed at the middle of her chest and gasped as though she had been drenched.

There was an opportunity here, of course, if he were to step forward and help her collect the beads, joking, making light of the accident; but he found he preferred the scene as it was. He stayed quite still as she knelt down, her hair dropping into her face and the umbrella falling away from her with a clatter.

After following her up the stairs at a safe distance he loitered among the shelves of the art history section, watching her take a book down and leaf through the stiff pages. At the end of the aisle a notice listed the contents of the room. He picked out a name he thought sounded familiar and browsed along the shelf until he was beside her.

'Excuse me,' he said. 'This artist, Albert Gaunt? Do you know, where would I . . .?'

Only a little alarmed, she showed him where to find the books. He thanked her in a warm undertone and touched her elbow for an instant. She looked up and down the aisle, then told him that Gaunt was one of her favourites. He said, his too. Someone further along the shelves exhaled disapprovingly. Simon caught her eye and made a mischievous face.

At that first meeting it had taken him a few minutes to grow restless in her company. He had watched her trying to conceal how nervous he made her. It had been obvious that he would always be able to predict what she was going to say and do, and yet when she had mentioned an exhibition on Gaunt's printmaking at one of the galleries in town he had suggested that they go together. He could not have explained why, but as soon as he had seen Florence he had known that he was going to speak to her about his aspiration.

It had been a long time since he had tried confessing to anybody what he wanted. It never went well. They didn't understand when he told them that the aspiration had been folded inside him long before he could put a name to it, and that he had spent years pretending he was like everyone else, years in which no plan worked out for him and he started getting migraines which left him blind and speechless. They always got the same look on their faces, as if they thought he'd made a joke so tasteless they could not have heard it right. For most people, what he wanted was just about the worst fate they could imagine. As a desire they found it unthinkable; their skin crawled. It wasn't even real, the Flâneur – it was just some folklore nightmare, some hallucination generated by the city. Why would you dream of seeking it out? That ancient, lonely thing, wandering the city forever in search of someone to whom it could speak its tale. No one knew what that story was, or what happened to those who heard it, but everyone knew that if you listened you were lost. You would never be the same again.

Weeks after the library, he and Florence had spent a bleak afternoon walking around Lizavet Heath while he tried to explain himself. As they skirted the pond, exposed between the damp dish of the heath and a low winter sky, she kept her overcoat wrapped around her small body and her gaze fixed on the rooftops, but she listened as he told her what his aspiration meant. He did his best to put it in terms she would find appealing. He said:

'We're always telling ourselves the story of ourselves, every waking moment, as if nothing matters more. Isn't that a selfish way to live? Shouldn't we try and get outside that?'

He knew he was doing himself an injustice by phrasing it that way, but it was as close as he could manage. He wanted to tell her: the beauty of this broke my heart at sixteen and it still hasn't finished breaking. But she turned her face to the grey disc of the water. She couldn't understand why he would want to do something like that to himself, she told him, and she didn't want to talk about it any more. Walking away, she said: 'You sound as though you don't want to be here at all.'

He thought that would be the end of it with Florence. As she moved past and left him standing by the pond, he was at a loss to understand why he had even tried. And yet when he left the heath she was waiting for him at the gate; she took his hand and asked him to walk her back to the house, and when they reached the three steep stone steps that led up to her front door she said she was going to take him out to dinner. She telephoned to make reservations at a restaurant on the Mile.

Later they walked through the Esplanade as the daylight failed. Simon offered his elbow and Florence folded her arm through it, taller than him in her heels. He was wearing a high-collared overcoat that she had found for him in one of her upstairs rooms, and he felt old-fashioned and graceful strolling among the carnation sellers with pigeons fussing around their feet. In the restaurant, a tiny underground place with three foreign waitresses who tended to them approvingly, they drank a whole bottle of red wine and found themselves talking a good deal. They did not mention his aspiration. She took him home in a taxi, led him up the steps of the house and pinioned him in the bed. Her mouth tasted of tannin and to his surprise they were not disappointed.

Thirst woke him early the next morning, with Florence curled towards him in the sheets sleeping deeply and giving off a powerful warmth. The room was bright because they had not closed the curtains, and he watched as a magpie arrived on the windowsill, snatched some morsel and leaped out of sight. For a while he lay there and tried to gauge the severity of his headache.

Ignoring the grey cat's keening, he went down to the hall, the timbers of the staircase popping under his feet. His migraine had not subsided. It was a sinuous thing which now opened its poisoned veils all through his head, now shrank into a pebble in his eyeball. No one could have blamed Simon if he'd gone back into the bedroom, drawn the curtains and given up on the day, but he refused to admit defeat. The season was here and his aspiration was within reach.

In the parlour Florence sat curled on the sofa, holding the black-and-white kitten against her chest. Her forearms were goosefleshed and her hair hung as if she had just dried it with a towel. She had been listening to music, it seemed, and a record still turned on the gramophone, the needle popping and crackling along the rim. Simon hated the corroded brass horn: its gross organic shape sprouting in the corner was so obsolete it was beyond ridiculous. It was like living with his grandmother, but along with everything else, Florence had inherited a superb vinyl collection – opera and lieder, piano concertos and string quartets – and she would never be able to give that up and start her own.

As Simon hesitated in the parlour doorway, torn between saying something and pressing on for the front door, the kitten wriggled free, dodged around his feet and sprinted upstairs. The fat ginger cat lifted its head and projected a perfect lack of interest from its copper-green eyes. The record crackled on. Florence took a cushion and drew her knees up around it, retreating deeper into the sofa, and Simon suppressed an impulse to cross the room and kick over the side table. All of this might have been planned specifically to prevent him from leaving. He wanted to ask if it was so hard for her to summon a couple of words or just a smile of assent; but she had never once given him that. He wasn't sure she would even recognise the idea. He marvelled, not for the first time, at how neatly she could put him in the wrong.

The elderly animal wailed from upstairs. Florence flinched, and Simon knew what she was thinking: the poor thing was suffering and she didn't know what to do, it couldn't clean itself any more, could barely eat without help; maybe she should ask the vet again; it was all too much to cope with. He saw these anxieties swell through her mind, then ebb as she returned to the main task of denying him any scrap of approval, of permission, before he left. His eye was a lump of gristle implanted in his head but he paid it no attention.

She could seem like a lonely spinster with the stink of catfood through the place and the shed hair everywhere. There was an atmosphere of shame about her empty house and its sodden, sunken garden where wrens flickered their tails and skipped tauntingly from the sills to the branches and back. If he stepped into the room, he could sit down and slide towards her along the cool, glazed cloth of the sofa, holding out his arms until their ribcages bumped like teacups. She would let him hook his chin over her shoulder to gaze into the warped gloss of the windowpane and the mass of tree-fingers beyond. She always let him, if he tried. A throb went through his back teeth and all at once he was desperate to get outside and walking, not having to think about Florence sitting in her parlour with her cats. It was time to go.

Florence drew a deep breath and dared another look into Simon's eyes. He opened his palms to her helplessly. The ginger cat made an approving noise.

'Don't go,' she said. 'Stay here.'

It took him a moment to make sense of the words. He opened his mouth, pushed the heel of his hand into his left eye and laughed at how completely she had failed to understand him. Then, shaking his head, he walked out of the house.

He could not understand how she had drawn him into the life of these past years. It was as if she had never doubted that he would join her for walks and shopping trips and cinema outings, that she was qualified to lace her fingers in his and lay her head on his shoulder, that he would let her cook him dinner in the evenings and would stay with her afterwards – and without quite knowing why, he had allowed her to carry on believing all this. He was good at the deception, talking with every sign of enthusiasm about the books and films she liked, making her laugh with his wry remarks when they went people-watching. He even took her into town and helped her buy some new clothes. He waited for her to notice how bored he was – that wherever his heart might be, it was not here – but she saw nothing. To dissolve her contentment would have been so easy that he couldn't bring himself to do it, even when he was ready to scream at her for the way she had entangled him.

One afternoon they parted on Ectarine Walk after she had spent half an hour debating with herself whether she dared make an expedition across the city to the Strangers' Market. She wanted to browse the bookstalls, but feared that the effort of doing so might prove too much for her; she could not make up her mind. Simon had listened in mounting disbelief, his expression portraying concern, and he had asked sympathetic questions just as if he had nothing more important to worry about. Once she had disappeared into the house his face twisted into an ugly mask which churned on his skull all the way along the street.

And yet a few days later he went with her to the

Market. Having finally made the decision, she was in a good mood, and as they surveyed the paperbacks she waved at the bald, flaccid man behind one of the smaller tables.

'I always find something here,' she said. 'Henry has good taste.'

Astonishingly, the man lowered his eyes and shuffled his feet, his patchily shaven jowls wobbling. Simon had not imagined she could produce such a response even from so raddled a specimen. As Florence took her time over the stall, the man's loose grey tongue pressed out between his varnished teeth and his eyes stayed on her. She glanced up and threaded a strand of hair behind her ear. When she looked away again the man's face turned to Simon and twitched in a sort of pantomime, servile and insinuating at once, as if he was trying to share some lecherous joke. Simon was surprised by how badly he wanted to overturn the stall and break that pendulous nose; but then he saw that Florence had moved to another stall, and he hurried after her without replying. The fat man's expression crumpled as he watched them leave.

The next time Simon was walking in Glory Part, fingers grasped his elbow, an oniony sweat smell enclosed him and the same sorry character greeted him like a bosom friend. It was a good thing they'd met again, he said, breathing heavily, because last time they had been interrupted. As Simon permitted himself a silent laugh at the kinds of difficulties she could get him into, the man launched into a story, some incoherent hard-luck tale about something bad which had happened to him: a mistake from which he had never recovered, the cause of his present state. Simon did his best not to hear, and after a few minutes he was able to get away by joining the flow of shoppers into the Part High metro – but he took with him the irrational unease that this meeting had somehow enmeshed him with Florence further.

Soon enough she wanted him to move into the house on Ectarine Walk, and although he squirmed when she asked him he was penned in by guilty obligation. He had let her continue happily in her fantasies for so long now. Besides, he had nowhere to go – a malicious landlord had given him notice on his tenancy – and Florence's house was big enough, too big: it was full of the impediments of the past, heavy furniture and leather-armoured books and brown oil paintings, and when you came in from the street the hall closed over you like woodland. The wallpaper was a diagram of an overgrown garden and a giant cobweb of shadow hung always across the upstairs landing. When he arrived with his rucksack he felt a tingle of excitement at the sense that these rooms might carry on unfolding indefinitely, that the house might be the secret entrance to an underground world of limitless dim galleries and stairs. Only as he was unpacking did he realise that if Florence's house had offered an image of escape, it had been nothing but a lure.

Living with her, he had grown baffled by the excuses she made for herself. In all this time he had never grasped what was really supposed to be the problem. The story, as far as he could make out, was that she had once had a viral infection and that ever since then she had been too tired to do anything. She suffered from an inconclusive catalogue of complaints – aching joints, the occasional fever – but all Simon knew was that she could lie despondent on the sofa for weeks on end.

Her more active periods were even more irksome. She fretted continually about tiring herself out, and was always fussing with a note-book in which she wrote down everything she did; she appeared to believe that walking to the shops was an achievement worth recording. The transparency of her tactics infuriated him as much as their success. When it suited her, she could manage well enough to go on daytrips into town, or cook complicated meals and insist that he eat them with her sitting up at the drop-leaf table in the dining room, but after a few weeks she would remember how tired she was meant to be and retreat to the sofa again. It still took Simon aback that she could behave like this in front of someone with a genuine affliction, but he said nothing. Soon enough, he reminded himself, it wouldn't matter.

*   *   *

He ran down the front steps and set a smart pace along Ectarine Walk. Branches shook droplets on him as he walked, acid daylight stung his eyes and he thought of returning to Florence: he could apologise and lie in a darkened bedroom for the rest of the day, letting her press cool flannels on his forehead. He cursed himself for a faint heart and kept walking until he saw the green glass canopies of Lizavet Heath metro station.

He bought a ticket and went down to the platform. When he was small, he had liked travelling on the metro, the tramcar jogging him along tracks that stitched themselves through the city and led off into the hidden maze of all the places you could go. He had tried imagining that one day he would own all the trams, so that all of those destinations would belong to him too, but the idea had not convinced him even briefly. It felt more like his father's than his own. His father had been a limited man who had made a lot of money in property and, having no real personality, had settled for the usual pretence: bluff, hard-nosed, no-nonsense. For years he had behaved as though Simon was incapable of managing anything for himself, but later he had refused to support his son in the smallest way, laying down platitudes instead about how we all have to learn to stand on our own two feet. Then he had gone bankrupt.

Simon rode the metro over to Sweatmarket

station and climbed through chipped tiling and wet concrete up to the streets of Glory Part. He crossed a footbridge and turned down Sluice Lane. He had lived in digs near here for a couple of months, at one time, and had never forgotten it. The landlady had chewed raw garlic for her blood pressure. The kitchen had barely been large enough for an electric kettle, a hotplate and a cupboard smelling of mildew; there was a view of the canal. Sliding open the drawer, he'd discovered a lone fork, the tines bent in four slightly different directions and the handle stamped *Not to be removed from hospital.* In the early mornings that room had been bright, and crammed with a sense of promise so pure it was hard to bear, like a sound pitched at the limit of hearing.

He was angry with Florence for spoiling his departure from the house. By rights, all he had to do was walk until the day ended – the afternoon was already dimming – and keep walking for as long as it took, a pilgrim thinking only of his journey, on faith, letting the rest of his life fall away. But instead he was rattled and distracted. She had done it again. To settle his mind he walked fast in no particular direction until he emerged from the alleys to the quays.

The waterfront was in the process of redevelopment. They had laid tiny, pastel-coloured paving stones, planted blue bollards, and put up a bronze image of a stevedore hauling a rope. Most of the gutted buildings were dressed with scaffolding, but a few restaurants and shops were ready, their dim interiors poised for customers. The sky, overcast and unsettled, was opening itself in an endless slow gesture to the waves. The waterfront was empty except for a man slumped on one of the benches. Simon cursed: he had grown accustomed to ducking down the side streets of Glory Part whenever he saw that grey face approaching, but this time he was caught in the open. Before he could turn on his heel, the figure on the bench raised a hand and began to get up. Simon walked on past, ignoring the cry of abject greeting and the snagging of fingernails on his sleeve. As he hastened away from the quays the fat man shambled after him, still calling out as if to start a conversation.

The streets were almost dark, the daylight retreating into the clouds where it would soon fade, and the evening was colder than he had thought. He pushed his fists into the pockets of his jacket but the wind went through the cotton and the pavement's chill had infiltrated the soles of his shoes. The migraine was a clenched fist behind his eye. As he stepped off the pavement on the Part High Street the front corner of a single-decker bus snapped at his sleeve and the driver leant on the horn, loosing a long peal of abuse. He looked up and down the road before trying again. Shopkeepers were hauling down loud steel blinds and some of the streetlamps had come on, their glow darkening the air.

On Dapper Street some youths were killing time by the ash-bins, bullying a dog that kept nosing around their ankles. Once he had slightly known a man who died when a group of boys and girls had knocked him down and jumped on his head. Having an aspiration was like carrying a wad of cash in your pocket: they knew by instinct there was something they could take off you. On these afternoons the city was nothing but cold brick and closed faces, and it made him feel that he was no different from the fat bookseller, a shabby clown wandering the streets in search of some delusion. But that was not true. His aspiration was not like that.

It was the earliest desire he could remember. He had always known that there were clues in the city, traces of what he was looking for, certain streets which he was sure would lead him where he needed to go. In childhood he had discovered that anything could be a signal: guano on red brick and white pavement, blackberries under a concrete walkway, water swirling into the mouth of a storm-drain. Gradually he had come to understand that hidden in some fold of every scene was the Flâneur, always moving on around the next corner, and sometimes he felt on the brink of understanding why he wanted so much to follow; sometimes he felt sure that the real mysteries do not conceal themselves but live beside us in plain view. Once he had seen the corpse of a blackbird splayed on the pavement

341

with its body scooped away, leaving the head, wings and feathered ribcage, a shaman's cloak. Another time it had been a one-eyed yellow tomcat whose punctured orb had shrivelled in the socket like dried egg in the bottom of a pan. These encounters were promises of a kind.

Two seasons ago he had come close, closer than before or since. It had happened at the end of an afternoon like this one when, heading back to Florence's house, he had lost his bearings. He had kept on walking as the dusk gathered, sure that he must soon recognise a street or a building, but it was as if he had chanced into another city where he saw only dead ends and locked metro stations. He had walked faster, his watering eyes smearing the streets with light. When he saw the figure, it was far off, standing at the other end of an echoing pedestrian tunnel whose walls angled inwards to give a false perspective. For an instant he thought it was another citizen out walking late, but it turned its pale head towards him while beside him a film of dirty water coursed over tiles like teeth, and in that moment his feet tangled so that he tripped and spun and slammed into the wall. He picked himself up and walked away, not quite daring to run, never once looking over his shoulder, half-expecting to hear a lame footfall close behind.

He had never found out where he had been that night, but since then he had been keeping to familiar parts of the city.

★　　★　　★

Now he crossed the Part Bridge and continued towards the Old Quarter until the Impasto Street metro came in sight. On days like this, days when he decided to leave Florence and begin his search for the Flâneur, it was here, more often than not, that he would change his mind and catch a tram back to Lizavet Heath. When he saw the yellow mouth of the metro station glowing among the smaller lights, he would discover that he was not yet ready for the pilgrimage, and, knowing that readiness was all, warmed by a certain wryness at his own expense, he would pass through the turnstile and buy a ticket home.

As he went down to the platform he thought of Florence. On dull days she often lit the fire to comfort herself and so that the cats could stretch out on the hearthrug. She might still be sitting on the sofa, not turning on the lamps as the room darkened, or she might be trying to read a book or cook a meal: but no matter what she did she would in truth only be waiting, purposeless as a ghost in her empty house, for him to come home. A couple of hours ago this thought would have exasperated him, but now it seemed not so bad. It wasn't her fault that every time he came back she would greet him with simple relief, unable to disguise how glad she was to have him with her again. He didn't blame her for that: it was sweet in its way.

This evening the tramcar was empty except for

an elderly man seated at the front, gazing into the glass. Simon sat close to the back and as the car began to move he realised that by blessed increments the throbbing in his head was letting go. The poisoned core of the migraine had drained out. It always happened at this point in the journey, he now remembered: it was strange how each time he forgot. The tram jogged, the old man swayed like a doll loose at the neck and Simon's body copied the movement. He felt good. When he got back to Ectarine Walk he would make it up handsomely to Florence. He would tell her how much she meant to him and do whatever was needed to make her happy, not out of guilt but because he felt now that it was true.

By the time he climbed up to the street at Lizavet Heath he could barely recall the ache in his head. The last of the daylight had trickled behind the rooftops, but a bright sensation spread in him as he walked, beginning as a spark in his chest and soon spilling through his body, translating him into a lighter substance. In a way he did all of this for her sake. He was impatient for the surrender that he would see in her face a few minutes from now.

The front windows were lit along Ectarine Walk, but Florence's house was dark. The curtains were open in the bedroom window above and he could see part of the room's ceiling in the glow of a reading lamp. Otherwise the house might have been untenanted. He mounted the steps to the front door and found a bulky object propped against the jamb. It was his old rucksack. His key would not go into the lock: Florence must have left hers on the other side. He rattled the key back and forth, trying to dislodge the obstruction, then rang the doorbell and waited, then rang again. He opened the rucksack, which was packed with his T-shirts and jeans, neatly rolled. He stepped back into the street and peered up at the window. As he watched, the light in the bedroom went out.

He stood for a long time in the street waiting for some further sign, and then no longer waiting but simply standing there below the dark house. He stood until he had established it fully, because if this was what she wanted then he was going to insist on it: there would be no mistake.

He could no longer see the house, having stared so long that it was only a group of dim flat shapes which hovered featureless behind the streetlamps. He had nowhere to go and night had fallen, but he climbed the steps, picked up his rucksack and, to justify himself the more completely, dropped his keys through the letterbox, becoming aware as he did so of the city's empty spaces lying open around him in every direction. From somewhere came the echo of an uneven footstep and for an instant he glimpsed water flowing across yellow-white tiles, but the street was deserted. The lamps tilted slow pinwheels of light. He paused and looked back before he turned the corner, but no one prevented him from leaving.

Florence woke earlier than usual. She lay for a few minutes listening to far-off traffic sounds and thinking her way into the morning and beyond it. Dismay stirred at the thought of how much would be required of her in the time ahead, but she told herself to keep her pace steady and spend her energy well. She could not be sure how much she had in reserve, but she was better than before, rested and prepared, and besides there was no delaying any longer. It had been six months of guilt and consternation.

She climbed out of bed and looked down into Ectarine Walk, where the last of the doctors and solicitors were disappearing towards the metro station and the elm trees were dropping their papery fruit to be swept along the street by a damp spring wind. While she stood at the bedroom window the sky seemed to grow a fraction dimmer as if dusk had been falling since before day began.

Downstairs she let the cats in and fed them while the kettle boiled. After a cup of tea she got dressed and tidied the kitchen. It was important to stick to the established rhythms and routines and still to keep building up gradually, always doing a little more but never too much, but today in spite of herself she found that each household duty was marked with an extra significance. She felt as if she was about to set out on a journey into unknown regions and this was the last time she would rinse the teapot or rub Misto's head when he came to sniff at her knee.

The kitchen compost box was full, so she stepped into her gardening shoes and carried it outside. The lawn would have been as tall as her waist if the grass had been upright, but it lay waterlogged and buckled under its own weight. The flowerbeds had become thickets and the silver birch was clogged with the pale threads of a climbing weed. She would put all this right eventually, but the discipline was not to worry about it now and only to do as much as she was able. At the bottom of the garden she opened the lid of the compost bin and upended the loose brick of tealeaves, eggshells and vegetable peelings into the hot mulch. Two months ago she could not have managed even this.

After turning him away she had relapsed worse than ever. The old pains had bloomed in her spine and shoulder and the familiar headache had settled back behind her eyes, throbbing with each pulse, indifferent to analgesics; over the days that followed his departure, her muscles grew dull and sore as stones and soon she was submerged and sinking, slowly flailing, into that tranced depth where pressure trapped her head, light rippled down too bright through the surface of the world and every noise was a dissolving concussion, at once muffled and too loud. It was hard to hear what people said, impossible to think straight, hopeless to imagine going outside or reading a book. Time swamped her. She shivered with fever. She wanted only to sleep but lying in bed was a day's hard work at the end of which getting up to feed the cats would cost her the last of her strength. If this carried on for long it would actually be the end of her: the house would fall into ruin, the unfed cats would leave in search of new homes and she would stay here forever, stranded, insomniac and mad with exhaustion.

She could not explain why things had turned out otherwise, but somehow she had begun to struggle her way back up from the depths of fatigue. It was impossible to imagine, now, where she had found the resources for such an act of will, but one day she had opened the old notebook she had used for her recovery plan the first time. In it she had mapped her life hour by hour, plotting the difference between what she had done when she was well and what she could manage now, forcing herself to be realistic, trying to think of ways to make her tasks easier, instructing herself that it must all happen at a slow pace, step by step. She did a little more each day. Over a week or a fortnight she would begin to feel better; then she would ask too much of herself, staying out too long or trying to set things straight in the house too quickly, and she would slip backwards and have to pick herself up all over again. The months had passed and with intolerable slowness she had improved. And as the fatigue had retreated, it had left behind the immovable, hurtful weight deep in her chest which she had buried there by sending him away.

The cats met her halfway down the garden and stalked her heels back up to the house. She scrubbed out the compost box in the kitchen sink and set it upside down in the rack. The weight hung in her chest now as always. It tightened her breathing as if she was about to panic – she had to remind herself that this was not panic but something harder to name – and now, as often, she asked what kind of person she must be to stand here with such a weight in her, drying her hands on the tea towel and gazing out of the window behind the sink. Questions like this did not help. She did not know whether she had the energy to spare for a walk to the grocer's but she had given the cats the last of their tinned food this morning, so she found a cloth shopping bag, put on her coat and went out. There was no need to hurry. Everything that needed doing would be done in its time.

Standing on the pavement she glanced up to make sure that the bedroom window was closed, and set off along the street, not trying to walk too fast. Through these last months there had been nothing of her to spare, she had been consumed by the work of recovery: but then one day she had looked back at that evening half a year ago and found that her guilt no longer scorched thoughts away to nothing. She could look steadily into the past and ask herself why she had done it. If she ever really caught a glimpse of herself it wasn't when life unfolded to plan but at those moments when she didn't know what in the world she was doing, when she was drowning in some hurt, some desire or resentment or regret. She knew it now: now that she lived this orderly life with one hurt swelling endlessly inside her.

She remembered the Gaunt exhibition, their first outing together. He had walked into the gallery as if he expected to be arrested – it had been obvious that he'd never heard of Albert Gaunt before that time in the library when he'd made her smile by using the printmaker's name so clumsily to strike up a conversation – but when they started looking at the pictures he had forgotten his nerves. He had studied the small, dense lithographs and pointed out details which Florence had never noticed. He'd taken no interest in the information placards beside the prints; she on the other hand was always reprimanding herself for reading the text first, as if she needed to be told what to see. When they walked along the river afterwards it was as if they'd already known each other a long time. Slow learner that she was, it had never quite occurred to her that you could walk around all afternoon and into the evening with someone you had known for a day and already liked better than you could understand. On her way home she had reflected that there must be certain people in the world, a very few, with whom you'll never need to search for what to say, and you know you'll never reach the end.

Turning on to Lizavet High Street she passed the veterinary practice and thought of Emmie, whom she had finally taken to the vet three weeks ago because along with the yowling the poor old thing had started wheezing painfully and dragging a paralysed back leg around the house. Florence had stroked her as the vet had given the injection. Simon would have refused to understand why she had waited so long.

She bought six cans of catfood in the grocer's and paused to rest in the café next door before going home. She sat in the window, at the table where they had often spent hours together looking out at the au pairs with their pushchairs progressing along the ten or twelve shopfronts which made up the high street. Once, after swallowing another in the series of espressos which he liked to drink while she took her time over a pot of tea, he had waved a hand dismissively at the street and told her that this place *wasn't real*. That had made her suddenly furious. She had wanted to argue with him and prove what a stupid thing it was to say, but as usual she hadn't. She knew he'd win because arguing made her tongue-tied and she would run out of indignation first; but as she fumed she had realised that he was not going to change. He would never completely believe in ordinary things, the things he could touch. That had been the moment at which she had betrayed him, she supposed, by losing interest in his point of view. She had done her best to be patient, and to wait for him to see that though he took such pains to demonstrate that his heart was elsewhere, his life with her told a different story. In the end, though, she had not been able to show him that he already had what he needed, that what was real was the heath, the house, their meals, their bodies, the days and years they spent together.

Well, it meant that he had something to forgive her, and she had something to forgive him too. If they could both manage it they would be able to begin.

She left the café and started for home. A week ago here on the high street she had run into Henry the bookseller, of all people, emerging from one of the charity shops with two plastic carrier bags full of paperbacks. When she had said hello he had shuffled and stammered and looked hopelessly shifty in the way that always made her first warm to him and then worry she was being patronising. He had kept on glancing up and down the street, seeming suspicious of the fundraisers with their clipboards and the paired policemen. Then, his brow creasing, he had leant closer and told her that he had seen Simon.

It had happened early one morning in the Grand Terminus: as Henry was queuing to buy a cup of coffee in the concourse, he had recognised a figure standing motionless in the flow of arrivals from the dawn train. There had been no mistaking who it was. He had appeared to be waiting, or listening, and when the station was quiet again he had cast around aimlessly for a while, peering at the floor as if he had lost something. Finally, after picking up a trampled carnation which had fallen from the flower barrow, he had disappeared into the metro. That was all Henry could tell her.

By the time she got back to the house she was beginning to flag, so she put the tins on the kitchen counter and lay down on the sofa. When she woke, she sat up in alarm to find it almost dark in the parlour and the sky outside the colour of slate, but she had only slept for an hour. The days were short but there was still time. She wouldn't go far at first. She would search for only a brief while today, but tomorrow she would continue for a little longer and then longer again the day after until she was searching all the time, and she would not stop until she found him. What would happen after that didn't seem to matter. No doubt by then he would have another story to tell, but she would not be anxious to hear it. She wanted no more tellings, no reiterations. She only wanted to begin.

She fed the cats and ate some bread and cheese standing at the counter. Wanting to feel that she was equipping herself for a journey, she dug out an old pair of boots from the back of the bedroom wardrobe. They had once been favourites and their insides were still shaped to her feet. As the rooms

353

darkened, early evening light came up in the windows and faded from blue to grey, offering a last view of the heath and the rooftops. She took the pocket street atlas from the drawer of the hall table, then changed her mind and put it back. She buttoned her coat, and, after consideration, left a lamp on in the hall. Then she locked the house and walked out into the city.